CHRISTMAS
for the
HOME FRONT
GIRLS

BOOKS BY SUSANNA BAVIN

CHRISTMAS
for the
HOME FRONT
GIRLS

SUSANNA BAVIN

bookouture

Published by Bookouture in 2024

An imprint of Storyfire Ltd.
Carmelite House
50 Victoria Embankment
London EC4Y 0DZ

www.bookouture.com

ISBN: 978-1-83790-790-8
eBook ISBN: 978-1-83790-789-2

In memory of Jason
And also to his parents, Ian and Beverley

CHAPTER ONE

DECEMBER 1940

'Do you think we ought to decorate the Andy?' Betty asked, looking around at the inside of their Anderson shelter.

'Is there room for Christmas decorations?' Andrew quipped. 'There's only just room for us!'

Betty laughed along with the others, but what Andrew said was true. Theirs was a standard-sized shelter, supposedly big enough for six, but it felt cramped with that many in it. Currently in the shelter in the back garden at Star House were Betty; her friend and colleague, Sally Henshaw, together with Sally's husband Andrew, a woodwork teacher, and his mother; Mrs Beaumont, the landlady of Star House, where the rest of them were billeted; and Lorna, who worked at the local salvage depot with Betty and Sally. After a shaky start there a few weeks ago, Lorna had found her feet and the other two girls had warmed to her. Today was the Friday before Christmas, and Lorna was going to leave her current digs and move into Star House over the weekend.

'Seriously, any decorations would get spoiled in the damp,' said Mrs Henshaw, who could always be relied upon to be practical.

The shelter was indeed prone to damp. As everyone joked, it always rained in Manchester. When the Anderson had been installed, sawdust had been chucked at the newly painted inside walls as protection against damp, and the lino contained runnels in case water needed to be drawn away.

'I hope we won't end up spending Christmas Day in here,' Sally remarked. 'It's my first Christmas as a married woman and I want it to be perfect.'

Andrew gave her a loving smile. 'It doesn't matter where we are. It'll be special because we're together.'

Betty sighed. Sally and Andrew made such a happy couple. An attractive couple too, who were certain to have good-looking children one day. Slender Sally had hazel eyes and neat features in a heart-shaped face and her fair hair was of a deep hue that made some folk refer to her as a dirty blonde, but Betty always told her friend she was a dark-blonde. As for Andrew, well, he was rather gorgeous, with his warm brown eyes and boyish smile.

Mind you, as handsome as Andrew Henshaw was, he wasn't a patch on a certain Samuel Atkinson. Happiness blossomed inside Betty. After being led well and truly up the garden path by that rat Eddie Markham, she had finally seen what had been right in front of her the whole time. Samuel was kind and trustworthy – two qualities Betty had never fully appreciated before she had fallen foul of Eddie – and he had a slight stammer that she found endearing. In fact, everything about Samuel was endearing, from the stubborn curls that fought back against the hair-cream he used to flatten them, to the serious hazel eyes behind the lenses of his glasses. Betty had made an utter fool of herself over Eddie but, with Samuel, she felt she had come home and would be safe for ever. She couldn't wait to introduce him to her dad.

Lorna nudged her. 'Wake up, Betty. You were a million

miles away.' She smiled. She was a real stunner. Her eyes were pure green, a rare colour that was very lovely, and her glossy hair was the darkest of browns.

'I expect she was daydreaming about Samuel,' said Mrs Henshaw. 'Weren't you, dear?'

Betty blushed but she smiled too. 'I was, actually.'

'Well, that's got to be better than listening to the bombs falling,' said Mrs Beaumont as a series of long, drawn-out whistling sounds told of strings of incendiaries falling to earth.

'While you were busy dreaming of Samuel,' Sally told Betty, 'Mrs Beaumont was saying that from now on, instead of bringing the biscuit tin into the Andy, she's going to prepare Christmassy snacks. She wants to get us in the festive mood.'

'A most welcome idea after all the raids we've had since the summer,' Mrs Henshaw remarked.

'What snacks do you have in mind?' Betty asked her landlady.

'To be honest, it isn't really my idea,' said Mrs Beaumont. 'I found it in a magazine. I was thinking of cream cheese spread with redcurrant jelly, or a bit of ham topped with watercress. And condensed milk isn't rationed, so I could make some coconut pyramids. It's easy to make cinnamon sweets too.'

Andrew laughed. 'This is making me hungry.'

'I'll be glad to help you, of course, Mrs Beaumont,' offered Mrs Henshaw.

'That's kind of you but there's no need,' Mrs Beaumont replied. 'You and your family are guests in my house and it's my job to look after you.'

Betty and Sally looked at one another. This polite exchange, or a version of it, had become a regular occurrence between the two women. Mrs Beaumont wasn't just a private individual whom the others had been foisted onto by the billeting officer. She was a professional landlady and her home was called Star

House because she had for years before the war provided accommodation for touring actors and music hall performers. Since the Henshaws had moved in, Mrs Henshaw had been keen to lend a hand and Mrs Beaumont had been resolute in declining every offer.

'What about Christmas dinner itself?' Lorna asked. 'I had a letter from Mummy and she's going to have mock-turkey. In other words, rabbit stuffed with bacon and herbs.'

'There are going to be a lot of mock-turkey dinners this year,' said Mrs Henshaw. 'And have you seen the Christmas cards in the shops? Talk about flimsy! Not that I'm complaining. All our resources are going towards building weapons, which is as it should be.' She placed her hand on Sally's arm. 'I thought I'd better say that, so you didn't have to.'

It was a gentle tease. Sally had been promoted to the position of manager at the salvage depot in October and she took her job seriously. She was a fount of information as to what the various salvaged goods could be turned into to boost the war effort. Betty enjoyed working at the depot and she worked hard to do her bit for the war effort, but she wasn't dedicated to salvage the way Sally was.

'How long have we been in here now?' Mrs Beaumont asked, fitting a cigarette into the end of her cigarette-holder.

Andrew shot back his cuff to check his wristwatch. 'Half past eight. Two hours.'

'How much longer?' murmured Mrs Henshaw.

It was normal for a raid to last several hours. Often the women brought their knitting with them to pass the time, but none of them had done this for a while. Betty had stopped bringing hers because she was knitting Christmas presents that she mustn't let the others see, and she suspected the same applied to them. Betty was knitting scarves for Sally and Lorna. She had already made a striped V-necked sweater for Dad, having found two jumpers of similar-weight wool on the market that she had unravelled so she could re-knit them.

Of course, making that for Dad had more or less obliged her to make a pretty cardigan for Grace, her stepmother. *Step*mother seemed an appropriate word because Grace had stepped into Betty's late mum's shoes less than a year after Mum's unexpected death. Stepped? Slithered, more like. Betty didn't blame Dad, even though his early remarriage had shocked her at the time. No, she laid the blame squarely at Grace's door. Grace Milburn-as-was had seen a vulnerable widower and made her plans accordingly. It hadn't been the first time either. She had previously set her sights on Mr Wainwright from round the corner, but he had skilfully evaded her. Mum and the other local women had all talked about Grace Milburn behind her back for that. Then Mum had died and Grace had ended up as the second Mrs Hughes.

Realising that thoughts of Grace had brought a frown to her brow, Betty eased her face. She wished she had enough time to knit a sweater for Samuel, but there was no chance of it. Christmas Day was next Wednesday. She still hadn't found him a present. Gifts were hard to come by this year because of the shortages. Sally had managed to find a shaving mirror for Andrew.

'It's not exactly a romantic present,' she had confided to Betty, 'but it's useful.'

'I'm sure he'll be pleased with it,' Betty said loyally.

'When you've been bombed out and lost nearly everything you possess,' Sally had replied, 'a useful present is best.'

The raid dragged on until gone midnight. When the all-clear sounded, everybody stretched out the kinks in their joints and headed back to the house, with Andrew carrying the air-raid box containing everyone's important documents – birth certificates, insurance papers and so on.

Betty sniffed the night air. You could tell a lot from sniffing. If your nose clogged with the smells of smoke, cordite and brick dust, you knew that somewhere close by had taken a direct hit. The sickly aroma of gas told you the mains had been ruptured nearby and you mustn't switch your gas back on yet. But just now the prevalent scent was the tang of crisp night air, which was something to be grateful for.

Betty sent up a quick prayer that Dad, Grace and Samuel were all safe. Dad and Samuel were both on duty tonight. Dad was a police sergeant and often worked nights. Samuel's voluntary war work was as an ARP warden and one of his duties was to hurry to the scene when a bomb fell and take stock of the situation so that the correct services could be sent for – fire, first aid, ambulance, a rescue squad, an engineer to see to ruptured gas or water mains, whatever was required. It was work that called for courage and a cool head, and Betty was proud of her Samuel.

Inside the house, before they could tumble into bed, they had to undo all the preparations they had swiftly put in place when the siren had sounded at half past six the previous evening. The gas, electricity and water had to be switched back on and the blackout, which had been lifted so that flames inside could be seen from the road, had to be reinstated.

When the light was switched on, Betty heard Mrs Beaumont huff a sigh. Everywhere was coated with a thin film of dust. This was a regular occurrence. If a high explosive detonated, all the household dust within a half-mile radius rose up and settled for all to see. It didn't matter how houseproud you were. It happened to everyone.

'I'll walk you home,' Andrew said to Lorna.

'It'll be your last night at the Lockwoods' house,' said Mrs Beaumont. 'You're moving in here tomorrow – today, I should say.'

Soon Betty was in bed in Marie Lloyd. That was the name

of her bedroom. Other landladies gave their bedrooms numbers, but Mrs Beaumont had named hers after the greats of the music hall.

As she snuggled down beneath the covers, Betty thought of her new-found happiness with Samuel. This promised to be the best Christmas since she had lost her darling mum.

CHAPTER TWO

Lorna came downstairs on Saturday morning to have her final breakfast with the Lockwoods. She had already packed most of her things and had only paused in this task because it would be ungracious to dash out of their front door straight after breakfast. It had been good of the Lockwoods to provide a billet when she was new in Manchester. Well, it had been good of Mr Lockwood, but his wife had definitely had an ulterior motive, though it had taken Lorna some time to realise it.

Mrs Lockwood, an erect, buxom woman whose air of energy and confidence endowed her with considerable authority, was a leading light in the local branch of the WVS and was their designated salvage officer. A formidable woman who liked nothing better than to organise and be in charge, she wanted to get Sally, the newly appointed manager of the salvage depot in Chorlton-cum-Hardy, under her thumb. That was why, when Lorna had been assigned to work there, Mrs Lockwood had been keen to have her under her roof. By leading Lorna to believe that Sally was merely a minion who looked after the depot on her behalf, Mrs Lockwood had tried to undermine Sally's authority and boost her own influence.

Having had no reason to question this, Lorna had unwittingly played along. It had taken her a while to see things as they truly were. It was one of the reasons she wanted to leave the Lockwoods' house. Moving into Star House with Sally and Betty would cement their new friendship and remove her from an uncomfortable position.

The Lockwoods were already at the table when Lorna entered the dining room.

'Ah, there you are, my dear,' Mr Lockwood said in his genial way. He was kindly and mild-mannered and clearly thought his wife was rather remarkable.

'I'm sorry,' said Lorna. 'Have I kept you waiting?'

'Not at all,' said Mr Lockwood.

Mrs Jenks brought in the breakfast. She was the Lockwoods' daily and had looked after their house for years.

Today being Saturday, breakfast was boiled eggs and soldiers followed by toast and marmalade. The soldiers were 'undressed' to save on the butter. Mrs Jenks was an expert at boiling eggs so that the white was firm while the yolk was runny, just the way Lorna liked them.

When Lorna had polished off her egg, she turned the shell upside down in her eggcup and bashed the bottom of it, just as she had as a child, so that the witches couldn't sail away in it.

'The memsahib and I will miss you when you move on to pastures new,' said Mr Lockwood, 'but it'll be nice for you to be in a house with company of your own age – won't it, m'dear?' he asked his wife.

Mrs Lockwood nodded. 'Yes, indeed.' She had taken Lorna's decision to leave on the chin.

'Thank you,' said Lorna. 'I know I've said it before, but I really am most awfully grateful to you both for taking me in. As long as I live, I'll never forget your pair of umbrella stands full of stout sticks and gardening implements in case Jerry marches up the garden path.'

'We'll give him what for if we get half a chance,' Mr Lockwood declared. 'Won't we, m'dear?'

'We most certainly will,' Mrs Lockwood declared.

Lorna didn't doubt it for a single moment. Whatever reservations she now entertained towards Mrs Lockwood, there could be no doubting her patriotism.

'What time shall you be leaving us?' Mrs Lockwood asked. 'We'll send you on your way in a taxi.'

'There's no need—' Lorna started to say.

'Nonsense,' Mrs Lockwood said in her forthright way.

Mrs Jenks came in again, bringing the toast rack and the first postal delivery of the day. There was a letter for Lorna, who recognised her mother's handwriting on the envelope.

'And this one is addressed to the two of you.' Mrs Jenks allowed her glance to slide between the Lockwoods.

With a movement of her chin, Mrs Lockwood indicated that it should be handed to her husband. He opened it using the knife off his plate, which made his wife roll her eyes.

Mr Lockwood scanned the page. 'It's from your mother, Lorna, thanking us for having you in our home. Jolly decent of her to write. Here, pass this to the memsahib, will you?'

Lorna passed the letter along, then read her own from Mummy.

What you said in reply to Daddy's offer was the last thing either of us expected.

When Lorna's father had sent her away from home, it had been to remove her from the public eye following a disastrous court case. Lorna had expected to be sent off to the West Country to see out the war in a five-star hotel, which was what some wealthy people had chosen to do. Instead Daddy had packed her off to Manchester to work in a grotty salvage depot, of all places. Then, at the beginning of this week, Daddy had at last written to offer her the longed-for West Country bolt-hole –

just when Lorna had chosen to stay in Manchester and do her bit, a decision she was proud of.

She had written back at once to explain this. Hence Mummy's letter today, filled with astonishment.

I'm coming down to see you, darling. I won't completely believe in your wish to remain where you are until you look me in the eye and tell me. I will travel by train as far as Bolton on Saturday and stay overnight with Marjorie Halburton (dear old soul – I haven't seen her since before the abdication) and then come to Manchester on Sunday, returning home on the teatime train.

Instructions followed for Lorna to meet her mother the next day.

Just before she finished reading the letter, an exclamation from Mr Lockwood, who was reading the newspaper, wrenched her attention in his direction.

'Good grief!'

'Whatever is it?' asked Mrs Lockwood.

'This – this.' He jabbed at the newspaper, making the page flop over. With a sharp rustle, he righted it. Then he lowered it and stared at Lorna. 'This is you, isn't it? This photograph. But it says here that your name is West-Sadler, not plain Sadler.'

Dread rolled in Lorna's stomach. She had known this was going to happen. Of course she had. It had been inevitable. From the moment she had stepped in to save Betty's bacon, she'd known this would have to be faced. She just hadn't allowed herself to think about it.

'You're the girl from the breach-of-promise case,' said Mr Lockwood, a look of disgust on his face. 'The girl the judge called unpatriotic – and you've been living here under our roof.'

CHAPTER THREE

It was Sally's Saturday to open the depot. Shortly before eight o'clock, she walked along Beech Road past the local shops to where the depot stood behind a brick wall on two sides and a tall wooden fence in the front. Set into the fence were a pair of big gates and a door with a keyhole. Sally took out her key and let herself in, automatically picking up her feet as she stepped over the plank across the bottom of the doorway.

Closing the door behind her, she made her way across the yard, much of which was open to the elements, though a strip down each side was covered over. Back in the late summer when she had started working here, all the salvage work had been done outside in the yard, but since she had taken over she had moved much of the work indoors.

She unlocked the building and went upstairs to get changed into her dungarees and headscarf. Under her dungarees she wore a warm knitted sweater. Before working here, she had been a clerk in the Food Office based in the Town Hall and had worn a skirt and blouse to work. Her mum had been so proud of having an office girl in the family. Although she tried not to let it show, it hurt Sally deeply that Mum didn't respect the work she did now, even though she was the depot manager. Mum would have liked it if, as manager, Sally had worn a smart jacket and skirt and sat behind a desk filling in forms and telling others what to do, but Sally wasn't like that. It was through choice as well as necessity that she donned dungarees every day and mucked in with whatever needed doing. It was just a pity that Mum didn't see that as something to be proud of in her only daughter.

Sally unbolted the front gates and hauled them open. Various Corporation vans as well as the van from the paper-mill visited the depot regularly to collect salvage and take it on its way. Also, members of the public often came by to hand in their own salvage. Sally was in the process of organising weekly door-to-door collections of household salvage by the Scouts.

A few minutes after eight, the daily salvage sacks arrived by van. The first task of the day was always to sort the sacks' contents, which was a bigger job on Saturday because whoever was on duty was on her own. Moreover, Saturdays could be busy with members of the public dropping in – but it wouldn't be like that today. On the Saturday before Christmas, people would have plenty of other things to do, mainly shopping for whatever they could find that would make this wartime Christmas a better experience.

Last year had also seen a wartime Christmas, though in a lot of ways it had still been like an ordinary peacetime festive season. Yes, the blackout had meant that the shop windows couldn't have lights on so window-shopping was impossible after dark, and the War Budget had raised prices; and of course, for many families, Christmas had been made poignant by the absence of husbands, fathers and grown-up sons.

But there had also been a feeling that it was important to enjoy Christmas and make the best of it. Women's magazines had been full of cheerful advice; and at that point food rationing hadn't yet started – and neither had the air raids.

It was very different now. This time last year Dunkirk hadn't happened; neither had the Battle of Britain. London hadn't suffered night after night of relentless bombing. None of the cities had. And Coventry was still standing.

Sally shook off those thoughts. It was everyone's duty to be determined and optimistic – though, to be honest, a certain amount of optimism at present was derived from the knowledge that, now winter was here, the danger of invasion had receded and wouldn't return until the spring of 1941.

Some Scouts arrived, carrying boxes and sacks of salvage they had collected.

'Let's get it weighed, shall we?' Sally said with a smile.

She led the boys to the weighing machine in the corner so they could weigh their booty. A sense of competition had quickly developed between the various Scout troops, and Sally was more than happy to foster it. When the door-to-door collections were up and running, there would be no stopping them.

Shortly after midday, a familiar figure walked in through the open gates.

'Deborah!' Sally exclaimed, surprised and pleased.

Aside from a difficult time earlier this year, she and Deborah had been close friends all their lives, and had even worked together until Sally had come to the salvage depot. Deborah and her family, the Grants, lived along the road from Sally's family, the Whites, in Withington, three or four miles from Chorlton, where Sally now lived and worked.

Sally couldn't have been more delighted to see her chum. She had always admired Deborah's looks, her bright-blue eyes, her attractive smile and her brown hair that was so dark it was almost black. Deborah wore a wool overcoat with a buckle-belt and a felt hat with a rosette on the side, and she looked very smart. Over one shoulder was her gas-mask box on its length of string.

'What brings you here?' Sally asked.

'I can always go away again if you prefer,' Deborah answered with a cheeky smile.

'Don't be daft. It's lovely to see you. I didn't know you were coming, that's all.'

'I worked overtime this week, so Mr Morland let me finish early today instead of staying until one,' Deborah explained. 'Instead of going straight home, I thought I'd come here and see if you're free to have your dinner break.'

'Now is as good a time as any,' said Sally. 'We can sit in the office. That way I can see into the yard. If anyone comes, I'll have to see to them. It's only me on duty today.'

Deborah pulled a face. 'The Saturday before Christmas – poor you. Drew the short straw, did you?'

'We take turns.' Sally led the way indoors. 'I started the fire about twenty minutes ago, so it should have lifted the chill from the air by now. It's that door along there. Make yourself at home while I pop the kettle on.'

Soon the girls were settled in Sally's office. Sally had provided plates and they opened their packets of sandwiches.

'Fish paste,' said Deborah.

'Grated cheese and chutney,' said Sally.

Without another word, each girl picked up one of her sandwiches and leaned over to place it on the other's plate. It was something they had started doing years ago.

'I wanted to be sure I saw you before Christmas,' said Deborah.

'What's new in the world of food rationing?' Sally asked.

'The meat ration is being reduced in the new year,' Deborah told her. 'And they're going to introduce a new kind of loaf containing more whole grain, which will be sold at a fixed price. What's new in the world of salvage?'

'We've just received new instructions about alcohol bottles,' said Sally. 'They have to be kept separate so they can be returned to the distilleries and breweries. Apparently there's a trade in illegal alcohol and this rule will help to combat that.'

'I can imagine you keeping on top of all the rules and regs,' Deborah said with a smile. 'Oh, it's good to see you again.'

'I'm going over to Mum and Dad's this evening,' Sally answered. 'I was intending to pop round.'

Deborah shook her head. 'I won't be there. I'm going out with some of the girls from work. We're going dancing at the Ritz.'

'I love it there,' said Sally, picturing the ballroom's famous revolving stage. The Ritz had two dance bands and, when it was time for one to stop performing, the stage slowly revolved while they played a number to reveal the other band, who would be playing the same music, so the dancing never had to pause.

'Come with us,' Deborah said at once.

Sally shook her head. 'I can't let Mum and Dad down. I hope you have a good time. Remember me to everyone.'

'I will,' Deborah promised.

Sally hesitated before asking, 'Are you... having visitors for Christmas?'

'You mean Rod and Dulcie?' Deborah asked bluntly.

'Well – yes,' Sally admitted.

She was curious about Dulcie, although she had no wish whatsoever to see Rod Grant ever again. Even the thought of him sent a shiver through her. Rod was Deborah's older brother, and he used to be Sally's boyfriend. He had been dead keen on her but she had realised she'd made a mistake; but with both families, not to mention all the neighbours, warmly approving of the relationship, it had become increasingly diffi-cult for Sally to extricate herself, especially after Rod had been sent off to Barrow-in-Furness to work in shipbuilding, which had made everyone at home regard him as a war hero. Then Sally had met Andrew, and in the same week Rod had proposed. When Sally had turned him down, nobody had believed she would have done this anyway and that it was nothing to do with having met Andrew. That had only added to the ill-feeling of the time.

Then, to everybody's astonishment, when Rod had returned to Barrow, he had met and married Dulcie in double-quick time. His family had yet to meet her.

'They're stopping in Barrow for Christmas,' said Deborah. 'Dad says it's probably for the best. We can't wait to meet Dulcie, but Dad reckons the neighbours need more time to forget the way Rod hammered on your mum's door and yelled in your face the last time he was here.'

Sally tried to make light of it. 'I'm sure that would be forgotten in an instant if he brought Dulcie here. Everyone must be dying to meet her.'

'It's strange having a sister-in-law I've never seen. I hope I like her when we do meet.'

'Have you sent her a Christmas present?' Sally asked.

Deborah nodded. 'A lipstick for her and cigarettes for Rod.'

Sally was impressed. 'Lipstick is a nice present. Everyone says make-up is going to end up being scarce.'

'Along with just about everything else,' Deborah replied gloomily. Then she smiled. 'My mum crocheted a cardy for Dulcie, so I hope she likes it. What's your mother-in-law getting you?'

'I don't know,' said Sally. 'I knitted a tea cosy for her – but now she doesn't own a teapot any more.'

Deborah reached across the desk and touched her hand, her pretty face softening in concern. 'I'm so sorry you were bombed out. So are Mum and Dad.'

'Thanks. I never thought it would happen to us.'

'Everyone thinks that.'

'Let's not be glum,' said Sally. 'Tell me something cheerful. Have you put your tree up yet?'

'We're doing it this afternoon,' said Deborah.

Sally arched an eyebrow. 'Complete with electric fairy lights?'

'Oh aye,' Deborah said airily. 'You know us. We're proper posh in our house.'

'My mum still has candles on her tree,' said Sally, 'or she will if she can find any this year. I bet they're in short supply—'

'—along with everything else,' the two girls finished in chorus.

They grinned at one another, then Sally sighed.

'I'm glad we're friends again,' she said.

'So am I,' said Deborah. 'It was horrid when we fell out. We'll never let that happen again, will we? Friends for always. That's us.'

'Friends for always,' Sally agreed.

CHAPTER FOUR

Betty helped Lorna to unpack. Lorna's room was called Vesta Victoria.

'I love being in Vesta Victoria,' Lorna declared. 'I remember my grandma singing "Waiting at the Church" and "Daddy Wouldn't Buy Me a Bow Wow" when I was small.'

Betty laughed. 'I thought you were going to say you love it because of the gorgeous satiny patchwork bedspread or the wallpaper with the roses.'

She handed Lorna's clothes to her to put away in the chest of drawers or the wardrobe. Lorna had some beautiful things. Well, that made sense now that Betty knew who she really was. She had come to Manchester as plain Lorna Sadler and had never said much about her background, but it had turned out that she was Miss West-Sadler, the society girl who had brought a breach-of-promise case against the man, an heir to a baronetcy no less, who had changed his mind and broken off their engagement. To say the judge had been critical would be putting it mildly. He had condemned Miss West-Sadler for indulging in a breach-of-promise case when the rest of the population was

busy with the war effort, and the newspapers had had a
field day.

Betty had been one of those who had lapped up the story.
The papers had been even more critical of Miss West-Sadler
than the judge had been and Betty had agreed with every word
– until Samuel had pointed out that journalists wrote stories in
such a way as to make their readers form a certain opinion. That
had given Betty something to think about.

When they'd finished unpacking, Lorna thanked Betty for
her help. Lorna was about to leave the room when Betty put out
a hand to stop her.

'Before we go down, I just wanted to say...' Betty's voice
trailed off.

'Don't tell me,' said Lorna. 'You've seen the article
about me.'

'You only gave that interview to help me, and I'm so
grateful.'

Lorna shrugged as if it didn't matter, but Betty could tell
from the glint in her eyes that it did.

'Geoff Baldwin wrote a *sympathetic* piece about me,' Lorna
said, emphasising the creepy reporter's own choice of word,
'which is a lot more than those other journalists did at the time
of the court case.' She turned fully to Betty, taking both her
hands. 'I don't regret doing it even for a moment, so you're never
to think that. Now let's go downstairs. I expect Mrs Beaumont
will want to grill me about it.'

Their landlady did indeed, though, when Lorna told her
frankly why she had given the interview, Mrs Beaumont let the
subject drop.

Betty felt a surge of admiration for Lorna. She was handling
this with such generosity and grace.

'Would you two help me get out the Christmas decorations?' Mrs Beaumont asked. 'I thought we could put up the

streamers today and then we can decorate the tree tomorrow afternoon when everyone is at home.'

'I'm afraid I shan't be here for that,' said Lorna. 'My mother is coming down to Manchester for a quick visit and I'll be with her.'

'You're welcome to bring her here,' offered Mrs Beaumont.

'Thanks, but there wouldn't be time. She wants to go home on the teatime train.' Lorna smiled. 'But I'm here now and more than happy to pin up streamers.'

'Help me fetch the boxes,' said Mrs Beaumont, 'and we can get to work.'

The decorations were stored in two stout cardboard boxes with lids. The box Betty opened was full of decorations for the tree. She would have loved to look through its contents, but that would have to wait for tomorrow.

The other box contained long paper streamers, faded with age, as well as tinsel and layers of shiny paper fastened together that opened up into 'lanterns'.

'I like to have streamers in the sitting room and the dining room,' said Mrs Beaumont. 'In the sitting room I have one from each corner to the ceiling rose in the middle, and in the dining room I like them hung in loops around the walls.'

'Not from the corners to the middle?' asked Betty.

'Not since the year one fell down and landed in the soup.'

That made the girls laugh, and they set about decorating with a will. Lorna was taller, so she stood on the chair and reached up to pin the end of each streamer to the picture rail, while Betty gently shook out each lantern.

'That'll be nice for the others to come home to,' Mrs Beaumont observed when they had finished.

'I know Sally's at the depot,' said Lorna. 'Where are Andrew and his mother?'

'Andrew is at the youth club he helps run,' said Betty, 'and Mrs Henshaw is on WVS duty.'

Mrs Beaumont was right about the Henshaws all being delighted by the decorations when they returned home.

'It all looks lovely,' Sally said appreciatively.

'It'll look lovelier tomorrow,' Betty answered happily. 'We'll be doing the tree.'

'I must get the meal started,' said Mrs Beaumont. 'Betty's going out with Samuel this evening and she doesn't want to be late, do you, dear?' she added with a twinkle.

'Let me help in the kitchen,' said Mrs Henshaw.

'Thank you for offering but there's no need,' Mrs Beaumont replied. 'You've been out all day at the WVS. That's your job and mine is running the house.'

For the Henshaws, who had all had a sandwich at midday, Mrs Beaumont produced macaroni cheese followed by lemon tart. For Betty and Lorna, who'd had that earlier, she made sardines on toast, with mince pies afterwards.

'Though I'm not sure they really count as mince pies,' said Mrs Beaumont. 'There's more prune in them than dried fruit.'

'Nice tangy taste,' Lorna commented.

'That'll be the marmalade I put in.'

Afterwards Betty ran upstairs to get ready. She wanted to look her best for Samuel. For a moment she wished she had beautiful tailor-made clothes like Lorna, but then she shook off the thought. Samuel liked her just as she was, an ordinary girl with nothing special about her.

She put on her tweed skirt and white blouse with the Peter Pan collar, and took out her cherry-red jumper to wear on top. Then she changed her mind. That jumper was her favourite because Mum had knitted it for her and she loved wearing it, but it was high time Samuel saw her in something different. Instead she wore a dark-green sweater with a large floppy collar and decorative buttons on one shoulder.

The doorbell rang and Betty hurried downstairs as Andrew let Samuel in, first switching off the hall light so as not to break the blackout by letting light spill outside. The three of them went into the sitting room. Unlike Eddie, who had always spirited Betty away toot sweet, Samuel liked getting to know the folk she lived with. Seeing how polite and affable he was in company made Betty all the more eager for him to meet Dad.

After a few minutes Samuel stood up, smiling at Betty, who rose also. He helped her on with her coat and she wound her scarf round her neck and tucked it inside the front of her coat before picking up her beloved asymmetrical hat. She thought of it as her film-star hat because it was so stylish.

Soon they were walking to one of the local cinemas to see *Law and Disorder*, a comedy thriller starring Alastair Sim and also Barry K. Barnes, whom Betty had loved in *The Return of the Scarlet Pimpernel*.

Samuel gave Betty a shy but loving kiss, then he offered her his arm and she tucked her hand trustingly in the crook of his elbow, proud and happy to be out with him in public. Not that anyone would be able to see them – not unless someone bumped into them. Even after all this time, it still surprised Betty how dense the blackout was. It was easy to understand how people sometimes got lost in places they had known for years.

'I s-saw the piece about Lorna in the newspaper,' said Samuel.

'I hate to think of her having to give that interview,' said Betty.

'At least this time the article was in her f-favour. Not like all those others after the c-court case.'

'I think she just wants to put it behind her,' said Betty. 'She wasn't keen to talk about it earlier on.'

'That's understandable,' said Samuel. On a brighter note he added, 'The d-decorations in Star House look very attractive.'

'Lorna and I put them up. It's good to have some Christmas cheer after all the weeks of air raids.'

'And so s-say all of us,' Samuel agreed.

'Was the shop busy today?' Betty asked him.

'It's s-safe to say I sold a fair number of C-Christmas presents, both new and s-second-hand. I have two regular c-customers called Mr and Mrs Linton. This morning Mrs Linton bought *The Power and the Glory* by Graham Greene for Mr Linton and this afternoon he w-wanted to buy the same book for her.'

'What did you do?' Betty asked.

'I had to persuade him to choose s-something else w-without being obvious about it.'

'It'll give them a chuckle on Christmas Day,' said Betty. 'We're decorating the tree tomorrow afternoon. Are you free? I'm sure Mrs Beaumont wouldn't mind you coming along to help.'

Samuel squeezed her arm. 'Just try to k-keep me away.'

On Saturday evening Sally and Andrew caught the bus to Withington to see Sally's parents.

'This time last year,' Andrew said as they walked hand in hand through the dark streets from the bus stop to the Whites' house, 'I had no idea it was my final Christmas as a bachelor.'

'Are you glad you married me?' Sally teased.

'I've never been happier,' was the serious answer. 'I've felt different since I met you – felt different about myself, I mean. I feel... complete.'

Stopping, Sally turned to him. She slipped her arms round him, ignoring the gas-mask box that had slid off her shoulder and down her arm. She lifted her face and he bent his to kiss her right there in the street, but, before his lips had done more than brush her mouth, they both stiffened as the melancholy moan of the air-raid siren lifted into the darkness.

Andrew seized Sally's hand and they raced along the pavement. As they turned the corner, they ran slap-bang into a man. The three of them bumped apart from one another, staggering backwards as they quickly regained their footing.

The man was an ARP warden, as his helmet and armband proclaimed.

'That way to the nearest public shelter,' he said, pointing.

'We're going to my parents' house,' Sally told him. 'We'll be there in two ticks.'

'Go straight there,' he ordered them before hurrying on his way.

When they arrived at Mum and Dad's house, Dad already had the front door open and was placing the buckets of sand and water outside by the step.

'Thank heaven you're here.' He sounded calm and cheerful, but Sally heard an edge in his voice that betrayed how anxious he had been as to their whereabouts. 'I'd never have got your mother into the Anderson if you hadn't turned up.'

'What needs doing?' Andrew asked. 'Shall I turn off the water? Where's the stopcock?'

Between them they finished getting the house ready, then headed for the Anderson. Dad had painted large white dots round the entrance to help them find it in the pitch dark. Arriving at the steep step down into it, Mum, carrying blankets and cushions, turned to hand them to Sally before, carefully holding the sides, she descended inside. Then she reached up so Sally could pass the bulky bundle to her before she too entered the shelter.

Once the door was shut and the hurricane lamps were aglow, Dad looked at Sally and Andrew.

'Good evening, you two,' he said in a pretend-formal voice. 'And how are you this fine evening? Thank you for coming.'

Sally hugged him, breathing in the sweet aroma of pipe tobacco that clung to his clothes and his skin. Then she wriggled round in the cramped conditions to give Mum a kiss.

Her parents were deeply precious to her. Mum with her salt-and-pepper hair and Dad with hardly any hair at all were considerably older than her contemporaries' parents; old enough, in fact, to be the parents of Deborah's mother. Sally was their only child and they thought the world of her. She had always felt special and much loved. It had taken two things in recent months to make her appreciate how important their approval was to her, because both of those events had placed that approval in jeopardy.

The first had been when she had turned down Rod's proposal and everyone had jumped to the conclusion that she had been two-timing him with Andrew. Mum had been desperately upset and had criticised Sally just when she was most in need of support. Dad had been kinder but even he had entertained doubts about her. Eventually Rod had shown his true colours and Mum and Dad, together with all the neighbours, had realised Sally had had a lucky escape.

The second event had been when Sally had been sent to work at the salvage depot, swapping her smart office clothes for dungarees. It sometimes felt as if Mum would never forgive her for that. Not even her being promoted to the post of depot manager had made Mum come round.

'This isn't what I wanted for this evening,' Mum said as they settled themselves in the small space.

'Nobody ever wants an air raid,' Dad said mildly, taking his pipe and tobacco pouch from his pocket.

'You know what I mean,' Mum replied. 'I wanted us all to have a nice evening together.'

'We still can,' said Sally. 'It's just that it won't be as comfortable.'

'Who knows?' said Andrew. 'Jerry might go home early.'

They played a few hands of whist, then Mum poured tea from the Thermos and they sat back for a chat.

'We saw your friend in the paper,' said Mum.

Sally's heart sank. Was Mum going to criticise Lorna? It took her a moment to realise that Mum didn't know enough about Lorna to associate her with the Miss West-Sadler who'd been in the papers after the breach-of-promise case.

'You mean Betty,' Sally said, relieved.

'Of course I mean Betty. Who else do you know who's been in the paper recently?'

'I'm glad you saw the article,' said Sally. 'It was good, wasn't it? Did you like the photograph of her sitting on top of the pile of tyres?'

'She has a very pretty smile,' said Dad. 'It looked like she was laughing.'

'She was,' Sally answered. 'She wasn't keen on climbing onto the tyres at first, but then it all turned into rather a lark.'

'The report was full of praise for her coming up with the plan to fool those looters,' said Mum.

'Looting is a shocking business,' said Dad. 'Stealing things from damaged houses.' He shook his head.

'Betty's a sweet girl,' said Mum, 'but I wouldn't have expected her to be that clever.'

Andrew gave Sally's hand a secret squeeze. 'She didn't come up with the idea completely on her own. All three girls pitched in.'

'Then why didn't it say so in the paper?' Mum demanded. 'I have to say that you haven't come out of this very well, Sally, when the girl who works under you turns out to be the one with the brains.'

'Now then,' said Dad in the equable voice he used when a spot of peacemaking was called for. 'Let's just be happy for Betty for getting her picture in the newspaper. That's something special, that is.'

'If all three of them came up with the plan,' Mum muttered, 'then they should all have been in the paper.'

'We wouldn't all have fitted on top of the tyres,' Sally said, trying to make light of it.

Dad rewarded her with a dutiful chuckle while Andrew firmly changed the subject, leading Mum to talk about her local WVS carol concert, at which home-made toys were going to be distributed.

'The Craft Council provided patterns for making soft toys out of oddments of material, so we've all been kept busy,' said Mum. 'And, of course, Andrew's wooden toys have been a godsend.' She smiled at her son-in-law.

Andrew had filled two cartons with small toys such as yo-yos, building bricks and sets of skittles. One carton had been sent to Mrs Henshaw's WVS group in Chorlton and the other had been brought here to Withington. Sally drew in a deep breath of pure pride. She was the luckiest wife in the world.

CHAPTER FIVE

On Sunday afternoon the residents of Star House, except for Lorna, who had headed into town to meet up with her mother, got together to decorate the tree. Sally had just taken the lid off the box of decorations when the doorbell sounded. Betty immediately jumped to her feet, her creamy skin radiant and her blue eyes shining.

'That'll be Samuel,' she said and hurried to let him in.

The others smiled to see her so happy, Sally in particular. She loved to see her friend so obviously in love with Samuel, who was the caring man she deserved.

Samuel greeted everyone, and said to Mrs Beaumont, 'I hope it's all right f-for me to be here.'

'Of course it is,' the landlady replied. 'You're very welcome. Let's get started. I've had a go at making a Christmas drink, using fruit cordial with cloves and spices. It just needs warming through.'

'It sounds delicious,' said Mrs Henshaw. 'You must give me the recipe. Shall I heat it up for you?'

'You stay here and watch the youngsters prepare the tree,' said Mrs Beaumont. 'It's an artificial one, I'm afraid.'

'No need to apologise,' said Andrew. 'I'm sure it'll look splendid.'

'I always used to have a real tree,' said Mrs Beaumont. 'I took pride in making Star House a home from home for my theatrical guests at all times, but it's so important at Christmastime. Then last Christmas I said to myself, "It's going to be hard getting a good tree if the war drags on," so I invested in an artificial one.'

She disappeared to sort out the festive drink while Andrew and Samuel set up the tree, ensuring it was stable. It was made of tinsel-covered wire. Then there was a big discussion as to whether the candles should go on first or last. Betty's mum had always clipped them on first, whereas Mrs Henshaw was accustomed to putting hers on last.

'It's a bit of a moot point,' said Andrew, 'since the candles in the box are little more than stubs and there aren't tree-candles in the shops.'

Samuel lifted his chin and sniffed. 'S-something smells good.'

A spicy-sweet aroma wafted into the sitting room. Mrs Beaumont looked round the door.

'Could I have a strong young man to carry the punch bowl for me?'

Andrew obliged, returning a minute later carefully bearing a large bowl of cut crystal containing a gently steaming dark-red liquid. Mrs Beaumont followed with a tray of matching glasses with handles, and a plate of mince pies.

'This is lovely, Mrs Beaumont,' said Betty. 'You're spoiling us.'

'I like to do things properly,' said the landlady. 'My theatrical ladies and gentlemen could always rely on me for those extra little details that made all the difference.'

'Shall we take the decorations out of the box and put them on the table?' asked Betty. 'Then we can see what we've got.'

While she and Samuel did this, Mrs Beaumont picked up a few decorations one at a time to tell the story behind them. The once-gleaming, now-dulled baubles that had originally hung from the late Mr Beaumont's parents' tree. The string of red beads she had frittered a disgraceful sum on for her first married Christmas. The box of four stars that had been presented to her by a troupe of chorus girls who had crammed in here one Christmas after their original digs had suffered burst pipes.

Sally listened, entranced. Then she noticed her mother-in-law looking down in the mouth. Sally unobtrusively took her hand.

'You must be remembering your own decorations.'

Mrs Henshaw nodded. 'It's a wretched business being bombed out. I know that what matters is that we're all alive, and our possessions are nothing compared to that, but sometimes I feel the loss of a particular thing.'

'You used to have tree decorations with stories behind them,' Sally said softly.

Mrs Henshaw smiled, her blue eyes misty with memories, her rather severe features softening. 'I too had baubles from my parents-in-laws' tree; and I had some balls that my husband made and polished to a high shine. Andrew made me some decorations as well.'

'He'll make more for us,' Sally whispered, having to push her voice past a lump in her throat, 'when we get another home of our own.'

Mrs Henshaw squeezed her hand. 'Yes, he will. Now we must concentrate on making the most of this afternoon.' All at once she was her usual brisk self. Leaning towards Sally, she murmured in her ear, 'Thank you, dear, for understanding.'

They took their time decorating the tree. Mrs Beaumont and Mrs Henshaw left the job to the young couples. Everyone chatted and sipped their drinks.

'Don't forget the mince pies,' said Mrs Beaumont.

'You must try one,' Betty encouraged Samuel. 'They're delicious.'

When the tree was finished, they all stood back to admire it.

'Since the candles have so little wax left,' said Mrs Beaumont, 'we'll save them for Christmas Day.'

'The tree looks beautiful,' said Mrs Henshaw. 'Just what we need in these difficult days.'

Sally smiled to herself as an idea came to her. She didn't say anything, so as not to spoil the surprise, but what Mrs Beaumont had said earlier about receiving decorations as a gift from the chorus girls made Sally want to present her with a decoration from herself, Lorna and Betty, her three wartime salvage workers.

With crystal glasses of tasty, fragrant cordial in their hands, the group gathered around the upright piano and Mrs Beaumont played carols as the others sang. Sally was impressed to hear that Betty had a pretty voice. The others wanted her to sing 'In the Bleak Midwinter' as a solo. Betty demurred at first, but when Samuel added his words of encouragement she agreed. Her voice was shaky with nerves to start with but then her confidence grew. Sally's eyes prickled with tears of emotion.

They all clapped warmly when Betty finished. She blushed, obviously delighted.

'Now we need something stirring,' Mrs Beaumont declared. 'How about "Angels We Have Heard on High"? And make those glorias as rousing as you can.'

Lorna made her way across the concourse at Manchester Victoria station. A ticket collector with a peaked cap and polished buttons gleaming on his jacket directed her to the correct platform. She purchased a platform ticket and walked through the barrier to wait for her mother's train to arrive. Presently it pulled in, slowing as it cruised alongside the platform. Even before it came to a halt, doors were flung open and passengers jumped out, hurrying to be the first to surrender their tickets and enter the concourse.

Mummy descended gracefully from a coach halfway along, looking elegant in a wool overcoat with a wide fur collar, gauntlet gloves and a felt hat trimmed with a pleated bow. Along with her handbag and her gas-mask box, she carried a smart leather valise, which must have last night's overnight things in it.

Lorna went forward eagerly to greet her. Mummy presented her cheek for a kiss. Lorna took the valise and they walked arm in arm along the platform.

They thanked the ticket collector as they surrendered their tickets, then walked onto the busy concourse.

'Where is the taxi rank?' Mummy asked.

'This way.'

Outside, they had to wait for no more than a minute.

'Where to?' asked the driver.

'A smart hotel with a nice restaurant,' said Mummy. 'And not too far away. I have to catch the six o'clock train. Do you know somewhere suitable?'

'The Claremont, madam,' the driver replied.

'You could have asked me for a suggestion, you know,' Lorna said mildly as they settled themselves in the rear of the vehicle and the motor pulled away from the pavement. 'I do live here now.'

Mummy glanced her way, raising a single eyebrow. 'And you know the best hotels, do you? The whole point of sending you here was for you to live quietly, not to go out gallivanting.'

'I haven't,' Lorna protested. 'But I've heard about the Claremont and the Midland and how swish they both are.'

'The driver is taking us to the Claremont, so what's the difference?'

'As a matter of fact, the WVS branch I'm with is busy organising a fundraising dance that will be held at the Claremont in the new year.'

'You'll be happy with the driver's choice, then, won't you?' Mummy said crisply.

Lorna frowned. It wasn't like Mummy to be tart. There was something more going on here.

The taxi drew up outside the hotel. Mummy paid the driver and the two of them went up the front steps. A top-hatted doorman stood at the doors to admit them. They entered the pillared foyer, with its gleaming woodwork, handsome armchairs and sofas. In the far wall were some alcoves, each with a pair of chairs and a table.

Mummy asked for the dining room and they were shown up a curving flight of stairs to a large first-floor room built around a gallery that looked down over the ballroom.

'It must be splendid to sit up here and watch the dancing below,' said Mummy. 'I can see why your WVS group chose this as your venue.'

An elderly waiter brought menus. It was wartime etiquette to choose two courses instead of three.

'Hors d'oeuvre or pudding?' Mummy asked.

'I rather like the sound of the parsnip soup,' said Lorna, 'especially on a chilly day like today.'

They both plumped for the soup.

'Then I'd like the beef hash,' said Mummy.

'And I'd like the vegetable casserole, please,' said Lorna.

After the waiter had withdrawn, Mummy leaned forward. Lorna knew what was coming – or she thought she did, so why did Mummy's eyes narrow like that?

'How could you, Lorna?' she demanded, her voice low but fierce. 'How could you do this to Daddy and me?'

'I know it must have come as a shock that I chose to stay in

Manchester instead of letting you send me to the safety of the West Country—'

'I don't mean that!' Mummy exclaimed. 'That has faded into insignificance compared to your latest escapade. Whatever possessed you to talk to the newspapers?'

Lorna's heart beat hard. 'I didn't – not to newspapers plural. It was just one journalist.'

'Oh, well, that's all right, then.' Mummy's voice dripped with sarcasm. 'What was I thinking to imagine this actually mattered?'

'Mummy, please—'

'Mummy, please, what? Just when everything had settled down after the court case, you've stirred it up again. I expect we'll have reporters crawling all over Lancaster, hoping to pounce on your father or me.'

Lorna lifted her chin. 'Daddy will see them off.'

This was so palpably true that Mummy couldn't deny it, but it didn't stop her onslaught. 'Why, Lorna? Just tell me why.' Her tone suggested that Lorna's explanation wouldn't be worth tuppence.

'I did it to help a friend.' Lorna took a moment to draw her thoughts together. 'Betty – one of the girls at the salvage depot – met a man who turned out to be a bad lot, though she had no notion, of course. He was a thief who looted bombed-out houses and he needed somewhere to store the stolen goods. He persuaded Betty to give him access to a room in the depot.' Cutting corners in the story, Lorna went on, 'When he was arrested, he put the blame on her, claiming it was all her idea, but the truth came out in the end and her good name was restored.'

'What has that to do with your newspaper interview?' Mummy's cool tone showed that she was a long way from understanding, let alone forgiving.

'The matter was reported by the *Manchester Evening News*

– not the business about Betty being the thief's girlfriend, just the fact that a villain had used the depot. Sally – she's the manager – let Betty take the credit for unmasking the thief.'

'Why?'

'Because they're friends. Because she wanted to give Betty a bit of a lift after she'd been treated so badly by the man she trusted.'

'That was a generous thing to do,' Mummy conceded.

'The next day another reporter came along. He must have had a pal in the police station because he knew the real story – that Betty had unwittingly been involved in hiding the stolen goods. You know what these people are like, Mummy, when they get the scent of blood in their nostrils. He wanted to write a piece about Betty's doomed romance with the villain. He said that if she would answer his questions, he'd write a piece that was sympathetic to her, but if she didn't, he'd write it anyway, only it wouldn't be sympathetic.'

'That was horrible for her, of course,' said Mummy, 'but I still don't see—'

'I made a deal with him,' said Lorna. 'I told him my real name and offered him an exclusive interview on the condition that he forgot he'd ever heard of Betty.'

Mummy released a breathy sound of disbelief. 'What about yourself – your reputation? After weeks of letting the gossip die away, you've brought it centre-stage again. Honestly, Lorna, I despair of you, I really do.'

'I did it to help a friend in a fix,' Lorna said in a steady voice.

'Well, I hope you think it was worthwhile.'

'I know what's it's like to be treated badly by the press,' said Lorna. 'I didn't want Betty to have to face that.'

'You're too soft for your own good.' Mummy sounded tetchy, but her features looked gentler.

'And you have to admit that Mr Baldwin's article about me was sympathetic.'

'I suppose so.'

'Actually,' said Lorna, 'it was a bit *too* sympathetic. He laid it on with a trowel, so to speak. I didn't say so to Betty, because I didn't want her to feel bad about it, but I'm not happy with some of what Mr Baldwin wrote.'

'If he has misrepresented you—' Mummy began.

'Please don't say we ought to object,' Lorna protested quickly. 'That would only string the story out for longer. I swear I didn't say a word against George. Mr Baldwin tried to get me to, but I wouldn't. But in the article, he has made George look like a cad for ditching me. And Mr Baldwin asked about the talk that went around London – you know, the gossip saying that you and Daddy took me there purely to bag a title. I said it was just a nasty rumour that had been deeply hurtful to us.'

She looked at her mother. It was no secret that her parents had taken her to London in the hope of finding a husband. Plenty of girls were brought to London for that reason. But Lorna had gradually come to wonder whether the gossip had been true that her parents, especially her father, had been set all along on her marrying into a titled family. Lorna had grown up a lot in recent weeks. Living away from home had provided her with her first taste of independence.

'There's one good thing,' said Mummy. 'The article didn't say you're living in Manchester.'

'I told Mr Baldwin he mustn't mention that, so I've hung on to that bit of privacy, at any rate,' said Lorna. 'And at least he didn't sell his piece to *The Times* or the *Daily Telegraph*, so let's hope that means George will never see it.'

CHAPTER SIX

Lorna saw her mother off on the six o'clock train from Victoria. A Salvation Army band was playing carols on the concourse and she stopped to listen, enjoying the way the notes rose and expanded in the vast space, creating an even richer sound. She ought to head for home but, at the end of each carol, she stayed for just one more... and just one more.

Finally, though, having dropped some coins in the collection box, she went on her way. Glancing up at the clock hanging from the gantry, she realised she had been listening to the music for nearly twenty minutes. Well, that just showed how beautiful it had been. She loved carols.

Outside, the blackout was in full force. She stood for a moment getting her bearings. She knew that she could get a bus from Piccadilly, but she wasn't familiar with the middle of Manchester. It wasn't long before she had to stop a passer-by to ask for directions.

'This is Albert Square, love,' the man answered cheerfully. 'The Town Hall's over yonder.' He waved a hand towards the deeper darkness. 'The back of Central Library is next to it. You need to walk around to the front of the library and carry on up the road.'

Thanking him, Lorna went on her way, walking briskly, which was a mistake because she walked straight into the huge plinth on which stood the statue of Prince Albert. Torn between feeling foolish and laughing at herself, she danced backwards a couple of steps. Then came the sound of the siren. Panic streaked through her, followed by a chilly sense of calm. There must be plenty of public shelters.

A massive explosion all but wrenched her lungs inside out as the power of the blast flattened her against the plinth, pinning her there, all but melding her with the stone. Then she was dropped to the ground in a stunned, gasping heap. There was light all around her. Looking over her shoulder, she beheld a great column of fire leaping up into the black sky.

Another explosion crammed her ears and sent her body jerking like a puppet as a wave of energy lifted the ground in a series of powerful ripples. Lorna curled up into a ball, protecting her head with her arms, until the quakes subsided.

Now the evening was twice as bright. A second column of flames stretched upwards on the diagonally opposite corner of Albert Square. Lorna's mouth went dry. She knew what those two fires meant: they were lighting the way for the Luftwaffe.

Lorna was astounded by how quickly it happened. She knew that the quiet of early evening, the carol-singing, the *Oh no, he isn't, Oh yes, he is* of the pantomime, the present-wrapping, the careful removal of mince pies from the oven – all the Christmas preparations had been swept aside by an air raid of tremendous proportions.

Bombs dropped in clusters, each of a dozen or more. Every explosion made a roof cave in, or brought down a wall or an entire building. The evening was filled with noise, smoke and heat.

Already there were fire crews and rescuers on the scene. Lorna ditched the thought of seeking a public shelter. If there was anything she could do, she was darned well going to do it.

'This way! Over here!'

The voice couldn't possibly be addressing her, but she followed it anyway and joined a group of men and women running towards a building on one side of Albert Square. The men were in the tin hats and armbands of the ARP and there were two women in the familiar uniform of the WVS. The women pushed a barrow heaped with blankets that would be used to keep people warm when they were in shock. They would also be used to cover the dead until their bodies could be removed.

The women halted for long enough to thrust a pile of blankets into Lorna's arms.

'Take these and go with those men. A rescue is needed. We've got to take the rest to the Town Hall. That's where all the work is coordinated.'

Lorna hurried on her way. Would she make it to the far side of the square before the next bomb exploded? Or was she running straight to a place that was about to be blown to kingdom come?

Before joining the group of men, she stopped and placed the blankets on a low wall for a minute while she quickly unfastened her coat, took one arm out and pushed the strap of her bag up onto her shoulder before shoving her arm back inside her sleeve. Then she grabbed the blankets and, with her gas-mask box banging against her, caught up with the ARP wardens.

They were grouped around the entrance to a tall, stone-clad building. Lorna moved in close, anxious to do her bit. The smell of smoke made her pull a face. If her arms hadn't been full of blankets, she would have wafted a hand in front of her nose and mouth. Not that it would have done much good, given the intensity of the stench.

An ARP man was speaking loudly, providing information and issuing orders.

'My name is Fairchild and I'm in charge of this rescue. The building might look all right from the outside but don't let that fool you. A high explosive went straight through the roof and the interior has collapsed. There are folk in there. They were taking shelter in the cellar. Our job is to dig a way through to them and fetch them out.'

'Do we need the fire brigade?' called one of the men.

'Some fire wardens have doused the flames but that doesn't mean the fires can't start up again,' said Mr Fairchild.

'So we need to be quick,' said another voice.

'Yes, we do,' agreed Mr Fairchild, 'but the most important thing is safety. We're no use to anybody if we make a hash of things.'

He handed out jobs – to the men.

'What about me?' Lorna asked.

'We'll need you and your blankets when we start bringing people out.'

Really? Did they expect her to stand here and wait patiently? Rebellion leapt up inside her, but she quelled it. She'd been given her orders and it was her duty to follow them.

A few minutes later, though, she was called upon to do more.

Mr Fairchild, his face grimy beneath his tin hat, came over to her. 'It's time for you to lend a hand, miss, if you're up for it.'

'I'll do anything,' Lorna offered at once.

'Good. Dump the blankets and put on your gas-mask. You don't want to be overcome by the smoke. We've nearly got through to the cellar, but we need someone slim to squeeze through a gap and unlock the door to the cellar belonging to the building next door. There are people trapped in there too, including children. While you make your way to the door, we'll unblock the way behind you so everyone can get out. Can you manage that?'

Lorna tugged her gas-mask out of its box. Her hat had vanished at some point. With her thumbs inside the gas-mask straps, she held her breath, thrust her chin into the mask and pulled the straps over her head.

Torch in hand, she entered the building, feeling her way through air thick with a mixture of smoke and plaster dust. Taking care where she put her feet, she carefully descended a staircase covered in debris. There was a handrail on one side but, when she took hold, it shifted position dramatically and she nearly came a cropper.

She'd been instructed to walk straight ahead once she reached the foot of the steps. The floor was inches deep in pieces of plaster and wood and she couldn't be certain she was maintaining a straight line. A few final stumbles brought her to the far wall. She found the door and, after a battle with the stiff lock, persuaded the key to turn. She pushed the door, but it wouldn't budge until she threw all her weight behind it.

From the inner darkness a group of people of various ages appeared. They surged towards her, all talking at once. Lorna pointed to her gas-mask to encourage them to put on their own. When they had done so, she led them back to the stairs. Would the rescuers have opened up sufficient space for them all to get out at the top? As they neared the top of the stairs, there was a distant *whump* that Lorna felt rather than heard. The staircase vibrated and then crumbled into pieces and everyone dropped with it to the floor, landing in a messy heap of limbs and stair-treads, not to mention a thick cloud of filthy dust.

Winded, Lorna couldn't move for a moment. Then she forced herself up, ignoring how wobbly she felt as she shoved pieces of timber aside and helped others to their feet. Oh, the temptation to wrench off the gas-mask so she could speak clearly! But goodness only knew what she would breathe in if she did.

Through her mask she dimly heard the wails of a young child, but nobody seemed to be badly injured, though no doubt they would all be discovering scrapes and bruises for days to come. After some moments the dust began to settle, and Lorna saw that the entire staircase had gone for a burton. How were they to escape now? A tiny hand slipped into her own and she looked through the large circular eyeholes of her mask at a little girl whose beribboned ringlets were matted with grey dust, as was her raglan-sleeved coat.

If only it was possible to smile through a gas-mask! Lorna crouched to give the child a hug, then straightened up and peered around. The space hadn't seemed all that big before, but now, with no way out, it appeared cavernous. As people stood up and started to move, they stumbled over the debris and had to right themselves.

Lorna experienced a surge of resolve. She'd been sent down here to rescue these people from the next-door cellar and lead them to safety, so now it was her responsibility to get them out of this new peril – but how?

The end of a rope dropped down beside her, making her exclaim in shock, the sound loud and underwatery inside her gas-mask. In order to look up, she had to lean back and tilt her head as far as she could. From out of the darkness came a figure, legs twisted round the rope, descending hand over hand.

Relief hummed through Lorna's veins. The gas-masked man reached the floor, or rather the thick layer of debris. He shifted, testing the steadiness of what lay beneath his feet, then he brought out a large torch from his pocket, aimed it upwards and clicked it on and off a couple of times. After a moment, the end of a second rope landed beside him.

He gestured to the woman nearest him and she went forward, holding her little lad by the hand. The man positioned them side by side. He lifted one of the ropes and doubled up the end to form a loop, skilfully tying a knot to hold it secure. After that he raised his arms to show the mother what to do. When she copied him, he passed the loop over her head and under her arms before taking her hands and showing her where to hold on to the rope. He repeated this with the boy, then gave each rope a tug, and the rescuers up above heaved the two people upwards.

As soon as she grasped the plan, Lorna started moving about, trying not to stumble, getting the other dozen or so people lined up ready. When the fourth pair were being hauled up, everything shook – floor, debris, walls, the air itself. Lorna flung out her arms in an effort to keep her balance. The two on the ropes dropped a yard or more. Lorna cried out in shock, hearing similar exclamations around her, muffled inside gas-masks.

The two people dangled for a few moments, limbs swinging, then the rescuers started pulling them up again. Lorna watched as they vanished into the darkness, then she took two youngsters by the shoulders and propelled them carefully forwards to take their turn.

At last there was only herself and the man left. He was coated so thickly in dirt that his own mother wouldn't have recognised him, not with that gas-mask on. Lorna raised her arms and let him position the rope's loop. When she grasped the rope, not needing to be shown where to hold it after seeing it happen so many times, the man seemed to hesitate in front of her, but she was too busy bracing herself to bother paying attention.

He reached above her head to give her rope a pull. A moment later she caught her breath as, with a small jerk, her ascent began. Clinging to the rope, she kept her legs together to make it as easy as possible for the men above to lift her. Even so, she swung round in a circle. Then hands reached out to help her onto the floor, though she didn't have time to find her feet before she was hurried away from the edge, through a room and up a steep flight of stairs. From here she was quickly taken along a passage, through a doorway and outside.

She wrenched off her gas-mask. Immediately her ears were packed with the deep drone of aeroplane engines and the bursts of firing as the ack-ack guns attempted to bring Jerry down. High above, the skies were criss-crossed with searchlight beams – and all around were fires. Dread tingled in Lorna's chest.

The people who had been rescued were now being hurried away.

'They're being taken to a shelter.' Mr Fairchild had appeared beside her. 'You go too.'

But Lorna had no intention of going anywhere without thanking the man who had shinned down the rope. Without him, there would have been no rescue.

Someone jostled her and she had to turn round to keep her footing. The man was emerging from the building. Like her, he evidently couldn't wait to rip off his gas-mask.

Giddiness struck Lorna and she went cold to her core. She couldn't believe what – or whom – she was seeing.

George.

* * *

Sally, Andrew, Betty, Samuel, Mrs Beaumont and Mrs Henshaw sat together in the Anderson shelter, where they had been since shortly after half past six.

'I hope Lorna's all right,' said Betty. 'Does anyone know which train her mother was due to leave on?'

'She might have got out of Manchester by the skin of her teeth,' said Sally. 'I hope so, anyway.'

'There are plenty of public sh-shelters in the middle of town,' said Samuel. 'Lorna w-will be in one of those.' He smiled reassuringly at the girls.

'Are you in charge of the fire-watching rota at the depot now that you're the manager?' Mrs Beaumont asked Sally.

Sally shook her head. 'No. It's still Mr Overton's responsibility.'

Mrs Henshaw snorted. 'Even though he doesn't work there any more. When will they learn that women are every bit as capable as men?'

'Probably never.' Mrs Beaumont slotted her cigarette into its holder and placed the end to her lips while Andrew held a match to the tip of the cigarette for her. 'You girls are on duty tonight, aren't you?'

'Yes,' Sally confirmed. 'Because of Christmas, Mr Overton changed the rota so that instead of working three or four nights in a row, we're all doing one at a time from now until the new year.'

As another explosion roared through the night and the hurricane lamps trembled, Mrs Beaumont commented, 'This is the heaviest raid we've had.'

'I agree,' said Mrs Henshaw.

'Maybe that means it'll be over soon,' Betty said hopefully.

'I wish I could believe that,' Andrew said, 'but the ferocity of this attack feels different. I'm on duty tonight and I think I should go now instead of waiting for my official starting time.'

'I feel the same,' said Sally. She looked at Betty, who nodded.

'I'm not d-due to go on duty,' said Samuel, 'but you're right. This is a bad one. I w-want to be out there. The services will need all the help they c-can get.'

Betty placed a hand on the sleeve of his tweed jacket. 'Be careful.'

'Y-you too,' he whispered.

The two young couples stood up, making the shelter feel distinctly crowded. Mrs Henshaw rose as well, which added to the attempts not to jostle.

'I ought to go too,' she said.

Andrew dropped a kiss on her cheek. 'Take care, Mum.'

Samuel opened the door and they climbed up the steep step one at a time. The night was cold, the world filled with noise and the smell of fire. Leaving Betty and Samuel to bid one another a hasty farewell, Sally, Andrew and his mother hurried inside to get ready. Sally and Andrew pulled on warm clothes, then clung together, Sally's heightened senses asking what if this was the last time? What if one of them went out into the dangers of the night and failed to come home again?

They shared a kiss of unbearable sweetness, then stepped apart from one another. As they hurried down the stairs, Mrs Henshaw opened her door and followed them.

Sally opened the front door. 'You two go. I'll wait for Betty. Take care. See you in the morning.'

She always said, 'See you in the morning,' as a kind of blessing, but a small part of her dreaded tempting fate.

No sooner had Andrew and his mother left than Betty came running downstairs. Beneath droning waves of enemy bombers, they raced along to the depot to take up their position. There could be no doubt that they had made the right decision in turning out early for their duty. Sally had never heard the sounds of war more loudly.

She scrambled up the ladder to the skylight and hauled herself out onto the depot roof, dragging her binoculars to her eyes even before she was standing upright.

Pillars of fire illuminated the night. The breath caught in Sally's throat and her heart forgot to beat. Slowly, she turned in a circle. More fires, more flames. More glittering strings of incendiaries spilling towards the ground. Another loud *crump*, and another, and another, as bomb after bomb landed.

Finally, she was looking towards town. Town, the Mancunian word for their city centre. Town, where you went to do your special shopping; where Gracie Fields and Stanley

Holloway, Margaret Rutherford and Two Ton Tessie O'Shea, and international stars such as Mae West and Danny Kaye had appeared at the Palace Theatre; where the Hallé Orchestra delighted audiences at the Free Trade Hall. Town, where Sally had worked in the Town Hall in Albert Square.

Town.

Town was aflame from one end to the other and the night sky was not black but red.

CHAPTER SEVEN

Albert Square was lit up as bright as day – brighter – by the huge fires surrounding it as Lorna ran with the other rescuers towards the Town Hall – and one of the rescuers was George. George! It was unbelievable. What could he possibly be doing here in Manchester? But there was no time to think about that. With the fires roaring and the ground shaking, all that mattered was focusing on what had to be done.

Even so – George.

Mr Fairchild led his group inside, where the lofty foyer was buzzing with activity. A warden came over and spoke to him briefly, then Mr Fairchild turned to his group.

'Those of you who are officially members of rescue groups, fire auxiliary groups and so forth, go and join up with your teams. Those of you who just happen to be in town, hand in your names at one of those tables over there. If you are trained for a particular duty, say so. We've got a lot of extra people in town at present, this being so early in the evening, and we need to know who is best equipped to help with what. Teams will be assembled from the information and lists will go on the noticeboard.'

There were long tables, each with several clerks sitting behind them, writing down details. Lorna joined one of the queues, deliberately refraining from looking around to see what other members of the group – in other words, George – were doing.

She sensed someone behind her. George? But then she heard two women in conversation. Should she be pleased or disappointed? The queue moved forwards.

'Excuse me.'

The male voice behind her brought a shiver to her insides.

'May I push in? This lady and I are old friends.'

'Lucky her,' said one of the women behind Lorna.

Lorna looked straight ahead, determined not to acknowledge George until the heat had drained from her cheeks. When she could trust herself, she glanced his way. She had never forgotten him, but now, seeing him at close quarters after all this time, it felt as though she were setting eyes on him for the first time. Every detail sprang out at her. The clever eyes that were more grey than blue. The lean face, the sharp cheekbones, the dark eyebrows. His clothes were coated with grime and plaster dust, but there was no disguising the broad shoulders and the upright posture.

'Hello, Lorna.'

For a moment, like a love-struck schoolgirl, she couldn't utter a sound. Then annoyance bubbled up inside her, lending her a voice.

'Hello, George. You're the last person I expected to see.'

'I didn't know you were in Manchester,' he replied.

She gave a small shrug.

'You were jolly brave back there in the cellar,' said George. 'After we all got out, I spoke to one of the people who'd been trapped and he sang your praises.'

'I only did what anyone else would have done,' she said quietly.

'You kept a cool head,' said George, 'and that counts for a lot in these situations.'

Lorna didn't answer. So what if he praised her? After the way he had jilted her, George Broughton shouldn't have the power to make her feel good about herself.

The queue advanced and Lorna stepped forwards a bit too eagerly, catching the heel of the man in front. He turned round. He was middle-aged with a fleshy face and a double chin.

'I'm sorry,' said Lorna.

'No harm done.'

The man turned away again, lifting himself on his toes to see how near the front of the queue he was.

'Has your family moved here from Lancaster?' George asked. 'Is that why you're here?'

Lorna wished he would go away. Learning to live without him hadn't been simple but she had forced herself to do it. The last thing she wanted was for the past to be stirred up.

'My parents are in Lancaster.'

'Lorna—'

But Lorna, finding herself at the head of the queue, all but hurled herself at the table and leaned over to give her details to the woman in the olive-green WVS uniform.

'We don't need any more WVS women in the Town Hall,' the woman told her, 'so you'll very likely be attached to a rescue group. The lists will be pinned on those boards over there in the next few minutes.'

'Thanks.'

Lorna moved away quickly, leaving George behind. This was a jolly bad air raid and she wasn't going to be distracted from her duty.

It wasn't long before a keen-eyed official rang a handbell for silence.

'The lists are up now,' he announced. 'Don't hang about in

front of them. Find your name and go straight to your allocated group.'

Everybody surged to the other end of the room. Lorna was caught up in the mass of bodies but others jostled their way to the front. When she got there, her gaze roamed swiftly across the pieces of paper. Two groups caught her eye because they each contained a crossing-out, with a new name added in capitals at the bottom.

It was in one of these groups that she found her own name – and the name added at the end was *GEORGE BROUGHTON*. Talk about bad luck. Then again, what did it matter? They were both here to do a job and, as far as she was concerned, she was going to do it.

She was in Group J. Looking around, she saw that in different parts of the room men were standing on chairs, each holding up a sheet of card with a letter on it. Lorna threaded her way through the crowd towards J.

'My name's Warrender,' said the man on the chair after counting heads. 'There's a bally awful raid in progress out there and our job is to render whatever assistance we can. Come on.'

He jumped down, grabbed two large cloth bags that clanked, and handed one of them to a member of the group. Wearing high heels and with her silk dress rustling beneath her dark-blue ribbed wool coat, Lorna had to hurry to keep up as they strode away, but she was determined not to fall behind or be any sort of drag on the others. Catching George looking her way, she put on a spurt.

Outside, the fires were more intense than before, flames roaring into the sky. High up at the top of a ladder attached to a fire engine, a fireman aimed the hose into the inferno, his form a stark black silhouette against the reds and oranges. In the next moment he was gone, swallowed up by the flames. Lorna's head jerked back in shock but there was no time to stop and stare, no time to try to accept what she'd just witnessed. She had to stay with her group and keep moving.

'Good grief,' came a voice from within Group J. 'The Free Trade Hall has bought it. Those buggers have demolished the Free Trade Hall.'

Footsteps slowed and necks craned at the mind-numbing sight, but nobody stopped and moments later the pace picked up again, debris and wreckage notwithstanding. Bombs and strings of incendiaries dropped in wave after relentless wave into a landscape of intense heat and ever-growing blazes.

Lorna crunched her way across shattered glass, staggering as the ground shivered, smoke stinging her eyes.

'Here! Over here!' yelled Mr Warrender, leading the way to where a human chain was lifting away chunks of rubble from what had previously been the front of a handsome building.

Group J joined the chain. When the first lump of rubble was dumped in her arms, Lorna thought she was about to fall over. Beside her she sensed rather than saw George move closer as if ready to remove the burden from her arms, but she kept her balance and braced herself for the next load of weight.

A lad of eight or nine came running up, looking frantic. Mr Warrender left the line to speak to him, then addressed Group J.

'You four,' he said, pointing, 'stop here and carry on with this. You three, come with me. This boy says his family uses their cellar as a shelter and now his mum is trapped in there with his little sister.'

Lorna, George and another man joined Mr Warrender. The boy was a scrap of a thing who, now Lorna could see him close up, was probably somewhat older than the eight or nine she had guessed at, just underfed thanks to poverty. He was practically dancing on the spot, desperate to bring help to his mother.

The adults followed him to the end of the road and round the corner, where, surprisingly near the grandeur of the city

centre, was a street of shabby dwellings, towards the other end
of which a house had collapsed. Lorna had to admire the way
Mr Warrender swiftly took stock.

'That looks like the cellar skylight – is that right, laddie? Is
that how you got out?'

'Yes, mister. I climbed up on the coal bunker and pulled
myself up.'

'Good-o. We'll squeeze in and get your mum out.'

'She's stuck, mister.'

'Stuck?'

'And there's water.'

George stepped forward. 'We need to get in there fast.'

'That's a small window.' Mr Warrender looked Lorna up
and down. Before she could volunteer, he said, 'We'll call
through first and find out what's what.' He stumbled across the
rubble to the window. 'What's your mother's name, sonny?'

'Mrs Flowers, and I'm Stan and my sister's called Patsy.'

Mr Warrender knelt down to shout through the window.
'Mrs Flowers, are you all right? Help is at hand. We'll soon have
you out of there... What's that?... I see.' He stood up. 'You –
Henderson – run to the ARP station in the next road and say
we need a pump urgently. Get gone!'

'Burst water main?' George asked as Mr Henderson
sprinted away.

'Worse than that,' Mr Warrender answered. 'The lady is
trapped by fallen debris and the water is rising.'

The hairs lifted along Lorna's arms. 'What about the little
girl?'

'Mother is holding her above the water level.'

'We can't wait for the pump,' said George.

'No, we can't,' Lorna agreed at once. 'I'll go in and get the
child.'

'Let's make more space for you,' said Mr Warrender.

He removed a pair of sturdy sledgehammers from his cloth

bag and handed one to George. Together, they knocked out the brickwork at either side of the window. Meanwhile Lorna dumped her gas-mask box and took off her shoes and coat as well as the handbag that had been hanging from her shoulder underneath her coat.

George stood back. 'Not too much or we'll bring down the wall above.'

'This will have to do,' said Mr Warrender. 'Can you get through there?'

Lorna didn't hesitate – well, in her heart she didn't. It was a different matter for her body, with all the rubble to negotiate. George joined her at the window.

'Sit down and slide your feet through,' he said. 'Keep one hand free and I'll hang on to the other one and lower you in, then I'll pass you a torch. Gloves off,' he added. 'They won't be any use to you in there and bare hands will make it easier for us to hold on to one another.'

For the second time that evening Lorna eased her way through a narrow space. George grasped her hand firmly in his. Would there be a return of the old tingle his touch used to create? But what Lorna felt was a sense of safety that increased her resolve as she slithered through the window and descended into chilly, moving water that, when her feet finally found the floor, was up to her hips. Standing on tiptoe, she took the torch George was reaching down to give to her, then turned to shine the beam across the cellar.

Two scared faces stared back at her. Mrs Flowers was on her feet. That was a mercy. Trapped she might be, but if she hadn't been upright, the water would already have swallowed her. She held her young daughter on her hip.

Lorna swished her way across to them.

'Hello there, sweetie,' she greeted the little girl. 'You're Patsy, aren't you? Stan is outside. Will you let me take you to him?'

Patsy clung harder to her mother.

'Go with the lady,' said Mrs Flowers, trying to unpeel the child from her.

Patsy clung harder still.

Mrs Flowers wasn't as tall as Lorna and the water had already reached her waist. Not only that but – oh, glory.

Lorna looked at Mrs Flowers. 'Are you in the family way?'

The woman nodded.

From behind came a shout of, 'The pump's here.'

'Good,' Lorna said to Mrs Flowers. 'They'll probably have to make the opening bigger to get it in, but it won't take long.'

She boggled at the confidence in her tone, all the more so because she didn't have a clue what she was talking about; but the important thing was to reassure Mrs Flowers.

'Lorna!' It was George's voice. 'Have you got the little girl?'

'Not yet,' she called, before saying to Mrs Flowers, 'Can you persuade her to come with me?'

'Come on, lovey. Time to let go,' Mrs Flowers said encouragingly to her daughter.

Wading closer, Lorna held out her arms. 'Come along, Patsy. The men are here to rescue your mummy but they need you to be safe first, so come with me.'

With some persuasion from her mother, who eventually resorted to a sharper tone of voice, Patsy gave in and allowed Lorna to take her. After being so reluctant to start with, she attached herself to Lorna like a barnacle. Lorna sloshed her way back to the window, where she had to prevail upon the child to let go so she could lift her up into George's waiting hands.

'Your turn now,' George called after he'd handed Patsy to someone else.

'No,' Lorna answered. 'I'm staying here with Mrs Flowers.'

'Lorna—'

'You aren't in a position to tell me what to do,' Lorna pointed out.

She returned to Mrs Flowers. In the short time that Lorna had been in the cellar, the water had risen by three or four inches. It was bitterly cold.

Plastering a smile on her face, Lorna said, 'Stan says you're stuck.'

'Aye. Part of the side wall caved in and I got caught in the debris. How long will it take to get that pump set up?'

'They're about to lower it through the window. They'll have it working in a jiffy.'

Two men dropped down into the water and the pump was lifted down. George, in just his undershirt and trousers, followed. He made his way towards Mrs Flowers.

'There's debris under the water,' Lorna warned him.

'Let's see what we can do to clear it. I'm going to duck down and have a feel about, so pardon me if I touch you by mistake, Mrs Flowers.'

He inhaled deeply. The water swooshed and Mrs Flowers uttered a small cry as he submerged. Exerting herself against the strength of the water, Lorna waded nearer, only to walk into an obstacle under the surface, barking her shins. Moving more cautiously, she edged closer to Mrs Flowers, noting anxiously that the water was still getting deeper.

Mrs Flowers was evidently thinking the same thing, as her widened eyes testified.

'Try not to be afraid,' Lorna told her. 'They'll have the pump working any moment now.'

Mrs Flowers folded her arms over her considerable belly, only the top of which was now visible.

The water surged as George reappeared. He took a couple of breaths and shook the drops from his face before giving Mrs Flowers a cheery smile.

'There's quite a bit of stuff down there but I've made a start at shifting it. Hang on and we'll have you out as soon as we can.'

'I'm not going anywhere,' Mrs Flowers replied drily.

'I'm just going to see how things are coming along with the pump,' said George.

He waded away, using his arms to help him move through the water. Lorna stayed with Mrs Flowers, putting her arm firmly round the woman's shoulders. She had to brace herself against the flow of the water as it burst up through the ruptured mains. She had almost lost sensation in her limbs because of the cold.

George returned, accompanied by another man, who blew out sharply a time or two before sucking in a huge breath and sinking beneath the surface.

Before George could do the same, Lorna made a grab for his arm.

'What's happening?'

Anguish twisted across George's face, there and gone so quickly that Lorna caught it only because she had once known him so well.

'A second pump will be here in a few minutes,' he said.

'If you mean the first one can't work fast enough, say so,' demanded Mrs Flowers.

George hesitated – which was answer enough.

'No, it can't, I'm afraid. I'd best press on.'

Lorna held Mrs Flowers more tightly. George's chest expanded as he inhaled, then he vanished beneath the water.

A knot of anxiety tightened in Lorna's chest. One of the men bumped into her underwater and she had to rearrange her footing as a hunk of rubble got shifted, creating a sudden insistent sucking sensation around her legs that seemed intent upon dragging her feet from under her. She and Mrs Flowers swayed.

The water level was at Mrs Flowers' chest height now. She had kept control of her fear before but now the tendons stood out at the sides of her neck and little whimpers emerged from her lips.

Lorna relaxed her hold on her. 'If I duck down, will you be all right?'

After receiving a wide-eyed nod, she took a few breaths, expanding her lungs a little more with each one. Finally, she drew in as much air as she possibly could and sank beneath the water, her flesh shrivelling against her bones as the raw chill enveloped her.

It was impossible to see. Everything had to be done by touch, using hands that were practically numb. Lorna bumped into George, or it might have been the other man, and lost her footing, which sent panic streaking through her. She thrust her feet downwards. One scraped the edge of a rough piece of rubble but the other made contact with the floor and she stood up, sucking in air.

George emerged, chest heaving. A man walked over from the pumps in what looked like slow motion as he fought against the water.

'We're holding the water in check for now. It shouldn't rise any further.'

'That's g-good,' said Lorna through chattering teeth.

'Of course,' the man added, 'getting that second pump through the opening means none of us can get out.'

George turned to Mrs Flowers. 'Well, that guarantees you a rescue, doesn't it?'

He smiled at her and his eyes crinkled. How did he do it? Lorna felt as if her own face was frozen solid, yet here was George, who had been underwater far more than she had, doing his bit to cheer Mrs Flowers' spirits with a tease and a bit of charm. It made Lorna feel she could cope with anything.

It took a further hour of feeling about under the water to remove all the debris that was keeping Mrs Flowers locked in position, by which time Lorna was so cold she had forgotten what warmth felt like. But that ceased to matter when Mrs Flowers, sagging with exhaustion, was carefully helped across the cellar. Once the second pump had been hauled out, a wooden chair on ropes was used to lift Mrs Flowers to freedom, where an ambulance was waiting.

Lorna looked up at where the window had previously been. She was tall and liked to think she was in good shape, but just now the aperture seemed impossibly high up and inaccessible. Besides, if anyone reached down to help her, she simply wouldn't be capable of grasping their hands because her own were numb.

'Let's get this rope round you and under your arms,' George said calmly. 'Just like in the other cellar earlier on.'

Lorna looked at him blankly for a moment. 'Of course. It's still the same evening.'

'And it's not over yet,' George said grimly. 'Jerry doesn't look like he's stopping any time soon.'

Now that she was in the street, Lorna realised what a massive effort she'd had to make when she was in and under the freezing-cold water. It wasn't just that she'd been chilled to her core. The water had displayed surprising strength below knee level and she felt as if every last ounce of stamina had been sucked out of her.

She thought it was standing on firm ground again that left her legs so wobbly that she fell over. It was only when she realised that people around her had also taken a tumble that she understood that the so-called firm ground had shaken under the force of a nearby explosion.

'Everyone who's been in the water needs to get to the nearest rest centre,' Mr Warrender ordered. 'They'll make sure you get dry and have a change of clothes.'

'There's too much that needs doing to worry about that,' George objected.

'Don't be a fool, man,' Mr Warrender retorted. 'The hospitals have enough to cope with without you going down with pneumonia.'

George nodded. 'Fair enough.'

Lorna and George, plus the other man who'd gone underwater with them, and the men who had worked the pumps, all gathered up their coats and other things and headed for the rest centre, led by a pump-man who knew the way. When George took Lorna's arm, she was too chilled to pull away, and in any case she was glad of the support.

The rest centre was in a school building. People with minor injuries were being seen to by WVS women wearing FIRST AID armbands. Other people looked stunned with shock, presumably having been bombed out.

Seeing their huge eyes and haunted faces – some grim, others slack with distress – made Lorna murmur to George, 'I feel like a fraud being here. There's nothing wrong with us except that we're wet.'

'I'm proud of you,' George blurted out.

Lorna blushed, but then her heart hardened. 'You've got no call to feel proud of me. We're nothing to one another now.'

She wanted to recall the words the instant they left her mouth – and that was before she saw the look of hurt and surprise in George's grey-blue eyes. Then his chiselled features stiffened.

'You're correct, of course,' he said in a formal voice. 'I merely intended to express my admiration, nothing more. I apologise for causing offence.'

'You didn't—' Lorna began, but her words were lost in the bustle as a pair of WVS women came to escort the group away.

The men were taken in one direction, Lorna in the other. Finding she had to strip off behind a blanket draped over a piece of rope, she dried herself off in record time using a scratchy towel, before dragging on clothes that weren't a bad fit. She'd been given a string bag to put her own clobber in.

'Are you decent?' came a woman's voice from the other side of the blanket. 'Come and have a hot drink. You'll feel better with some tea inside you.'

'Thanks for the clothes.' Lorna pushed aside the blanket. 'I'll make sure they're returned.'

'You can take them to your local WVS station.'

'That's easy.' Lorna smiled. 'I'm in the WVS.'

'Which branch?'

'Chorlton,' Lorna answered.

'On-Medlock or cum-Hardy?'

'Chorlton-cum-Hardy.'

'My sister lives there. Whereabouts do you live?'

'I've just moved into a new billet in Wilton Road beside the rec. I'm in a place called Star House.'

'Pretty name,' the WVS lady commented.

'My landlady used to let rooms to the stars of the music hall.'

'Come and get that cuppa.'

She took Lorna back into the main room, where the lady manning the tea urn thrust a mug into her hands. Spying a free chair in the corner, Lorna took the weight off her feet, enjoying the sensation of warmth that came from wrapping both hands round the mug. Her shoulders relaxed.

'You're meant to drink it,' George said casually, appearing beside her. 'It'll get you warm on the inside.'

She glanced up. He wasn't looking at her. His gaze was directed into the room. If she didn't respond, would he move away? That was what she wanted, wasn't it? That was the safe thing to want.

'I'm sorry I was sharp with you before,' she whispered. 'It was rude of me.'

He looked down at her, kindness showing in his face. 'You were right. It's not my place to feel pride in your achievements. I no longer enjoy that privilege.'

Lorna looked away. What was there to say? She took a sip. 'You're right about the tea, anyway. I didn't think I'd ever feel warm again.'

A passing WVS woman stopped to say, 'When you've finished that, come and lend a hand, will you?'

'Of course.' Lorna gulped down her drink and stood up.

She turned to George. For a moment everything seemed to go still as she drank in the sight of his lean, handsome face. Jerking her chin, she looked away. This man had jilted her. It had been hard moving on from the ruins of their relationship and she wasn't going to slide back into unhappiness now.

'It was good to see you, George,' she said formally.

'You too. Unexpected but good.'

'I'd better go and help out.'

'And I must join another rescue team.'

'Oh.' Why was she surprised? Had she really thought he would stay in the rest centre? 'Yes, I suppose so.'

'Well – goodbye, Lorna.'

Was he about to say something more? Lorna turned away, heading for the first place she saw, which happened to be the kitchen. When she reached the doorway, she looked back.

George had gone. Good.

So why did it feel as if her heart had gone with him?

CHAPTER EIGHT

Six o'clock on Monday morning came and went but Betty and Sally stayed put on the depot roof. It had been a night of horror. Manchester had suffered, was still suffering, an ordeal by fire. Their job on the roof was to watch over the yard and also a stretch of Beech Road, but it had grown harder and harder to do their duty because their eyes were constantly drawn back to the fires eating the city centre. The flames were so extensive, reaching so high, that the light from them reached all the way to Chorlton, where the depot roof, which should have been swathed in inky blackness, was illuminated by the glow.

'It's not just Manchester either,' said Betty. 'It's Salford an' all. I hope Dad's safe – and Grace.' Her heart swelled with worry. 'And Samuel's out on duty in all this. What a daft thing to say. Thousands of folk are on duty. You and me are on duty. Everyone is in danger.'

'But it's the people we care about who are at the forefront of our minds,' said Sally. 'It makes us care about them even more. I know how concerned you feel about Samuel because I feel exactly the same about Andrew.'

'He's probably worrying about you an' all,' Betty said ruefully.

'I imagine he's too busy for that,' Sally answered. 'He can't afford to lose his concentration in the middle of a rescue, and I expect there are a great many rescues going on.'

Just before half past six, the all-clear sounded, but it was still some minutes before the girls could drag themselves away from the distant scene that held their attention.

Finally, Betty looked at her wristwatch. 'We ought to be heading home. Mrs Beaumont will be worried. She'll think we must have been blown to bits. Sorry,' she added. 'That sounded like a joke and I didn't mean to make light of what's happened.'

'I know,' said Sally. 'It was the simple truth. That's exactly what Mrs Beaumont will be scared of.'

Betty followed Sally to the open skylight, waiting for Sally to climb all the way down the ladder before she stepped onto it. The ladder was inclined to bounce if two people used it at the same time.

Downstairs, they locked up the building and closed the large gates that had to stand open all night in case others needed access to assist in an emergency. Then they let themselves out through the door in the wooden fence and hurried along Beech Road.

Sally put on a spurt. 'I know in my head that Andrew won't be home yet, but I still keep hoping.'

Andrew wasn't home. Sally's face fell, though if Betty hadn't been watching at that exact moment, she wouldn't have known, because a second later Sally pinned a smile in place.

Mrs Beaumont fussed over them and made a pot of tea before letting them go upstairs to get changed. They came down to porridge followed by a flaked-fish fritter.

'Has there been no sign of Lorna?' Betty asked.

Mrs Beaumont shook her head gravely. 'Let's hope she spent the night in a public shelter.'

'Knowing her,' said Betty, 'I wouldn't be surprised if she helped out in some way.'

'Either way,' said Sally, 'she won't have left to come home until after the all-clear, and the journey will be anything but straightforward. It'll be a while before we see her.'

The front door opened. Sally jumped up and left the dining room. Betty listened, hoping for the sound of Andrew's voice. Instead she heard his mother. Betty and Mrs Beaumont went into the hallway, where the two Mrs Henshaws were hugging one another.

'Is Andrew back yet?' his mother asked.

'Not yet,' Sally answered. 'He must be in the middle of a rescue.' She sounded cheerful and down to earth, but Betty didn't miss the flicker of anxiety in her hazel eyes.

Betty gave her friend's arm a squeeze and Sally shot her a grateful look.

'Why don't you rush round to the bookshop and see if Samuel is back yet?' said Sally. 'Don't worry if you're late for work. I can hold the fort.'

It was Betty's turn to be grateful. What a good friend Sally was. The two of them had got off to a rocky start but now they couldn't be closer.

Betty dashed about fetching her things.

'Don't forget your sandwich,' Mrs Beaumont called.

'And wrap up warm,' Mrs Henshaw added, then she laughed. 'Sorry – I do tend to speak to you young ones as if you're children.'

Heading out again after a night on duty was normally the time when tiredness washed over Betty, but not this morning, not with the possibility of seeing her dear Samuel.

She hurried to his shop, her heart dipping in distress as she breathed in the smell of smoke and saw workmen examining a crater that had taken a chunk out of the road as well as a section of the pavement, causing the brick wall in front of a pair of semis to collapse into it. Still, that was better than the houses falling in.

As Samuel's shop came into view, she saw him walking towards it. His shoulders were rounded with exhaustion but when she called his name he immediately stood up straight, his smile appearing as a white streak in his otherwise grimy face.

Betty ran to him and would have flung her arms round him, but he held up his hands.

'D-don't come too c-close or you'll get covered in d-dirt.'

'A rescue?' she asked.

Samuel nodded. 'We c-could hear voices calling from under the rubble, but by the time we d-dug down far enough...' His voice faded away.

'Too late?'

Another nod. 'Poor blighters.'

'I'm so sorry to hear it. Let's go in and I'll make you a hot drink.'

Samuel put the key in the lock and opened the door. Inside were rows of bookcases and the counter with the cash register. As he shut the door behind them, Betty took a moment to appreciate the comforting aroma of wood and books.

Behind the shop was a room she called the parlour-office. It had started out as a parlour, as you could see from the wallpaper with its pattern of cabbage roses and the tiled fireplace with the three over-mantel shelves. But Samuel, living on the premises on his own, had let his work creep into what was supposed to be part of the living accommodation and now the room was populated by bookcases. One of his wartime duties was to house donated books and sort them out for sending to bombed-out libraries and also to the troops.

One of the three doors on the other side of the parlour-office led to a narrow kitchen with a scullery beyond. Samuel switched on the water and gas supplies and Betty filled the kettle, feeling a little thrill as she did so. She loved being in Samuel's home and feeling that it was her place to make tea. It wasn't her being forward or taking advantage. It was her being safe and comfortable in the home of the man she loved.

After a night like the one they and all of Manchester had just lived through, that feeling of being in the right place with the right person was more important than ever.

When Betty got to the depot, Lorna hadn't arrived. It was gone nine before she finally walked in through the depot's open gates. Betty and Sally flew across the yard to hug her.

'It's such a relief to see you,' said Sally. 'How are you?'

'Were you caught in it?' Betty asked.

Lorna nodded. Her beautiful green eyes, which Betty admired so much, had lost their sparkle. 'It was quite a night.'

'We watched the fires from the depot roof,' said Sally.

'It was pretty bad,' said Lorna.

'Did you find shelter?' Betty asked.

'No. I kept busy. I helped in a couple of rescues and ended up in a rest centre. Information was coming in from other WVS branches shortly before I left. You wouldn't believe how many have been left homeless.'

Betty hugged her again. 'I'm just glad you're safe.'

'The fires were still burning when I left.'

'I know,' said Sally. 'Betty and I went up onto the roof to look a few minutes ago.'

'First off, Jerry dropped two bombs, one on each side of Albert Square,' said Lorna.

'Albert Square?' exclaimed Sally. 'I used to work there – in the Town Hall.' Her voice quietened. 'Is it still standing?'

'As far as I know. I ended up somewhere else, though I've no idea where. Anyway, the first bombs lit up Albert Square and that showed the way for all the rest.'

All the rest. Betty pressed her lips together. The all-clear hadn't sounded for a whole twelve hours. Twelve hours of destruction raining down from the skies.

'Twelve flaming hours,' she muttered. 'Aye, and they were flaming an' all.'

News came their way throughout the day as locals dropped in, seeking company and moral support as they shared what they'd heard. There hadn't been enough local fire crews because many of Manchester's brigades had the previous night gone to help Liverpool survive a raid. Last night fire crews from all over the North-West and even further afield had streamed in the direction of Manchester and Salford.

The Free Trade Hall, Cross Street Chapel, Victoria Buildings, part of Deansgate – all gone. Chetham's Hospital had been severely damaged. The cathedral was all but a skeleton.

The fires burned all day. Every so often, the girls went up onto the roof to see them. According to the driver of the lone salvage collection van that arrived that day, all the warehouses around Piccadilly were either aflame or in danger of becoming so.

By the end of the day, Betty was almost at screaming point with the need to hear about Salford. It was then that Mrs Gill from Claude Road came into the depot yard.

'You know my daughter's a clippie? She dashed to see me in between shifts. The buses are going as close to town as they can today, but they can't get all the way in because of the bomb damage and the fires.'

'Did she say anything about Salford?' Betty asked hopefully. 'I imagine the drivers and conductors and clippies pass information around.'

'Aye, they do. She didn't say much about Salford, just that

thousands of incendiaries were dropped and there's been so much damage that there's been talk of fetching in soldiers to help with the clearing up. Four thousand are homeless. Someone told our Rita about a Salford bus that took shelter under a bridge when the raid started, and then the bridge took a direct hit.'

'No,' breathed Betty, her heart thumping.

'It destroyed the bus and killed everyone on board,' said Mrs Gill.

Betty went cold all over. Those poor people. At least it would have been quick – or would it? Had the passengers died slowly of their injuries before help arrived?

'There's bound to be another raid tonight,' Mrs Gill was saying. 'Jerry will want to finish what he started.'

When the siren sounded a few minutes after seven on Monday evening, it came as no surprise. The Manchester skyline was still aglow from the previous night, making the city and its suburbs an easy target for Jerry. Andrew had already set off for town on a borrowed bicycle. The word had gone out to heavy and light rescue teams in the outlying areas, asking for any men they could spare.

'It can't have been an easy decision to ask for reinforcements,' Andrew had told Sally while he got ready to go. 'It wasn't just the centres of Manchester and Salford that took it last night. It was all over the place in both cities.'

'The men who go to town now,' said Sally, 'do so knowing their own local areas might be hit tonight. I'm not saying that to put you off,' she added hastily. 'I was just thinking it through.'

Lorna and Mrs Henshaw were both going on WVS duty.

'Are you two fire-watching tonight?' Mrs Henshaw asked Sally and Betty.

'No,' said Betty.

'Then you can come with me.'

The four women set off together along Beech Road in the opposite direction from the depot, making their way to MacFadyen's, the church hall that was the base for the local WVS. When they arrived, Lorna peeled off from the little group to attend to her own duties. Mrs Henshaw introduced Sally and Betty to Mrs Callaghan, who was in charge. She was a tall though by no means willowy woman with dark eyes in a pale, strong-featured face. She looked tired about the eyes but the moment she spoke, her grit and determination were obvious.

'You can stay here and help in the rest centre,' she told Sally. 'Would you mind if we call you Mrs Sally to avoid confusion? And Miss Hughes can go out with the mobile canteen. Mrs Ashley!' she called. 'This is Miss Hughes, who will be coming out with you tonight.'

Sally barely had time to say goodbye to her friend before Betty was whisked away. Mrs Callaghan showed Sally round at top speed.

'First-aid station in the corner. Blankets and rolled-up palliasses over there. Clothes on the racks. Many people turn up literally with nothing but the clothes they stand up in. Kitchen through there. We provide tea and sandwiches all night and a hot breakfast in the morning. Everyone who comes through the door is asked for their details. Name, address, what's happened to the house, the names of the injured who have been taken to hospital, and if they can tell us which hospital all the better. Unfortunately, we also have to ask for the names of any known fatalities. You can start in the kitchen, Mrs Sally, and after that I'll put you where you're most needed.'

* * *

'It used to be a removal van,' Mrs Ashley informed Betty. 'It's

been modified to carry a tank with five hundred gallons of
water—'

'Five hundred!' Betty exclaimed. That sounded more like a
fire engine to her.

'—as well as urns and a counter on which to make sandwiches. The canteen is driven by Mr Rutledge because even the
ladies who can drive have never driven anything as big as this.
But that will soon change. I'm being trained to drive this and
then there'll be no stopping me.'

Hoicking up her tweed skirt and treating Betty to a flash of
sturdy legs, she swung herself up into the cab and scooted along
the bench seat for Betty to follow.

Their first destination was near a surface shelter that had
taken a direct hit. Dust-covered figures were emerging from the
rubble, some of them clearly walking wounded. Ambulancemen
carried others out on stretchers. After that Betty had no time to
look because she was kept busy pouring tea and making meat-
paste butties. She also handed out cigarettes to people in shock.

'Here,' she said to folk who were ashen-faced beneath the
dust. 'One of these will buck you up.'

After that they went to a road in Seymour Grove, where six
houses – six! – had been walloped.

'They're flat as pancakes,' Betty whispered. 'Oh my goodness, those poor people.'

'No time to gawp,' said Mrs Ashley. 'We've a job to do.'

'It made me think of my friend,' said Betty. 'Her family lost
their home not long ago. Such a dreadful thing to happen.'

'Did she and her family survive?' asked Mrs Ashley.

'Yes, they're all fine.'

'Well, then, that's what matters. From what the ARP
warden said, not everyone from these houses was so lucky.'

Their next stop was outside a school into which the residents from eight roads had been evacuated when a gas main had
been ruptured. A faint bad-egg whiff drifted through the air.

'Lots of tea,' said Mrs Ashley. 'Sandwiches if they want them, but no ciggies.'

Mr Rutledge chuckled. 'It's bad enough being blown up by the Luftwaffe – we don't want to blow ourselves up.'

When they left the school, they drove past more damaged houses and stopped at the end of a road where a bomb had landed right in front of a pair of semis, swiping off both frontages before making a huge crater that both houses had toppled into. More butties, more tea and cigarettes. More stunned residents and tired but determined rescuers.

Mr Rutledge drove the canteen away, fires leaping up nearby, very close to the van – too close, as far as Betty was concerned.

'Drat,' said Mr Rutledge. 'Another hole in the road.' This was how he referred to craters large enough to swallow a double-decker bus. 'Not to worry.'

Swinging the steering wheel, he expertly turned the van and set off back the way they had come.

'It's like Blackpool Illuminations,' he muttered. 'Fires all over the show.'

High above, a vast barrage balloon changed from eerie silver to deep red and then burst from the heat. Betty automatically ducked, but the other two didn't so much as flinch.

'We saw that happen several times last night,' said Mrs Ashley. 'Don't worry. You'll get used to it.'

'Never mind the barrage balloons,' said Mr Rutledge. 'It's the parachute mines you want to watch out for.'

They were finishing up outside a public shelter, from where everyone had now been taken off to nearby rest centres, when the all-clear sounded. Betty was astonished to see it was only a little after midnight.

'I was expecting another twelve-hour raid,' she said.

'So were we all, love,' said Mr Rutledge.

'Just because the Luftwaffe have gone home, that doesn't

mean the Blitz is finished,' Mrs Ashley pointed out. 'There are fires everywhere.'

'If anyone for twenty miles around was ever in any doubt as to where Manchester is,' said Mr Rutland, 'they'll know now. Come on, Miss Hughes, back in the van with you. Jerry might have legged it but we've still got hours ahead of us.'

CHAPTER NINE

'I'm so sorry,' whispered the old lady, distress showing in her eyes. She had been dug out of the rubble a couple of streets away and brought here to the rest centre.

Sally crouched beside her. 'What are you sorry for?' she asked gently.

'Just look at the state of me, covered in filth. What must folk be thinking? I'm a clean person, you know, I really am.'

Sally's heart melted. This old lady had spent four hours pinned alone under the ruins of her little house, but what she cared about was letting herself down by being seen in public covered in dirt. It was partly the shock speaking, Sally knew, but beneath that there was a very real pride.

'Let me fetch you a flannel and a bowl of water,' she said, coming to her feet.

She hadn't stopped for breath, let alone a cup of tea, all night. She had developed a new respect for her mother-in-law.

'I hadn't appreciated how hard you work when you're here all night,' she told Mrs Henshaw when they ended up in the kitchen at the same time. 'It makes me feel I have it easy up on the depot roof.'

'That's a nice compliment,' Mrs Henshaw replied in her usual sensible way. 'We all do what's needed. But do I have to remind you of how you and Betty saved the depot from burning to the ground a few weeks back?'

As Sally returned to the spacious hall, the doors opened again. She looked round, ready for more homeless to arrive, but instead in walked a group of WVS women.

'This is the next shift,' said Mrs Henshaw. 'You'd best go now, Sally. You've got a job to go to, remember. That doesn't stop because of this. There'll be plenty of us here to see to what needs doing.'

Sally felt reluctant to leave, but she knew her duty. She walked back to Star House, stunned with tiredness now she had stopped working. The smell of smoke clogged her nose.

Mrs Beaumont sent her straight upstairs for a strip-wash. 'I'll have breakfast on the table when you come down.'

Sally washed and dressed. The front door opened – Andrew? Her heart leapt. She flew across the bedroom to open the door, only to see Betty coming up the stairs.

'I'm sorry it's only me,' said Betty.

'Don't say that.'

'I know who you were hoping to see,' Betty replied.

'Yes, and it was silly of me. Andrew's been in town all night, so goodness only knows when he'll be back. It's not as though he has to go to work today – unlike you and me,' Sally added, trying to inject a light-hearted note into her voice. 'We have to open the depot.'

Betty seized her hand. 'He'll come home safe. You'll see.'

Sally nodded. 'Go and get changed. Mrs Beaumont is preparing the breakfast.'

Sally was on edge all through the meal. It didn't matter how sure she was in her head that Andrew was most unlikely to appear before she went to work. That didn't stop her hoping.

She and Betty were just about to set off for work when Lorna came in.

'Is it time to go?' she asked, looking at them.

'Time for them, yes,' said Mrs Beaumont, 'but you have to get washed and changed and have breakfast. You aren't going anywhere without something inside you.'

Lorna smiled. 'Yes, ma'am.' She saluted before running upstairs.

The others went to the depot. Lorna arrived forty minutes later while Sally and Betty were sorting some mixed salvage. She headed indoors to change.

'This feels peculiar,' she commented as she rejoined the others in her dungarees and thick woolly jumper, her dark hair covered with a silk scarf. 'After the – the intensity of the past two nights, carrying on with normal life is just plain weird.'

'What duty were you given last night?' Sally asked.

'I was out in an ambulance-car.'

'I didn't know you could drive,' said Betty.

'I can't – but I'm jolly well going to learn, I can promise you that. When I saw my mother – not on Sunday, the time before that when I went to that party in Lancaster – she said the same. Daddy would never let us learn before the war. He said driving is for men.'

'Honestly!' Betty exclaimed. 'When you think of the jobs women are doing now that most of the men are away fighting.'

'I know,' Lorna agreed.

'What did you actually do last night?' Sally asked her.

'Every motor had to have two people, a driver and one other. I was the "other". The ambulances are saved for the seriously injured, so they need a fleet of motorcars to ferry the broken ankles and concussions and so forth.'

Betty giggled. 'You make it sound as if the broken ankle isn't accompanied by the rest of the body.'

'That's how injuries are referred to,' Lorna told her. 'You don't say, "Mrs Smith has a broken collarbone. Can you take her to Withington Hospital?" You say, "Can you take this broken collarbone?" Apparently, that's the way doctors and nurses refer to sick people.'

'Betty was out and about last night as well,' said Sally.

As they worked, Betty and Sally told Lorna about their experiences of the previous night.

'Have you seen Andrew since he went off last night?' Lorna asked.

Sally shook her head. 'It's only to be expected. I keep reminding myself how lucky I am to have him at home when all the other young wives have had to say goodbye for goodness knows how long.'

'I feel lucky an' all, having Samuel here,' said Betty. 'Being able to see one another is a real blessing.'

Sally felt a pang of conscience. 'I know Betty and I are always going on about Samuel and Andrew. I hope it doesn't upset you, Lorna. I wouldn't want you to think we've forgotten about your romantic disappointment.'

'Disappointment? Catastrophe, you mean,' Lorna said breezily. 'Seriously, I know you haven't.' She bit her lip. 'I haven't known whether to say this, but...'

'What is it?' Sally asked.

'Look, you're not to read anything into it,' Lorna insisted, 'but I'll burst if I don't say something.'

'Now you've got to tell us,' said Betty.

'Not last night, the night before, when I was in town... George was there.'

'George?' said Betty, startled. 'Your old fiancé?'

'I was in a rescue where we were all wearing gas-masks,' said Lorna. 'When we got outside, everyone took them off – and there was George.'

'Gracious,' said Sally. *What an inadequate thing to say*, she thought.

'After that we ended up in the same rescue group and took part in another rescue together.'

'I'm sorry if this sounds shallow after the dreadful hammering Manchester and Salford have taken,' said Betty, 'but that sounds very romantic.'

'Believe me,' Lorna replied, 'romantic is the very last thing it was.'

'How extraordinary to meet one another again like that,' said Sally.

'I assumed he was still in London,' said Lorna. 'Or I would have done if I'd thought about it.'

'Are you going to see him again?' asked Betty.

'What a question!' said Lorna. 'No. Absolutely not.'

'I've got good news for you, Sally,' Mrs Henshaw said, appearing in the hallway, when the girls got home after work. 'Your mother got word to the WVS in Chorlton that she and your father are both safe and well. She said the Grants are too.'

Something inside Sally sagged in relief. 'That's wonderful news. Thank you.'

'Come and sit down, all of you,' said Mrs Henshaw, leading the way into the sitting room.

Sally's gaze went straight to the Christmas tree. 'Was it really only on Sunday afternoon we decorated it? Such a happy time.'

'Yes, it was,' Betty said with a misty look in her eyes. 'Now it's Tuesday, but it feels as if a fortnight has gone by because so much has happened.'

'It's not just Tuesday,' said Lorna. 'It's Christmas Eve, as bizarre as that seems.'

'Well, it won't seem bizarre for much longer,' said Mrs

Henshaw, taking control, 'because the WVS and plenty of others are going to do something about it. We're going to make Christmas Day into something special for all the people who've been made homeless in the Blitz.'

'But there are hundreds of them,' said Lorna. 'Hundreds upon hundreds.'

Mrs Henshaw didn't show a flicker of uncertainty regarding what was planned. 'It's being said that if you add together all the houses in Manchester, Salford and Stretford that were destroyed, and those that are beyond repair, and those that can be repaired but can't be lived in for the time being – if you add them all together, it's something like fifteen or sixteen thousand homes. Fifteen or sixteen *thousand*. And that's before you count the houses that are damaged but live-able-in.'

Sally stared. She couldn't think of any words that could adequately express her shock. Everything that had happened since Sunday evening felt too huge to be encapsulated in words.

'All those people need feeding,' said Mrs Henshaw, 'as do all the firemen, the rescuers and so forth. There's going to be a heck of a lot of canteen cooking going on and I'm going to be helping with that. We're going to start tonight by preparing Christmas dinners for all those people.' She looked at her listeners.

'Count me in,' Sally said at once.

'And me,' said Lorna.

'Me an' all,' Betty added.

'Good,' said Mrs Henshaw. 'I knew you'd all want to muck in. The Christmas dinners will be simple, just hotpots and meat pies, with sultana puddings instead of Christmas puddings.'

'I'm sure it will all be splendid,' said Lorna.

'I'll tell you what will make it splendid,' said Betty. 'All those folk who have lost their homes will be shocked and distressed, but they'll know that an army of women got together to make them all a Christmas dinner. In its own way, that will take the edge off their problems, even if it's only for a while.'

At the sound of the front door opening, Sally jumped up. She dashed from the sitting room straight into Andrew's arms. They clung together for a long time, not speaking, not kissing, just holding one another, being together, needing one another.

At last Sally stepped back from her husband, reluctant to let him go. He smelled of smoke, dirt and brick dust. He was covered in grime and ashes. He smelled of the Blitz.

He gave his mother a hug, then went upstairs. Sally heated up some water and took it up to him. After Andrew had had a strip-wash, Sally took the bowl of dirty water downstairs. When she returned, she tried to persuade him to go to bed and sleep.

'You must be exhausted,' she said.

'I am, but after everything I've seen—' His face twisted. 'Dear heaven, Sally.'

There was a long, charged silence. Andrew's brown eyes were almost black with anguish. Sally drew him to the bed, wanting him to sit, but he didn't even when she did.

'Jerry might have been aiming at the buildings,' he said, 'but they wanted to destroy our morale as well.'

'They'll never do that,' said Sally.

'They sent down landmines by parachute. They don't make a sound when they come down that way. They're enormous, those mines, Sally, as big as telephone boxes. I've seen men running towards them because in the dark they could only make out the 'chutes, so they thought it was soldiers being dropped, and then the mines exploded. I've seen dead bodies. I've seen arms and legs. I've seen a head, just a head, rolling down the road like a football.'

'Oh, Andrew,' Sally whispered.

'I've seen men vanish into thin air. There were these firemen with their hoses trained on the warehouse fires near Piccadilly. Then there was an explosion and I was picked up and dumped twenty feet away. When I next looked, there was nothing where those men had been. Nothing. No limbs. Just – nothing. They'd been blown to smithereens. There was nothing left of them.'

Sally reached out to touch him but he didn't respond.

'Ever since Sunday night,' he continued, 'a wall of flames has engulfed the middle of Manchester. The hotels on Deansgate. Parts of Market Street. Corporation Street was flattened. At one point I thought it was raining but it was water from the hosepipes. And the heat – the buildings that weren't on fire were red-hot. You couldn't touch them. One whole side of Piccadilly was a heap of rubble. And there were rats all over the place.'

'Rats?' Sally asked.

'They don't just desert sinking ships. They desert warehouses that have gone up in flames. All the cotton mill warehouses down by Piccadilly. The warehouses along the Irwell. Everything was ablaze. And just when—' He smashed one fist into a cupped palm. 'Jerry cleared off about midnight and, just when our lads might have been able to bring the fires under control at last, the wind changed. There were strong winds from the north and they kept the fires spreading.'

Now he finally did sink onto the bed, bending over with his head in his hands. Sally was about to stretch an arm across his back and gather him to her, but he reared up and gazed at her, the expression in his eyes startling her as it went from wild to dull in an instant.

'They don't know for certain yet how many have died,' he said, 'but the ARP reckon it's going to be the best part of three thousand people at least. In two nights. Not to mention all the injured.'

'And we survived,' Sally whispered. 'You and me and your mum. Our family. My parents. Betty, Lorna, Mrs Beaumont.

We're all still here. We need to be together. We need one another.'

'They're talking about mass burials, you know,' said Andrew.

'This is why we stayed in Manchester when Mum wanted us to see if we could get evacuated to the country with your job. We said we wanted to stay here and see things through.'

'Aye, we did,' said Andrew.

CHAPTER TEN

After tea, Lorna was in the sitting room with Betty. Lorna stood in front of the Christmas tree. The string of red beads caught her eye, as did some oval-shaped baubles with pointed ends.

'You all did a good job with the tree,' she told Betty.

'I'm glad you like it.'

'Before the war, my father always arranged for a twenty-foot tree to be set up in our hall. My mother decorated it – and when I say "my mother", I mean the maids. They had to climb up stepladders and stand on the top. Years ago, my mother bought a big box of white and silver baubles, and we always had those and white clip-on candles.'

'It sounds beautiful,' said Betty.

'It was,' Lorna confirmed, 'but this tree is better.'

'Really?' asked Betty, surprised.

'Just look at it,' said Lorna. 'Lots of colours. Different types of decoration. Mummy's tree was stylish and perfect, but this tree tells a story. I bet Mrs Beaumont can remember where every single decoration came from. And d'you know the best thing of all?'

'What?' Betty asked.

'It's in the sitting room. It's not facing the front door, looking grand and demanding admiration from everybody who walks in. It's where you can sit by the fire and enjoy looking at it. When I have a home of my own, that's going to be my rule for the Christmas tree.'

What sort of traditions did George's family, the Broughtons, have for their Christmas tree? If she hadn't been jilted, this would have been Lorna's first Christmas as Mrs George Broughton. Would they have spent a few days at the family seat with Sir Jolyon and Lady Broughton?

Oh, what mad thoughts! Seeing George had done her no good at all.

Sally walked in. 'You two look deep in thought.'

'I was thinking about decorating the tree and what a happy afternoon we had,' said Betty.

'I know,' said Sally. 'We're so lucky to live here. I'm grateful Star House is still standing. I don't think I could bear to lose a second home.'

'But if Star House did take a direct hit,' Lorna replied matter-of-factly, 'you would bear it. We'd all take it on the chin because that's how we're going to get through this war.'

For all her fine words, she had to look away. She hadn't exactly taken seeing George on the chin, had she?

Mrs Beaumont and Mrs Henshaw walked in.

'It's almost time to go,' said Mrs Henshaw.

'Are you coming too, Mrs Beaumont?' Lorna asked, pleased.

'I am indeed. Usually I prefer to do my war work at home, knitting for the bombed-out or sewing little gifts to raise money, but after the time we've all had, it's important to get involved in this.'

'Andrew is getting ready to go out on duty again,' said Sally, 'so I'll hang on and see him off. I'll catch up with you in a while.'

Lorna, Betty, Mrs Henshaw and their landlady wrapped up warm and, taking care with the blackout, slipped out of the front door and set off for one of the local schools, where tonight the kitchen was to be used for preparing Christmas meals. Outside, the building was in darkness as if empty, but once they were indoors they found thirty or forty women chatting as they awaited instructions. There were some men as well.

The person in charge was – oh, glory – Mrs Lockwood.

'Don't worry,' Lorna whispered to Betty, seeing how her face fell. 'She's got loads of people here to boss about, so it won't be just us on the receiving end. And to give her her due, she is very good at organising.'

Mrs Lockwood soon set everybody to work. Groups of women were put on hotpot duty or pie duty. As the meat was sealed in hot oil, an appetising scent lifted into the air.

Lorna and Betty were in the group assigned to the sultana puddings. They worked in a human chain. On the other side of the long counter, women weighed the dry ingredients and put the correct amounts on saucers. On Lorna and Betty's side, each woman added 'her' dry ingredients to each bowl and passed it on.

Lorna's ingredient was breadcrumbs and Betty's was flour.

Betty giggled and gave Lorna a nudge. 'We've got the easy jobs down this end. All the interesting stuff – the syrup and suet and sultanas – is happening up the other end.'

'I'm perfectly happy to have an easy job, thanks very much,' Lorna replied. 'I was dreading being given the job at the far end where they're pouring in the milk and mixing everything together. If I did that, it would end up either like a lump of plaster or else as a heap of slop.'

'Sounds interesting,' said a new voice that made Lorna catch her breath and she jerked round to see George, his wool over-coat unbuttoned to reveal his suit underneath.

'George...' Hideously embarrassed, she bent over the bowl in front of her and quickly passed it along.

'This is just oatmeal,' said Betty, handing it back. 'You haven't put in the breadcrumbs.'

Drat. Lorna picked up a saucer of breadcrumbs and tipped it into the bowl, which she then thrust in Betty's direction again. What on earth was George doing here?

'You, sir.' Mrs Lockwood marched purposefully down the room. 'Are you one of my volunteers? I'm Mrs Lockwood – and you are?'

'Broughton, George Broughton, and I'm here to assist.'

'Good,' said Mrs Lockwood. 'There are cartons of ingredients to be carried through from the storeroom. Follow me.'

As she and George walked away, some of the women on the other side of the counter openly watched George.

'Talk about handsome,' said Mrs Vine, a rosy-cheeked, square-faced brunette. 'If I'd known the likes of him would be here, I wouldn't have turned up in my rollers and a turban. I'd be showing off my best Norma Shearer curls.'

'Very appropriate,' a petite redhead beside her said, 'given that Mr George Broughton looks like a matinee idol.'

Honestly! Some women! Put a good-looking man in front of them and they went to pieces.

Betty moved closer to Lorna. 'Is that your George?'

'No, he isn't *my* George.' She bent her head so she could speak into Betty's ear. 'Yes, that's George, but please don't let on. It's bad enough that he's here, without everyone knowing.'

Lorna had been enjoying herself before this, but now her skin crawled with self-consciousness. How had George ended up here? They had found one another by chance on Sunday, but this time it couldn't be a coincidence. It wasn't possible.

The pace of work in the large kitchen was brisk, with everybody all too well aware that the Luftwaffe might come calling at any

moment. But for once Jerry stayed away, and the cooking operation looked like being a success.

'As long as Jerry doesn't pitch up just when everything is in
the oven,' said the woman who was in charge of the baking. She
was a professional cook. 'If we have to switch off the ovens to go
to the shelter, the meals will be spoiled, and that's the polite
word for it.'

But the siren remained silent. Mrs Lockwood sent her
workers – there was no question in Lorna's mind that she would
see them all as 'her' workers – in groups to have a cup of tea and
a cigarette.

When the women from Lorna's part of the counter were
despatched, Sally, who was working elsewhere, darted across
for a quick word.

'Lorna, did George find you?'

'Oho – *George,* is it? So you *do* know the man with the film-
star looks?'

It was Mrs Vine. Lorna could have crowned her. She could
have crowned Sally too.

'You do know him, don't you?' Mrs Vine demanded.

'No,' Lorna replied immediately, giving Sally the evil eye to
stop her saying yes. She pulled Sally away so they could have
some privacy.

'I'm sorry,' said Sally. 'Have I done the wrong thing? But
you did those rescues together, and then he turned up at Star
House looking for you, so I sent him here. It seemed like the
right thing to do.'

'I told you I didn't want to see him again.'

'But you must have given him your address,' said Sally.

'No, I didn't. I don't know how he could have got it. He
came to the house?'

'Yes. I'm sorry but I need to get back to peeling carrots
before Mrs Lockwood sees me.'

Sally hastened away. The girls and women Lorna was due

to have her break with had disappeared into a room further along a green-tiled passage, but before Lorna could follow, George called her name.

Reluctantly she turned to face him. She'd been prepared to see him in his suit and she wouldn't have batted an eyelid if he'd taken off his jacket. But here he was, with his smart waistcoat unbuttoned and hanging open, his silk tie loosened and his sleeves rolled up, showing off his muscular forearms.

No wonder Mrs Vine and her chum had been smitten. It wasn't just that George's lean face was handsome, his grey-blue eyes intelligent: he had an eye-catching figure, and he held his shoulders in a way that conveyed self-confidence.

Could she really have forgotten how attractive he was?

Irrelevant, she told herself. Being well worth a second look hadn't prevented him from giving her her marching orders. She hardened her heart. Her stupid heart.

George came closer. A slight frown made him look uncertain, even vulnerable. 'Could I have a few minutes?'

'Why?' she asked, hating that her voice trembled. 'I don't understand why you're here. How did you find out where I live?'

'I went to the rest centre where I last saw you. You gave your address to one of the WVS ladies and I persuaded her to give it to me.'

'She had no business doing that,' said Lorna.

'Please don't blame her. I was very persistent.' He smiled but Lorna refused to smile back. 'I told her about the lady we rescued – Mrs Flowers. I said I wanted to let you know how she was getting on. That wasn't a lie. I went to see her in hospital, and I'm pleased to tell you she's none the worse for her ordeal.'

'That's good. Thanks for letting me know.' She started to turn away, not wanting to show George the tears in her eyes.

'The two children, Stan and Patsy, are being cared for by

their auntie. Mrs Flowers is to stay in hospital for a couple of days to be on the safe side.'

'It was kind of you to find out,' said Lorna.

An ease slipped into place between them, a feeling of familiarity, of remembered harmony and compatibility.

Lorna took a step backwards. 'I should join the others.'

'I didn't seek you out just to tell you about Mrs Flowers,' George said quickly. 'I wanted to see you.' He waited and, when she didn't answer, he said, 'I hoped you might want to see me.'

'Says the man who broke things off between us.' Lorna spoke sharply to hide her hurt.

'I know this might appear inappropriate,' George said wistfully, 'but I had to take the chance. I'm going to be in Manchester for a while. I've got a suite in the Claremont Hotel. I hope we might see one another. I'd like to know what you've been doing since I last saw you. I'd like to get to know you, the real you, away from all the pressures of London society, away from—'

'From my family,' Lorna finished crisply.

'And mine,' George answered immediately, surprising her. 'On Sunday night I saw a side of you I've never glimpsed before. I'd like the chance to know that brave, determined girl. Do you want the whole truth, Lorna? On Sunday evening, when the lists were pinned up on the Town Hall noticeboards – I fiddled with the lists.'

'You did what?' she exclaimed.

'You and I had been put in different groups, so I did some crossing out and rewriting and put us in the same group. And now I'm so very glad I did. I was already impressed by how you conducted yourself in the first cellar. I came late to that rescue and all I saw was this girl in a gas-mask, keeping her cool and putting other people first – and that turned out to be you. So I altered the Town Hall lists so I could stay close to you – and now I very much hope you'll agree to see me again. What d'you say, Lorna? Will you at least consider it?'

CHAPTER ELEVEN

Even though the two nights of what was now being referred to as the Christmas Blitz, followed by being up until all hours on Christmas Eve preparing hotpots, pies, vegetables and sultana puddings, had left Sally deeply tired, she kept waking up after she collapsed into bed for a few hours before Christmas Day began. Anxiety about Andrew made it impossible to succumb to sleep. Finally, she awoke from a light doze when the front door opened softly. She threw aside the bedclothes, swinging her feet to the floor, toes scrabbling about to locate her slippers. Switching on the bedside lamp, she looked at the clock: it was just gone half past six.

She pulled on her dressing gown without bothering to tie it and ran downstairs into Andrew's arms. He smelled of smoke overlaid by the aroma of something oily and rather sickly, but Sally didn't care. She held him tightly, pressing herself as close to him as she could as her worry for him faded away.

'You'll end up all stinky if you hang on to me,' he murmured, continuing to hold her.

Eventually Sally broke away. 'Let's get you out of those clothes.'

'I like the sound of that.'

'So I can hang them in the back garden to air,' she said in a pretend-severe voice. 'You need to have a good wash and then get some sleep. You must be worn out.'

From above them came Mrs Henshaw's voice. 'Good – you're home. You're safe.' She came halfway down the stairs, then stopped. 'Sally will look after you.'

Ever since Sally had first moved in with Andrew and his mother as their lodger before she and Andrew got married, Mrs Henshaw had made a point of giving way to Sally in the matter of taking care of Andrew, something that Sally appreciated deeply, and all the more so because she knew that Deborah's mother regularly sent unsolicited advice to her new daughter-in-law about Rod's likes and dislikes.

Andrew smiled up at his mother. 'I'm a bit whiffy at the moment.'

'More than a bit,' she answered.

'Let me get cleaned up and grab a bit of shut-eye. Then, as the lone male in the house, I'll regard it as my duty to dispense hugs in all directions.' Andrew reached for Sally's hand. 'This isn't what I'd envisaged for our first Christmas together, but I want us to have the best day possible in the circumstances.'

'So do I,' Sally whispered, her voice catching.

'Though I warn you now there may be some festive snoring this afternoon.'

'I'll wake you up if it gets too loud,' Sally answered. 'We can't have a passing ARP warden setting off the siren because it sounds like enemy aircraft overhead.'

* * *

Mrs Beaumont prepared a special breakfast of devilled herrings for Christmas morning.

'It's delicious,' said Lorna, 'but it makes me feel guilty when

I think of all those homeless people we were cooking for last night.'

Mrs Beaumont dealt her a stern look. 'That's enough of that. It's a great shame for all those who've lost their homes and their belongings, of course it is, but there's no call for guilt. A sincere appreciation of your own good luck is much healthier.'

After breakfast, they all put on their outdoor things to go to church.

'You all sit where you like,' said Mrs Beaumont, 'but I'll sit at the back so I can slip out before the end and do the dinner.'

'We'll all help,' Mrs Henshaw began.

'There's no call for that, thank you,' Mrs Beaumont replied. 'I peeled and chopped the potatoes, carrots and parsnips yesterday afternoon and left them in pans of water, so there isn't much to do.'

Mrs Henshaw sighed, then quickly put a smile on her face.

The Christmas service was a poignant affair, with prayers for the dead and injured of the terrible Blitz. Local people from Chorlton-cum-Hardy were mentioned – Dorothy Bryan of 316 Wilbraham Road, Ernest and Gene Carr of 549a Wilbraham Road, Anastasia Watterson of 2 Silverdale Road, the Smith family of 18 Cheltenham Road, Annie and Daniel Paton of 66 Newport Road, who had all lost their lives; and Charles Foster of 18 Albemarle Road, the Ogilvys of 4 Silverdale Road, Ethel Weeks of 210 Brantingham Road and what felt like numerous residents of Cheltenham Road, who had all suffered serious injuries. The road names meant little to Sally, not being a local girl, but when she saw members of the congregation bow their heads or swipe away a tear, a pang of sorrow smote her.

It made her think of Withington, where she had grown up. She yearned for the news from there and she ached to see Mum and Dad, and Deborah and her parents. She and Andrew were going over there tomorrow. That had been the arrangement all along, from before the Henshaws' house had been hit: Sally and

Andrew would spend Christmas Day with Andrew's mother and Boxing Day with Mum and Dad.

The thought of all those families who would never share another Christmas Day was suddenly overwhelming, and Sally dropped her chin to her chest to hide her emotion.

At the end of the service, they walked home. The chilly breeze held a real bite. Sally left Andrew to accompany his mother while she walked with the other two girls. Lorna looked very dashing in a plum-coloured wool coat with wide lapels and deep turned-back cuffs with top-stitching.

'I'm lucky to be able to spend today with Andrew,' Sally said to Betty. 'What about Samuel's family?'

'His brother and sister are both in the services,' said Betty. 'John is abroad and Samuel isn't sure where. Valerie is a nurse with the Queen Alexandra's and she's working over Christmas.'

'I wish you could be with Samuel – or rather, I wish he could spend the day with us at Star House.'

'So do I,' Betty agreed, 'but he was invited ages ago to go to the Kendalls' for Christmas. Have I mentioned them to you before? They're his elderly neighbours and he helps them out by doing their shopping and running errands. Inviting him for Christmas Day is their way of paying him back. He wouldn't dream of putting them off – and I wouldn't want him to. When Samuel agrees to do something, he does it and I like that. He always keeps a promise. Not everyone does.'

'That's true,' said Lorna.

'Are you thinking of how George let you down?' Betty shivered. 'It must be horrible to be jilted.'

'What made him turn up at the school kitchen yesterday?' Sally asked, quickly adding, 'You don't have to say if you don't want to.'

'He wants to see me again,' said Lorna.

'Crikey!' Betty exclaimed. 'Are you going to?'

Lorna didn't reply immediately.

'Would you like to?' Sally asked quietly.

Lorna shrugged her slender shoulders. 'I honestly don't know. Part of me wants to and part is yelling at me, telling me not to be so ridiculous. I don't want to set myself up to get hurt all over again, but on the other hand...' Another shrug, this time accompanied by a don't-care tilt of the chin that wasn't as convincing as it might have been.

They arrived home to a mouthwatering herby aroma that suggested Mrs Beaumont was preparing the stuffing.

'Can I do anything to help?' Mrs Henshaw called amidst the bustle of taking off outdoor things.

'I'm on top of everything, thank you,' came the reply from the kitchen.

'I can at least sort out the dining room,' Mrs Henshaw said in a quietly determined voice.

'We'll help,' Lorna offered.

But when they opened the door they found that Mrs Beaumont had already pushed together all the small tables to make one huge one, which she had covered with a vast snowy tablecloth with scalloped edges of heavy lacework. The table was set and each place had a linen napkin hand-embroidered with springs of holly.

It wasn't long before Christmas dinner was on the table. It might not have been the hearty, meaty meal of pre-war days, but Mrs Beaumont was nothing if not an excellent cook and, with the memory of the Christmas Blitz still raw, the dinner was one to be savoured.

After the main course, Mrs Beaumont brought out the Christmas pudding.

'This is lovely,' said Betty.

'I never imagined I'd one day put mashed potato and cider into a Christmas pud, but it hasn't turned out badly at all,' Mrs Beaumont replied.

'Congrats, Mrs Beaumont,' Lorna said at the end of the

meal. 'That was a wonderful feast. How you managed to pull it off with all the shortages, I don't know.'

'Now you must put your feet up,' said Mrs Henshaw, 'while I clear away.'

'I've told you before,' replied Mrs Beaumont. 'I'm a professional landlady. Clearing away this number of dishes is nothing to me.'

While she set to work in the kitchen, Betty and Lorna picked up the *Radio Times*, with its jolly picture on the front cover of Father Christmas in a tin hat with BBC on it, and started to examine the listings. Seeing the fed-up look on her mother-in-law's face, Sally took her aside for a quiet word.

'I do wish Mrs Beaumont would permit me to help,' said Mrs Henshaw. 'I've looked after my own home all my adult life and I miss it.'

'It's like Mrs Beaumont says. She's a professional landlady,' said Sally. 'You should relax and let yourself be looked after. You deserve it.'

But Mrs Henshaw looked at her as if she was mad. Sally smothered a sigh. She didn't want to be piggy-in-the-middle. She loved and respected Andrew's mother and could see her point of view. She was also increasingly fond of Mrs Beaumont and could see things through her eyes too.

'There's music by the Orchestre Raymonde,' said Betty, looking up from the *Radio Times*. 'Shall we have that on while we open our presents?'

The gifts were under the tree. Some were wrapped in Christmas paper Mrs Beaumont had saved from last year, others in brown paper or even newspaper since proper wrapping paper, being far from essential, was now hard to find.

Everything was unwrapped with little exclamations of delight. For the women Lorna had managed to buy a large jar of rose-scented bath salts, which she had decanted into jam jars tied with pretty ribbon. Mrs Henshaw had knitted scarves for

Betty and Lorna and embroidered a tray-cloth for Mrs Beaumont, who had sewn needle-cases and pincushions for the girls.

Andrew received cigarettes and toffee, as well as the shaving mirror from Sally, which he made a big fuss over. As well as the tea cosy Sally had knitted, Andrew and Sally gave his mother a set of eggcups.

'For when you eventually have your own home again, Mum,' said Andrew.

But the best gift of all was from Mrs Henshaw to Sally and Andrew.

'You open it.' Andrew handed it to Sally.

She removed the paper – and caught her breath in a huge gulp of astonishment as she recognised the photograph frame that had once stood on the mantelpiece in the Henshaws' old house and which she had last seen among the stolen goods that Eddie Markham had stored in the depot. The frame had been empty then because Eddie had chucked away the photograph – but now the picture was back in its rightful place. Sally couldn't tear her gaze away from the photograph of herself and Andrew on their wedding day.

'You've given us back our wedding picture,' she whispered. 'I thought this photograph was lost for ever.'

'It isn't the original,' said Mrs Henshaw. 'Andrew's uncle took the picture, and he still had the negative, so I asked him to have a copy developed.'

Sally's vision misted. 'It's perfect. Thank you. I couldn't have dreamed of a better present this Christmas.'

On Boxing Day morning Sally and Andrew went for a walk. It was another cold day and a stiff wind carried the smell of smoke everywhere. Sally wrinkled her nose.

'It feels as though the smell has been hanging in the air for ever,' she commented.

'I ought to go back into town,' said Andrew. 'Even if there are no more rescues, there's plenty of rubble to be shifted and ruined buildings that need to be made safe.'

'Don't forget we're going to Mum and Dad's this afternoon,' Sally reminded him. She was looking forward to it and wanted him to as well.

His smile didn't quite reach his eyes. 'Yes, of course.' Then he stopped walking and faced her, his smile now genuine. 'We'll all have a good time together. Your mum has invited the Grants to drop in, hasn't she?'

'You'll enjoy seeing them all, won't you?' Sally asked as they started walking again.

'Yes – as long as Rod isn't there,' Andrew added wryly.

'You and me both,' agreed Sally. She gave a little shudder at the memory of Rod holding her hand a fraction too tightly or drawing it through the crook of his arm and clamping it to his side.

'He made you unhappy, didn't he?'

'He did,' said Sally, 'though it was a while before I realised it, what with everybody saying what a wonderful couple we made. Then the powers that be sent him off to work in Barrow, which made it possible for me to ignore the problem for longer.' She sighed. 'I do wish I'd handled it better.'

'You coped as best you could,' Andrew said loyally. 'Part of it was that you didn't want to upset your family and Rod's family.'

'I'm so glad you understand,' Sally said. 'You're the only man I have ever really and truly loved and the only one I could have married.'

'That's handy,' said Andrew, 'because you're the only one I could have married too.'

When they returned to Star House, Mrs Henshaw was on her way out, dressed in her WVS uniform.

'I'll see you later,' she said. 'I hope you both enjoy this afternoon.'

Lorna and Betty were getting ready to go out as well.

'There's a day of games, stories and simple crafts at St Clement's,' said Betty. 'It's to keep the children busy while their parents work at removing furniture and other things from bombed-out houses and get them put in storage. The over-twelves will be helping the adults while the under-twelves are being kept busy in the church hall. Me and Lorna are going along for an hour or two.'

'That sounds worthwhile,' Andrew commented before turning to Sally. 'Would you mind if I went out and helped with the clear-up? Not in town, but locally. I promise to be back in plenty of time to go to Withington.'

'You can come with us, Sally,' said Lorna.

Sally couldn't help feeling disappointed. She had hoped – assumed – that she and Andrew would have the whole morning together before they went out, but of course the war effort was more important than anything. Andrew's dedication to his war work was something she deeply respected.

Raising herself on tiptoe, she placed a little kiss on his cheek. 'Of course. Just make sure you're not late back,' she said with a smile, determined to keep her disappointment to herself.

Sally and Andrew got off the bus in Withington and walked briskly through the streets to the Whites' house. The day had grown colder and Sally stamped her feet as Andrew rang the bell.

Dad opened the door. 'Come on in out of the chill. Happy Christmas.'

'Happy Christmas, Dad,' Sally responded.

She stepped indoors, giving Dad a kiss. Mum was in the hall as well.

'Strictly speaking,' she said, 'it's Happy Boxing Day.'

Sally glanced at her. A little reminder that their only daughter hadn't been with them on Christmas Day itself? That would be just like Mum. But no, she was smiling, her hazel eyes warm and approving.

'Take off your coats and come into the parlour,' she added. 'It's jolly parky outside.'

'It certainly is,' Andrew agreed.

'We've got a good fire going,' said Dad. 'We've been saving a couple of lumps of coal each day for this.'

'Oh, Dad, you didn't.' Sally was concerned.

'We'd do anything for our girl,' said Dad. 'And you're not to go imagining that we were sitting here freezing, because we weren't.'

The parlour was cosy, the fire cheerful. As she sat down and made herself comfy, Sally looked around her childhood home with a feeling of affection – the dark-green three-piece suite that her father had inherited not long after he and Mum got married, Mum's knitting basket on the floor by her armchair, the standard lamp with the fringed lampshade, Dad's pipe-rack, the ashtray.

'Are you admiring the tree?' Mum asked.

Sally focused on it. 'This is the tree I grew up with,' she said to Andrew.

Standing on a table by the wall, it was about three feet tall, decorated with baubles that were years old and tinsel that was almost bald in places. It looked the same as it always had and gave Sally a sense of continuity, though she didn't say so in case it sounded daft.

They exchanged gifts. Sally had got a pair of gloves for Mum and a second-hand book from Samuel's shop about growing vegetables for Dad, who was very keen on his vegetable plot.

'I told you not to get us anything, you naughty girl,' said Mum.

'I'll take them back again, shall I?' Sally asked with a laugh.

For her from her parents was a jumper knitted by Mum and a box of talcum powder with a large powder puff.

'It's gorgeous,' Sally exclaimed, sniffing the talc.

'Don't use it all at once,' warned Mum. 'Things like that are going to be impossible to get before long. This one is for you as well, Sally.'

'Mum, you shouldn't have.'

'Open it.'

Mum had knitted a white shawl with a lacy pattern.

'It's beautiful,' said Sally. 'You are clever. It'll be perfect for when Andrew and I go out dancing.'

For Andrew, Mum had knitted a V-necked sweater in dark-brown wool with cable stitch down the front. He immediately took off his jacket and put it on.

'It's champion. Thank you, Mrs White.'

'My pleasure,' said Mum, pleased. She looked at Sally. 'The Grants will be here soon. Let's put the kettle on and warm up the mince pies.'

They went into the kitchen.

'Thanks for the presents, Mum,' Sally said. 'Thanks for knitting a sweater for Andrew.'

'I like knitting,' Mum said over her shoulder as she filled the kettle in the scullery.

Sally started getting out the crockery. 'And my shawl is heavenly. It's so fine, it's like gossamer.'

Mum stood in the scullery doorway, looking at her. 'You do realise it isn't a shawl?'

Sally frowned. 'Yes, it is.'

'It's a christening robe.'

Sally had cups in her hands. She quickly set them down before she could drop them.

'It's a... But I'm not...'

'Well, you ought to be.'

'*Mum.*'

'Anyway, you've got the christening robe for when the time comes.'

Sally didn't know what to say. Then the bell rang and she put the conversation to one side as she rushed to admit the Grants. She had loved the family all her life and Mrs Grant was a second mother to her. She opened the parlour door for them, then returned to the kitchen to help Mum load two trays and carry them through.

'It's good to see you, Sally,' said Mrs Grant. 'I hope you managed to have a pleasant Christmas Day.'

'We did, actually,' said Sally, 'though we were all tired from the cooking the previous night.'

'We did that as well,' said Deborah. 'I hope everyone got a meal that needed one.'

'I'm sure they did,' said Mum. 'It all seemed very well organised.'

'I'm just glad that Jerry stayed away the past two nights,' said Mr Grant.

'Well now,' said Dad, 'I think we should concentrate on something else. Having us all here together is special and we could do with a bit of jollity. How about a game of cards?'

The Grants stayed for an hour and Sally was sorry to see them go. She hugged Deborah when it was time to say goodbye.

'I wish we'd had a chance to talk.'

Or maybe it was just as well that they hadn't had the chance to be alone. She would probably have told Deborah about the christening robe – and what if Deborah had then told her mum – and if Mrs Grant had mentioned it to a neighbour... No, it was far better to keep the lid on all that.

Sally and Mum made mock-turkey sandwiches, using the leftover mock-turkey from Mum and Dad's Christmas dinner.

Sally wondered if they had stinted themselves yesterday, because there was certainly an ample amount today.

After they had eaten, it was time for the Henshaws to catch the bus home.

Sally wondered whether to tell Andrew that her beautiful shawl really had a different purpose. What would he say? She couldn't suppress a flicker of excitement. Even so, she decided not to say anything. It wasn't all that long since Mum had done her best to get her and Andrew to move to the countryside, and now here she was dropping a hint the size of a ton of bricks that she wanted a grandchild. Sally didn't want Andrew thinking he had a managing sort for a mother-in-law.

When they got back to Star House, they went upstairs to change out of their shoes and into their slippers. Andrew hadn't said much on the way home. Now he turned to Sally with a serious look in his brown eyes. For a moment she imagined that the christening robe conversation in the kitchen must have been audible in the parlour, even though she knew it couldn't have been.

Andrew took her hands. 'Sally, there's something I have to tell you.'

'That sounds serious.'

'It is,' he confirmed. 'I didn't intend to say anything yet but I've known since the second night of the Blitz and I can't keep it from you any longer. I'm going to join up.'

Something cold and hard thumped Sally inside her stomach. 'You're what?' she whispered.

'I told you what the Blitz was like, what I witnessed.'

'I know. It was terrible for you. It was terrible for everyone.'

'It was, but "everyone" doesn't build coffins like I do – and not just coffins. Smaller boxes, too, for – for limbs and body parts that have been retrieved. I didn't choose to do this, Sally. I was ordered to. I was told it was essential war work – and it is. I can see that. But I talked to you before about how it feels as though I'm inviting death to come.'

'You didn't invite the Christmas Blitz to take place,' said Sally.

'Yet I seem to have spent a lot of time preparing for its aftermath,' said Andrew. 'The numbers that have died...'

'I know how it tears at your heart to build all those coffins,' said Sally, 'but...' But what? She didn't know how to finish the sentence.

'I don't want to stay here and make coffins.' Andrew's voice was flat. 'I want to join up. I *have* to join up. After everything I saw in the Christmas Blitz, I have to fight for my country.'

Sally's heart cracked from top to bottom. She wanted to say, 'Don't leave me.' She wanted to say, 'What will I do without you?' She wanted to say, 'Please stay.'

Instead she uttered the words she knew she had to say.

'The very last thing I want is for you to go, but if you're determined then I'll support your choice. Of course I will.'

Andrew's arms slid round her, pulling her to him. Sally laid her cheek against his chest and stared, eyes wide, at nothing. Supporting his decision was her duty as a good wife, but even so... what had she just done?

CHAPTER TWELVE

On Friday, the day after Boxing Day, the siren commenced its mournful wail at a quarter to one in the afternoon. Cold fear washed through Betty. Was this to be another prolonged and merciless onslaught like on the two nights of the Christmas Blitz?

She was in the depot yard, standing on top of a vast crate filled with empty tin cans and other random pieces of metal along with odds and ends of rubber. For the past hour, she'd been balancing on the shifting heap, bent over so she could chuck everything into smaller crates, metal one side and rubber the other. As far as the salvage girls were concerned, it was an extra job because the factory that had sent the large crate ought to have kept the two types of salvage separate in the first place.

Stepping across the salvage was like walking across a sand dune. Everything shifted beneath Betty's feet. Sally came running across the yard to help her climb down.

Glad to be back on firm ground, Betty looked around. 'Where's Lorna?'

'She'll join us in the cellar. Come on.'

They entered the building, and met Lorna at the head of

the cellar steps. She carried a tray of tea. They walked halfway down and sat on the steps, nursing their hot mugs and smoking.

'As if there hasn't been enough damage done already,' Betty said. 'Those two nights before Christmas...' She shuddered as her words trailed away.

'Chin up,' said Lorna. 'We'll get through it.'

'There's going to be a funeral with a mass grave tomorrow in Southern Cemetery,' Sally said soberly, and they were all silent for a moment.

'I'm sorry this has happened to your home town,' said Lorna.

Sally bowed her head. Betty assumed she must be deep in thought, but then – did her shoulders twitch? She sniffed.

Betty hastily put down her mug and dumped her cigarette in the saucer they used as an ashtray, then bumped down a couple of steps to gather Sally in her arms. 'What is it? You're crying! Tell us what's happened.'

Sally lifted her chin and took a couple of gulps of air. 'I didn't mean to say anything but I'm so worried. It's Andrew. He wants to join up – and when I say "wants to", I mean he's going to. He's set on it. It's because of everything he saw in the Blitz.'

'When did this happen?' Lorna asked.

'He told me on Boxing Day.'

'Oh, Sally,' said Betty, picturing how she would feel if Samuel were to make such an announcement. Not that he could, because he had a medical exemption, but all the same... 'You must feel wretched.'

'You could say that.' Sally sat up straight, brushing away her tears, and Betty loosened her embrace, leaving one arm draped round her. 'But he's determined to go and I'm determined to support his decision. We haven't told his mother yet, so please don't say a word at home.'

'Of course not,' Lorna promised.

'I asked for a few days to let me get used to the idea,' Sally explained, 'but I feel more unsettled with each passing hour. I can't bear to think of him going away. Then I feel guilty because there are thousands upon thousands of women whose husbands were called up right at the start.'

'It's hard on everybody who's left behind,' said Lorna.

Sally nodded. 'Ever since I met him, I've felt so lucky that he's in a reserved occupation.'

'Won't that mean he won't be allowed to go?' Betty asked.

'If a man in a reserved occupation wants to join up,' said Sally, 'he can generally get permission as long as there is a suitable person to take over from him at work.'

'Many male teachers have joined up,' said Lorna, 'so presumably Andrew will be allowed to.'

Betty pulled Sally closer again and planted a kiss on her cheek. 'It'll be hard for you, but we'll take care of you – won't we, Lorna?'

'Definitely,' said Lorna.

The Friday dinnertime raid lasted three-quarters of an hour. No bombs were dropped but Betty still felt anxious.

'I hope this won't be the start of a spate of daytime raids,' she said to Lorna that afternoon while they were tying the heap of paper into bundles ready to be taken to the paper-mill while Sally was in the office returning some telephone calls. 'I'm taking Samuel to meet my dad and stepmother this Sunday and I'd hate it to be spoiled.'

'Meeting the family.' Lorna smiled. 'That sounds serious.'

'It is important,' said Betty, 'not just because I truly love Samuel but also because it's not all that long since I was keen on Eddie.'

'But he turned out to be a crook,' said Lorna, 'whereas Samuel is honest and respectable. Your parents are bound to appreciate that.' Betty must have reacted without even realising it, because Lorna added, 'Sorry. Have I said the wrong thing?'

Betty huffed a sigh. 'No, it's just me being daft. It was when you said "parents". I don't see Grace as my mother.'

'Don't you get on?'

Betty chewed the inside of her cheek. If she talked freely about Grace, would that be disloyal to Dad? She adored her lovely dad and had always bent over backwards to shield him from the truth about her and Grace, but surely there was no harm in confiding in a trusted friend? Frankly, it would be a relief.

'We do and we don't,' she said. 'On the surface we do, and we definitely do in front of Dad, but underneath it's different. She's always wanted to get rid of me. She never said it in so many words, but I could always tell. You know how I came to lose my previous job. It was Grace who got me fixed up with this job, and the billet at Star House, miles away from her and Dad. And when Eddie was arrested and he tried blaming it all on me, Grace came round to Star House and told me I could never go home again because of the disgrace I'd brought on Dad.'

'What did your father say to that?' Lorna asked.

'Nothing. I never told him. It would have hurt him dreadfully.'

'And that would have been the last thing you wanted,' Lorna said, nodding her understanding. 'You're a good daughter, Betty. I'm sorry I referred to Grace as one of your parents. She doesn't deserve that title.'

'She takes care of my dad,' said Betty, feeling she ought to play fair. 'She looks after the house and she's a good cook. It means a lot to me that Dad is looked after.'

'I'm sure your mother would have wanted him to be taken care of,' Lorna said gently.

'But not by Grace!' Betty exclaimed. 'She was a widow on

the hunt for a new husband and I know exactly what Mum thought of her.'

'Which gives you another reason to feel iffy about her. What d'you think she'll make of you and Samuel?'

Betty sighed. 'When I was going out with Eddie, she was very keen and made a big fuss of me. I enjoyed it, even though I knew that what she really wanted was for me to get married so there'd be no chance of me going back home to Dad's in the future.'

'Then it's in her interests to approve of you and Samuel,' said Lorna.

'Put like that, yes. To be honest, I'm more concerned about what Dad thinks.'

'He means a lot to you,' Lorna said softly.

'He's always been my hero,' said Betty.

* * *

That evening, Lorna invited Betty into her bedroom to take a look through her wardrobe to see if she'd like to borrow something to wear on Sunday when she took Samuel to Salford to meet her father and Grace. Tomorrow was Betty's Saturday for opening the depot, so Lorna had chosen to do this now, thinking it would feel more relaxed than if she waited until tomorrow evening.

Lorna had never received much of a personal allowance from Daddy, but he had always been generous when it came to footing the bill for clothes. He liked Lorna and her mother to look expensively dressed because that reflected well on him.

Lorna watched as Betty admired her things, though she could tell her friend felt awkward about borrowing.

It was time to take charge. Lorna plucked a royal-blue dress from its hanger. It had a collarless neckline, patch pockets and buttons down the front of the bodice.

'This would go well with your colouring,' she said. 'It's always been a bit roomy as I'm so straight up and down, so it should look lovely on you. You're curvier than I am. Try it on.'

The sparkle in Betty's eyes showed how tempted she was, and she didn't require much encouragement to slip out of her own clothes and into the jersey wool dress, which skimmed over her figure to the waist before the skirt flared a little.

Smiling, Lorna turned Betty to face the mirror. 'Take a look at yourself.'

Betty breathed a sigh of pleasure. 'Are you sure it's all right for me to borrow it?'

'I wouldn't have offered otherwise,' said Lorna. At a knock on the door, she looked in that direction, calling, 'Come in.'

Sally entered. 'I've brought— my goodness, Betty! What a beautiful dress. Where did you get it?'

Betty grinned. 'From Lorna's wardrobe. She says I can borrow it on Sunday.'

'I hope you're going to accept the offer,' said Sally. 'It's perfect on you.'

'Thanks, Lorna,' said Betty. 'I'd love to borrow it. It'll be a treat to wear something so lovely.'

Sally handed Lorna a knitting pattern. 'This is the one I told you about. I'm glad you're here too, Betty, so I can tell you both together how much I appreciated your kindness when I was upset about Andrew joining up.'

'It's what friends are for,' said Lorna.

Betty smiled at her. 'You were kind to me an' all, listening to me banging on about Grace. It helped.'

'Any time,' said Lorna.

'And you must feel able to talk to us about George if you want to,' said Sally.

Lorna hesitated before admitting, 'I've been thinking about him a lot, to tell you the truth. I've told myself that with you, Betty, taking Samuel to Salford and you, Sally, dreading

Andrew leaving, it's only natural for me to think about George. But I know that's not the real reason. He's in my mind because... because he's George.'

'It sounds to me,' said Betty, 'as though you'd like to see him again.'

'It's what he wants too,' Sally added. 'Think of the trouble he went to to track you down so he could tell you.'

'How do you feel?' Betty asked. 'Be honest.'

'How do I feel? Excited. Intrigued. It would be impossible not to. But it's also impossible not to curse myself for being interested. Anyway,' Lorna added, trying to sound dismissive, 'it hardly matters whether I'm interested or not, because I told him on the night of the Christmas cooking that I didn't want to see him again.'

'Is that what you truly want?' Sally asked.

Lorna nodded. 'Yes.'

CHAPTER THIRTEEN

On Saturday morning Sally took down the blackout frame that covered the bedroom window and peeped through the curtains underneath. Frost made a lacy pattern on the inside of the panes, which told her all she needed to know about the sort of day it was going to be. Wrapped up inside her dressing gown, she hugged herself as she left the window and smiled at her drowsy husband. He had a firm jawline but sometimes there was something vulnerable in the set of his mouth, and never more so than at moments like this.

He blinked a couple of times, then his gaze settled on her, his smile making his brown eyes crinkle.

'Morning, Mrs Henshaw.' There was still a dreamy heaviness in his voice.

Sally perched beside him, leaning down for a kiss. 'Morning, Mr Henshaw.' She rested the side of her face against his chest. 'We need to tell your mother that you're going to join up.'

'Are you sure you're ready to?'

Sally said lightly, 'If you wait for me to be ready, you'll wait a jolly long time.' Sitting up, she looked at her husband. 'There's nothing to be gained by putting it off. She'd be hurt if she thought we'd kept it from her.'

'True,' Andrew agreed.

'She's going over to your Auntie Vera's this afternoon,' said Sally. 'What if we tell her this morning? Then she can talk it over with Auntie Vera.'

Andrew nodded. 'Good idea.' He drew in a breath that inflated his chest, then let it out.

'I know,' said Sally. 'I don't want to upset her either, but there's no way round it. It's Betty's Saturday for the depot and Lorna has a WVS shift, so I'll ask Mrs Beaumont if we can have the sitting room to ourselves for a while.'

Part of her boggled at what she was doing. She was helping to make it possible for Andrew to go off to war. She must be mad! She would do anything to have him stay here with her. But if he wanted to fight for king and country, then it was her duty to give him every encouragement. She knew his mother would feel the same once she had recovered from the shock.

Sally was careful to behave normally at the breakfast table, until she realised she was behaving *too* normally, being too chatty, and reined herself in before anyone could notice.

Soon Betty and Lorna disappeared, and Mrs Beaumont picked up her wicker shopping basket.

'Time to go and stand in a queue,' she joked.

Sally and Andrew looked at one another.

'Mum,' said Andrew, 'come into the sitting room. We've got something to tell you.'

Mrs Henshaw's face brightened. 'Oh...' she breathed, blue eyes shining.

Good grief, she wasn't hoping for a baby announcement, was she? First Mum and the christening robe, now this.

'Come and sit down,' said Sally. 'This is important.' She used her most serious voice, anxious to quell the baby idea without having to say the actual words.

When Mrs Henshaw sat on the sofa, Andrew took the place beside her. Mrs Henshaw looked from him to Sally and back again. 'What is it?'

'Mum, there's no easy way to tell you this—'

'Just tell me.' There was no smile now.

'I'm joining up,' Andrew said, taking his mother's hand. 'After what happened at Christmas, I can't stay here any longer. I've got to go and do my bit.'

'You're doing your bit here,' his mother protested, her natural strength and authority vanishing as maternal anguish came to the fore. She stared at Sally. 'What do you think of this?'

Sally pushed back her shoulders. 'I understand why Andrew wants to do this and I wouldn't dream of standing in his way. He has my full support.'

Mrs Henshaw's eyes widened, then she pressed her mouth tight shut before giving a crisp nod. To Andrew she said, 'If you're sure, then obviously it's what you must do. Sally and I will stand by you.'

'Yes, we will,' said Sally.

Letting go of his mother's hand, Andrew enveloped her in his arms and held her close. Mrs Henshaw clung to him for several moments, then wriggled free.

'Well,' she said, resuming her usual briskness, 'it's going to take a bit of getting used to. Is it a secret or can I tell Auntie Vera?'

'Tell her,' said Sally. 'The reason we're telling you now is because you're seeing her later on.'

Mrs Henshaw gave her a sharp look. 'Oh aye? You've got it all planned, haven't you? I'm sorry, I shouldn't have said that. I know you both mean well – and you're right. It will be a comfort to talk to Vera.'

Sally and Andrew exchanged looks of relief.

When they were alone, they hugged one another.

'Thank you,' Andrew whispered.

Sally held him tighter. She knew she'd done the right thing in supporting him – but, oh, it was hard.

Andrew went off to spend the afternoon working on the massive clear-up operation following the Blitz. Sally wished he'd chosen to spend the time with her now that their time together was limited, but she knew him better than that. His duty was an important part of who he was and she respected that. Besides, she had her own duties. As a fire-watcher, she had to help fill more sandbags and distribute them.

Before they went their separate ways, she made Andrew promise not to be late back.

'Your mother has to be our priority this evening. Our news will have sunk in properly by then and she may be upset.'

But when she returned to Star House, Mrs Henshaw had, in her characteristic efficient fashion, set aside her worry and distress, and was all focus.

'I don't want you to go, Andrew, but what mother does? I've had a long discussion with Vera this afternoon and that's helped me sort things out in my head.'

'That's good,' Sally said, wondering what was coming.

'I've decided that if you're not going to be here, Andrew, then I'd be happier leaving Star House. Don't look so surprised. I appreciate Mrs Beaumont's generosity in taking us all in. If she hadn't, we'd have been split up, so I'll always be grateful to her for that, for giving us a bit longer together. But the truth is that living here doesn't really suit me.'

'Mum, I had no idea...' Andrew began.

'Which goes to show how unobservant you are – just like your father. I was a bride at eighteen and we were lucky enough to have a home of our own right from the start. I've been the lady of the house, responsible for everything, doing all the housework and the catering, my entire adult life. Now I live in Star House, which is comfortable and spotlessly clean, and I don't have a bad word to say about it – but I'm not permitted to lift a finger, other than to make my own bed and keep my room tidy.'

'Mrs Beaumont is a professional landlady,' Sally said. 'She sees it as her job to look after us.'

'I'm well aware of that, thank you,' Mrs Henshaw answered crisply. 'The fact remains that Star House doesn't suit me and, when Andrew leaves, it will be time for me to go too.'

'To Auntie Vera's?' Andrew asked.

'We've arranged it all between us,' his mother assured him. 'With her boys away fighting, there are two bedrooms going begging. I'll have one of them and Vera and I will divvy up the cleaning and the shopping.'

Sally was taken aback. This was the last thing she'd foreseen, but if she was going to support Andrew's decision, she had to support his mother's too.

'It's a great shame that you want to leave Star House,' she said, 'but I can see why. It sounds as if this is the right thing for you.'

'I'm pleased you think so.' Mrs Henshaw smiled at her.

'Not that I want you to go,' Sally added. 'I'll miss you.'

'No, you won't, you silly thing,' said Mrs Henshaw. 'I said there are two spare bedrooms, didn't I? You don't imagine I'd leave you behind you, do you? You're coming with me, of course – the two Mrs Henshaws sticking together.'

* * *

By the time she reached Star House after the end of her WVS shift, Lorna had made up her mind, even while she asked herself how she could contemplate anything so crazy. She'd spent the day thinking of Sally bravely accepting Andrew's decision to join up. She'd thought too of all those who had suffered bereavements in the Christmas Blitz. If she had the chance to see George, even if it was just for one more time, shouldn't she seize it with both hands?

Maybe she ought to talk it over with her friends – but when she got home, she found the Henshaws in a state of family upheaval, because Mrs Henshaw had informed Mrs Beaumont that in due course she would be moving out. Not only that but she expected Sally to go with her. Sally looked shocked and upset but was keeping quiet on the subject.

'Leave them be,' Mrs Beaumont advised Lorna and Betty, who had also just come home. 'Nothing is going to happen in a hurry. It will depend on when Andrew gets permission to go.'

'It all sounds very upsetting,' Betty commented.

'They'll sort it out,' Mrs Beaumont replied.

Lorna and Betty went upstairs. Lorna needed to change out of her WVS uniform and Betty had to change her shoes for slippers. Lorna was hanging up her green uniform when there was a tap on the door and Betty opened it.

'Can I come in? What a thing to happen. I expected Mrs Henshaw to be upset about Andrew but I never imagined anything like this.'

'It makes it even more of an upheaval.' Seeing the worried look on her chum's pretty face, Lorna gave her hand a squeeze. 'All we can do is lend a sympathetic ear.'

Betty nodded. 'I'm seeing Samuel this evening. I made him promise not to volunteer for an additional ARP night. He needs a break.'

'Good idea.'

'Would you like to come out with us? Samuel won't mind. He thinks the world of you and Sally after the way you helped me when the police suspected me, thanks to Eddie. It would save you from being here while the Henshaws are having a to-do.'

'It's sweet of you to offer but I've made plans for this evening.' Lorna's heart beat harder. 'I'm going to see George.'

Betty's blue eyes widened. 'Really? I thought you'd decided not to.'

'I did and I'm still not sure if it's the right thing, but...'

'How did you get in touch with him to arrange it?' Betty asked.

'I haven't,' said Lorna. 'He told me he has a suite in the Claremont Hotel and I'm simply going to turn up.'

'He might not be there.'

'I know, but I don't want to make a proper arrangement. The only way I can do this is by turning up accidentally on purpose.'

'It's a lot to put yourself through if he isn't there,' Betty pointed out.

'Let's not think about that,' said Lorna. 'Come and help me choose what to wear.'

Betty had been all in favour of Lorna getting decked out in a shimmering evening gown, but Lorna's stubborn streak had woken up unexpectedly and she'd decided to put her WVS uniform back on. It was smart but plain. To arrive at the Claremont looking glamorous might suggest... Lorna wasn't going to dwell on what it might suggest. Her uniform made her feel safe.

She took a taxi there. She entered the pillared foyer with its handsome furniture and headed across to the long reception desk, where an older gentleman, possibly brought out of retirement, was on duty. Before she got there, a man on the curving staircase caught her attention. Her heart leapt.

She turned to watch him, observing his tall figure and his lean-faced good looks. He wore evening dress and was adjusting his cuffs as he made his way downstairs. Even from this distance, Lorna could make out the way his dark eyebrows were drawn together, showing he was deep in thought.

If she wanted, she could turn and walk away and he'd never know she'd been here.

Lorna didn't move.

As George reached the bottom step, his head turned and his gaze locked on Lorna's. Had he sensed he was being watched? For a moment he didn't move, then a surprised smile flashed across his face as he came purposefully towards her.

'Lorna – I don't know what to say. I never expected—'

He stopped speaking. His blue-grey eyes became more blue as the strong angles of his face softened.

Lorna had planned what she was going to say but now she couldn't for the life of her remember what it was.

'I'm expecting some acquaintances presently,' said George. 'Until they come, won't you please join me?'

He escorted her to an alcove with a table and a pair of chairs. Lorna was powerfully reminded of all the occasions when he had escorted her across a ballroom or a theatre foyer or a restaurant. How proud she had always been to be seen on his arm. It wasn't just that he was handsome. He had presence. There was something about him that drew the eye.

When she sat down, George remained on his feet to order drinks from a young waitress who had followed them. Then he looked down at Lorna with a smile.

'If I go and tell the man on reception where I'm sitting so he can direct my visitors, will you still be here when I get back?'

Lorna couldn't help smiling in return. She nodded.

While George was at the desk, the waitress brought their drinks. She was a sweet-looking girl with fair hair.

'Thank you,' Lorna said.

'He's very handsome, isn't he?' the waitress whispered.

Lorna's father would have slapped the girl down for being familiar, but Lorna was amused.

'It's exciting to have a man-about-town staying here,' the waitress added.

Lorna was startled. 'A man-about-town?' That was the last thing George was.

'Oh yes,' said the girl. 'That's what all the staff call him.'

As the waitress departed, Lorna looked at George. Man-about-town? That wasn't the way she thought of him at all. He wasn't a swell who could be seen hobnobbing with the right people and going to nightclubs. He had far more substance than that. But then, how well could she say she really knew him? They had met, got engaged and then separated all in a matter of weeks. Hotel staff must get to see all kinds of people and must be experts at summing them up. The idea of George as a man-about-town drew a heavy sigh of disappointment from her. She'd thought more of him than that. She'd thought he had more about him. She hadn't been wrong – had she?

She pushed the uncomfortable thoughts aside when he returned and sat down. He looked jolly pleased to see her and she couldn't help but be glad of it. He offered her a cigarette and she accepted one, letting him light it for her, the little pantomime meaning words weren't necessary for a few moments. But she couldn't push the tricky thoughts away entirely.

'Well, you know why I'm in Manchester,' she said lightly. 'What about you? I didn't know the War Office had a Manchester branch.'

'Ah.' George shifted in his seat. He took a glug of his Scotch before saying, 'If you must know, they gave me the boot. I'm not at liberty to say why, but I'd be grateful if you kept it to yourself.'

He'd been sacked? George had? *George?* It went against everything she knew of him. But, as she reminded herself, how much did she really know? Even so – *George?*

What was she supposed to say? She settled for, 'I wouldn't

dream of gossiping. I've been on the receiving end of gossip and I know all too well the damage it can do.'

'Indeed yes – the gossip in London before we ended our engagement.'

'Before *you* ended it,' Lorna said coolly. She gave George a level look. 'Anyway, I shan't gossip about you and I'm offended that you thought I might.' Before he could reply, she asked, 'So what brought you to Manchester?'

'I'm kicking my heels for a spell before I join up. Lying low, you might say. Like you.'

Lorna lifted her chin. 'Daddy sent me here to hide me away from the newspaper people.' Was George about to mention her recent interview? It was a relief when he didn't. He mustn't have seen it. A sense of having dodged a bullet loosened her tongue. 'I wasn't at all happy to be here at first, but now I can't imagine being anywhere else. It's important to do war work.'

She met his eyes in a silent challenge to open up about what had gone wrong for him at the War Office, but George merely inhaled on his cigarette and tilted back his head to blow out the smoke.

'Tell me about your work, Lorna. I'm interested.'

He was, too. As she explained about salvage work, he asked relevant questions. Lorna relaxed. This wasn't so difficult after all. She remembered how much they used to talk when they first knew one another. She wanted – she actually wanted to move the conversation onto more personal ground.

'Mr Broughton? Your visitors are here, sir.'

'What? Oh – yes, of course.' George looked as if it was a wrench to remove his attention from their conversation. 'Thank you.'

Looking round, he raised a hand in acknowledgement to a pair of well-dressed men near the reception desk. Lorna looked too. The men were togged out in evening suits. One had a thin, bitter-looking mouth and the other had red-veined cheeks and a self-important strut.

George stood up. 'Lorna, I'm sorry to have to cut this short. My business associates have arrived.'

Business associates?

'I'm sorry to have barged in,' she answered.

'If I'd known you were coming...' said George. 'Never mind that now. May I see you again?'

'I don't know. I—'

'Please. For old times' sake.'

And somehow that made it possible to say yes.

CHAPTER FOURTEEN

Betty put on the blue jersey wool dress and gazed at her reflection. What a treat to wear something so beautifully made. How lucky Lorna was to have such gorgeous clothes – and how lucky she, Betty, was to have such a generous, caring friend.

As she went downstairs, feeling very glamorous, Mrs Beaumont came out of the sitting room.

'Look at you,' she said. 'Don't you look a picture?'

'Thanks,' Betty said, pleased. 'I can't wait for Samuel to see me in this.'

'Don't be too disappointed if he doesn't notice,' Mrs Beaumont advised. 'Men don't always.'

But Samuel did. When he arrived to collect her, his serious features softened in admiration. Betty was thrilled. She put on her coat and her 'film-star' hat with the asymmetrical brim and they set off to catch the bus.

'I could have caught the bus and you could have got on a few stops later,' said Betty. 'You didn't have to fetch me.'

'Yes, I d-did,' he replied. 'I w-want to look after you and spend every minute I can with you.'

It was a long journey into town because the bus had to follow a round-about route to avoid craters. When it drove up Oxford Road, it slowed and pulled into the kerb.

'This is as far as we can take you, folks,' the clippie called to her passengers. 'After this there's too much damage for vehicles to get through.'

The mood was sombre as everyone filed off.

'W-we'll have to walk across to the other s-side of town to get the bus to S-Salford,' said Samuel. 'Be prepared for s-some distressing sights.'

'Andrew and Lorna have both talked about what they've seen,' said Betty, 'so I'm ready.'

But she wasn't. Nobody could imagine it who hadn't already seen it. Buildings reduced to rubble; shattered glass everywhere; roofs dumped on the ground. Streets under several inches of water. The stench of burning lingered in the air. ARP wardens were around and about, giving pedestrians advice on the safest way through to where they wanted to go.

By the time they reached the bus stop, Betty was tearful. Without a word, Samuel produced a snowy handkerchief, and Betty bestowed a watery smile on him. He was so attentive in small ways and always made her feel cared for.

When they alighted at the other end, Betty held her head high with pride at being on her home soil with Samuel by her side. It didn't take long to reach home – her old home. Grace would make sure it would never be her real home again.

Grace answered the door. Her conker-brown hair was neatly arranged and her light-brown eyes flew over Samuel, who politely removed his trilby. All at once sadness swept over Betty at the knowledge that Samuel and her darling mum would never know one another.

Betty performed the introductions and Grace led them in. Dad appeared from the parlour, his serious brown eyes alight with a mixture of curiosity and concern. Betty went to him and kissed his cheek, feeling the faint rasp of his moustache against her skin. He smelled of soap and pipe tobacco.

Hanging on his arm, Betty turned to face Samuel so she could introduce the two men who meant so much to her – but Grace got in first.

'Trevor, this is Betty's new boyfriend, Samuel Atkinson.'

Dad thrust out his hand and grasped Samuel's. 'How do. I'll be honest with you, young man. It's not long since our Betty was looking forward to bringing another fellow home to meet us, but he turned out to be a bad 'un.'

'*Dad*,' Betty whispered, mortified.

'And now here she is w-with me,' said Samuel, meeting Dad's gaze squarely. 'I c-can understand your concern, Sergeant Hughes, but I assure you w-what is between Betty and me is real.'

'Samuel is the person who led the police to Eddie Markham's secret hoard,' said Betty. 'He did that because he cares about me.'

Dad looked at Samuel as if sizing him up, then nodded. 'That was a fine thing you did. I heard about it on the police grapevine. Thank you for what you did for my little girl.'

'*Dad*,' Betty said again, but this time she was laughing.

'Really, Trevor,' trilled Grace. 'You make Betty sound like a child. Now what are we doing standing out here in the hallway? Trevor, go and sit down while these two take their coats off. Hang up Samuel's things, will you, Betty? Then you can come and help me make tea.'

Betty knew only too well that any other visitor would have been fussed over and settled into a seat, but Grace was incapable of letting Betty and Dad have even five minutes together without her.

In the kitchen, Grace said bluntly, 'I hope you're not on the rebound, Betty.'

Heat poured into Betty's cheeks. 'I'm not.'

'Because that would be a big mistake,' said Grace. 'It would lead to all kinds of problems.'

'I'm not on the rebound,' Betty said with all the dignity she could muster.

'Well, let's hope you aren't.'

It was time to take a stand. 'Grace, I made an awful mistake over Eddie. I wish I'd never clapped eyes on him. My relationship with Samuel is completely different. He's a good man. He's honest and dependable. Instead of worrying that I'm on the rebound, you ought to be glad that I've found the right man so soon after Eddie turned out to be a rat.'

A thoughtful look entered Grace's light-brown eyes. It wasn't a warm look, more a calculating one.

She nodded. 'Fair enough.'

After that things went smoothly and Betty enjoyed herself, feeling proud of Samuel and happy to see him getting along well with Dad and Grace. She and Grace might have their moments, but having Grace on her side made a difference, just as it had when Grace had been so keen on Betty's romance with Eddie.

'I believe you have a shop,' Grace said to Samuel.

'That's right. I have my own bookshop.'

'Samuel is an expert on books,' Betty said. 'Customers write to him from all over asking him to help them find something in particular. He does war work with books an' all, sending them out to the troops and to bombed-out public libraries. He knows exactly the right books to send.'

'It must take education to do what you do.' Dad sounded impressed.

'Every sh-shopkeeper has to have expertise in their own area,' Samuel said with characteristic modesty.

'And do you have a home of your own or are you in lodgings?' Grace asked, and Betty could have crowned her for the personal question.

'I live above the sh-shop.'

'Really?' Grace practically purred in delight. 'That must be very convenient for you. How big is the flat?' She smiled sweetly, apparently unaware of Betty looking daggers at her.

'My predecessor lived there c-comfortably with his f-family,' said Samuel. 'Part of the living accommodation is downstairs in the back of the sh-shop.' He smiled wryly. 'What used to be the parlour is more of a s-storeroom these days, I'm afraid.'

Grace trilled a little laugh. 'Oh, you bachelors! No domestic sense at all.'

Betty was ready to sink through the floor. Grace couldn't have been any more obvious if she'd tried.

Fortunately, Grace stood up. 'Come along, Betty. It's time to make the sandwiches.' With a final simper in Samuel's direction, she led Betty out. In the kitchen, she turned to her with a look of warm approval.

'Well! You've got a good catch there, my girl.'

It wasn't the most tactful way of putting it, but Betty felt pleased all the same.

'But you're going to have to be careful, Betty.'

'How d'you mean?'

'Isn't it obvious?' asked Grace. 'Samuel is an educated man. He's a gentleman. He's clearly stuck on you, Betty, but he's way too good for you. You need to reel him in quick before he sees sense.'

Mrs Beaumont had organised what she called 'a little do' for New Year's Eve afternoon.

'I'd have liked to have it in the evening but there's more chance of a raid then,' she explained. 'Also, of course, we don't have to worry about people having to go off on night duty.'

As well as her house guests, she had naturally invited Samuel. It thrilled Betty to think he was such an accepted part of their household.

'Why don't you ask if you can invite George?' Betty suggested to Lorna when the three girls were having their tea break at the depot on Monday. 'I bet she'd say yes.'

Lorna shook her head.

'But you said you were going to see one another again,' Sally pointed out.

'We are,' said Lorna, 'but only for old times' sake. It wouldn't be appropriate to ask him to Star House. It would cause... complications.'

Betty exchanged a look with Sally. It was clear Lorna didn't wish to discuss the matter.

'On the subject of extra invitations,' said Sally, tapping her cigarette against the saucer to shake off the ash, 'Mrs Beaumont asked me if I'd like to invite Auntie Vera. She said she'd like to show there are no hard feelings about Mrs Henshaw deciding to leave Star House.'

'That was good of her,' Lorna observed.

'Yes, it was,' agreed Sally. 'Maybe it wasn't good of me, but I said no.'

'Why?' Betty asked. 'I thought you liked Andrew's Auntie Vera.'

'I do – but I don't want to go and live with her. If she came to Star House, who knows what direction the conversation might take? I don't want any awkwardness.'

'Haven't you told Mrs Henshaw you want to stay put?' asked Betty.

'Not yet. I want to let things ride for now. I know how cowardly that sounds, but at present everything feels very emotional. Mrs Henshaw isn't the sort to show her feelings but she's deeply upset about Andrew's decision—'

'As are you,' Lorna put in.

'—and I want to wait a while before I rock any more boats,' Sally said, adding briskly, 'So Auntie Vee hasn't been invited. I'm just grateful Mrs Beaumont suggested it to me and not to Mrs Henshaw.'

Lorna laughed. 'So she isn't coming and neither is George. Thank goodness for Samuel, that's what I say. At least one of us has a straightforward life.'

Betty felt an inner glow of pure happiness.

'What did your father and stepmother think of him yesterday?' Lorna asked.

'And what did he make of them?' Sally added.

'It went very well – except for Grace asking some pointed questions.' Betty rolled her eyes. 'She might as well have said, "It sounds like you can provide the perfect home for Betty." Honestly! I didn't know where to look.'

'What about Samuel?' Lorna asked. 'Was he fearfully embarrassed?'

'He seemed to take it in his stride. On the way home, he said he was glad to have everything out in the open.'

'Did he and your dad like one another?' Sally asked. 'That's the most important thing.'

'Yes,' Betty was able to say with certainty.

'It's good to see you looking so happy.' Sally stubbed out her cigarette. 'Time to get back to the grindstone.'

As Betty got on with her work, she felt bubbly with happiness. The trip to Salford had been a success and it had proved – not that proof was needed – how much Samuel cared for her. He'd been as keen as she was for him to meet Dad and Grace. It was the opposite in every way to how Eddie had behaved, stringing her along with his excuses as to why now wasn't the right time for him to meet Dad.

Why on earth hadn't she fallen for Samuel in the first place instead of being taken in by Eddie Markham's silver-tongued flattery? But the main thing was that she and Samuel were together now. That was all that mattered.

A movement caught Betty's eye and she turned to see the upright figure of Sergeant Robbins walking through the open gates.

'Morning, Miss Hughes,' he greeted her.

'Good morning, Sergeant,' she answered.

Lorna and Sally appeared and stood one on each side of her as if she needed protection.

'I have some news for you,' the policeman told Betty. 'It's about Eddie Markham.'

'Do you want to go into my office?' Sally asked Betty.

Betty stood up straight and looked at the sergeant. 'You can say anything in front of my friends.'

'It's to do with the depot and so it concerns all of you,' said Sergeant Robbins, 'but you most of all, Miss Hughes.'

'What is it?' Betty asked.

'Eddie Markham is going to plead guilty when his case goes to the Crown Court. So is his accomplice, Leon Hargreaves. That means none of you will be required to appear in court to give evidence.'

'Oh, Betty,' breathed Sally.

'You're going to be spared that ordeal,' Lorna added.

Betty shut her eyes and covered her mouth with her hand. As she lifted her hand away, she whispered, 'What a relief.'

'I heard this morning,' said Sergeant Robbins. 'I knew you'd want to know right away.'

'Thank you, Sergeant,' said Sally. 'This is good news for all of us – but especially for you, Betty.'

Good news? It was *wonderful* news. It meant that she could put Eddie Markham behind her for keeps.

. . .

Mrs Beaumont's New Year's Eve party was a lovely occasion. As well as the residents and Samuel, Mrs Beaumont had invited some of the neighbours – and also, without mentioning it to the girls, she'd asked Stella, Lottie and Mary. Betty squealed in delight when they walked in, all rosy-cheeked from their brisk walk through the sleety afternoon. They had lived here when she had first moved in and, although the three of them were great pals as well as colleagues, they had made a point of making her welcome in her new home. She'd been sorry when they left in order to live closer to the munitions factory in Trafford Park. On the other hand, it was because they'd left that Mrs Beaumont had ended up having rooms to offer to the Henshaws and Lorna.

Betty introduced Samuel to the munitions girls and they chatted for a while. Then, when Samuel was talking to Andrew, Stella, a tall redhead, gave Betty a nudge.

'He's nice,' she said in a low voice.

'Yes, he is,' Betty agreed. 'He's kind and hard-working.'

'Good-looking too,' said sandy-haired Lottie.

'But in a modest sort of way,' added Mary, her blue eyes thoughtful. 'He's not full of himself like some men.'

Hearing Samuel being praised made Betty's day. She enjoyed the afternoon. The neighbours chatted about who'd had mock-turkey for Christmas, and who'd had mock-goose – salted cod.

Betty helped pass round the sardine puffs and oatmeal crackers Mrs Beaumont had made. Everyone admired the food.

The munitions girls left first because they were due to start their next shift that evening. Betty hugged them all.

'Happy new year,' they all said.

'Or a better new year, at any rate,' Stella said.

'It couldn't be worse than what happened just before Christmas,' said Mary.

'That's enough of that,' chimed in Mrs Beaumont. 'We should part company on a cheerful note, not a glum one.'

'You're right, Mrs Beaumont,' Lottie said with a laugh. 'We'd better start the goodbyes again and do them cheerfully.'

There were more hugs and good wishes, this time accompanied by smiles and expressions of hope.

After the front door had shut behind the munitions girls, Samuel appeared in the hallway.

'Come and s-sit on the s-stairs with me,' he said softly to Betty.

She willingly complied. 'It's been such a good afternoon. Have you enjoyed it?'

'Very much, thanks, and I c-can tell that you have. You haven't stopped s-smiling. You'll wear out that dimple if you're not c-careful.'

Betty laughed. 'You daft ha'porth.'

'Seriously, I've enjoyed w-watching you enjoying yourself.'

Betty leaned against him for a moment.

'Are you f-free this evening?' Samuel asked her.

'Early evening, yes, but Sally and me are on fire-watching duty at the depot. We're on duty tomorrow night an' all.'

'I w-was hoping we'd have the whole evening together today, but never mind.'

'We'll have lots of other times together,' said Betty.

Samuel slid an arm round her shoulders and dropped a quick kiss on her temple. 'You c-can count on it.'

A short raid brought in the new year of 1941, but there was a worse raid the following night. It was bitterly cold up on the depot roof. Betty and Sally had barely arrived before the air-raid siren started, and they had run up through the building to the ladder that gave access to the flat roof. Already the night sky was criss-crossed with searchlights and the low thrum of aeroplane engines could be heard.

'Are they heading for town again?' Betty asked.

'Difficult to say,' answered Sally. 'I hope not. They've caused so much destruction there.' She stopped talking and looked at Betty.

'I know,' Betty said soberly. 'If they haven't got the middle of Manchester and Salford in their sights, then somewhere else is going to get it.'

It didn't take long to find out where. Strings of brilliant lights whistled their way to earth, and high explosives produced massive explosions that echoed across the miles, as the two girls trained their binoculars on the affected area. Not Chorlton, thank heaven.

'Is that Withington?' Betty asked. 'Oh, Sally.'

'Could be.' Sally's voice sounded hollow. 'Or it might be West Didsbury. Not that I want West Didsbury to cop it,' she added, her voice shaking, 'but please don't let it be Withington.'

Removing the binoculars from her eyes, Betty looked compassionately at her friend. She knew how Sally felt. Everybody knew how it felt to worry about their home territory and their loved ones during an air raid.

It was a long night. The raid, which had started before ten, went on until two. Only then did Betty venture downstairs to put the kettle on.

As they sipped their tea, Sally said, 'My mother said a little while back that she'd never felt the need of a telephone in the house before, but she wishes she had one now.'

'Only rich folk have their own telephones,' said Betty.

'What I wouldn't give to use the office telephone to ring my mum and hear her voice.'

'Maybe it wasn't Withington,' Betty suggested gently. 'Maybe it was West Didsbury.'

But it had indeed been Withington, as the girls discovered the next day when Samuel came round to the depot.

'I sh-shut the shop for an hour s-so I could c-come and tell you about last night. I knew you'd be anxious to hear.' He looked at Sally with such kindness that Betty guessed what was coming next. 'W-Withington had it bad last night. I'm sorry.'

Sally's face paled but she said steadily, 'Do you know any details?'

'I took the liberty of c-contacting the Withington ARP. The chap I sp-spoke to was in shock. Do you know Burton Road? There's a s-surface shelter there – or there was. It took a d-direct hit. Nine were killed, several of them ARP wardens.'

'Oh,' breathed Betty.

'I'm sorry to hear it,' Lorna added.

'The building next to it was badly d-damaged too,' Samuel went on, 'and a bomb landed in the garden of St Paul's Rectory. In all, twenty-nine people were k-killed and twenty-one seriously injured.'

'Do you know the names of any other roads that were hit?' Lorna asked with a glance at Sally.

Samuel named some and Sally drew in a quiet breath. Was that good – or bad?

'Not our road,' she whispered.

Betty gave her a hug. 'Do you want to bunk off and go and see your mum? Lorna and me can look after the depot.'

Sally shook her head. 'If everyone bunked off to visit loved ones, no work would get done.' She turned to Samuel. 'Thanks for coming. I appreciate it.'

'I'd better get back,' he said.

'I'll walk with you to the gates,' said Betty.

They crossed the yard and stopped in the open gateway. Betty would have loved a bit of time together, but she didn't want to take advantage and Samuel had to return to his shop.

'It was good of you to come,' she said.

'I knew Sally w-would be worrying. May I s-see you later? I'm not on d-duty tonight. Are you?'

Betty shook her head.

'Good,' said Samuel. 'I know w-we're lucky to be able to s-see one another regularly, but I really need to spend s-some time with you, just the two of us. Things f-feel right when I'm w-with you.'

'Where are we going?' Betty asked Samuel as he opened Star House's garden gate for her and then followed her onto Wilton Road. She tucked her hand in the crook of his arm.

He tilted his face to smile down at her. 'You'll see.'

It was another chilly evening. Above them the sky was dotted with stars. Just the sort of night Jerry liked. Betty hoped fervently that her special evening with Samuel wouldn't be interrupted.

Where was he taking her? He hadn't told her to skip her evening meal, so they weren't going for something to eat. Perhaps he was taking her to the pictures, though actually she would prefer to go to a place where they could talk and make the most of one another's company.

Samuel took her to the bus terminus.

'W-we're not going far,' he said, 'but I thought we'd d-dodge the cold by going on the bus.'

They got off after just a few stops. It took Betty a moment to orient herself in the blackout.

'We're near your shop,' she said.

'S-so we are.'

He guided her to the doorway and unlocked the door. Once they were inside, he switched on the light. The door and the large window were both swathed in blackout fabric.

Betty automatically walked through the shop to the parlour-office at the back, and stopped in surprise in the doorway.

'Notice anything?' Samuel asked. Betty wasn't looking at him but she could hear the smile in his voice.

The parlour-office had undergone something of a transformation. A number of bookcases had vanished and those that remained, instead of standing in the middle of the floor, lined the walls. The large square of carpet seemed much bigger now. Over by the fireplace stood a pair of armchairs with a table between them.

'Wh-what do you think?' Samuel asked, wrapping his arms round her from behind.

'You've turned it into a proper parlour.'

'There's more to d-do but I've made a good start, though I do s-say so myself.'

'I never realised how big this room is,' Betty said wonderingly, turning to face him. *It's perfect for a family.* The thought popped into her head and she glanced away, pretending to look around so as to conceal a blush. 'Where have the other bookcases gone?'

'You w-walked right past them when we c-came in. I squeezed them into the sh-shop.' Samuel indicated the remaining bookcases. 'These w-wouldn't fit into the shop, but there's a box room upstairs. I thought maybe I could turn it into a st-storeroom.'

'I like the thought of you having a comfy parlour,' said Betty. 'That's much better than being surrounded by bookcases, no matter how much you love your job.'

'I'm glad you w-want me to have a c-comfy parlour,' said Samuel. 'I... I'd like you to have a c-comfy parlour too.'

A little frown tugged at Betty's brow and her heart banged like a big bass drum. Did Samuel mean...?

'I w-was thinking of you here in this parlour,' Samuel said. 'W-with me. I d-don't want to be presumptuous but I'm trying to c-create a proper home here – f-for you, for us.'

'For us?' Betty repeated.

'I know we haven't been a c-couple for all that long, Betty, but I've known you w-were the girl for me ever s-since I met you. You're kind and loyal and principled and brave. After everything that happened w-with the Christmas Blitz, I d-don't want to let another minute go by without telling you how much you mean to me and – and w-what I hope for our future.'

To Betty's astonishment, he sank onto one knee, taking her hand in his.

'Betty Hughes, you're the most sp-special girl in the w-world. Please will you marry me?'

'Oh, Samuel.' Betty's heart almost leapt out of her chest. 'Yes. Yes!'

Rising, he took her in his arms and kissed her.

CHAPTER FIFTEEN

Lorna got ready to go on duty. She had just put on her WVS uniform when she heard the front door open. A minute later, her bedroom door flew open and Betty dashed in without so much as a by your leave.

'Come down right now, Lorna. We've got something to tell you.'

And Betty rushed out of the room and down the stairs. Lorna was intrigued. At least Betty hadn't appeared upset, so presumably nothing bad had happened. She hurried after her.

Andrew had set off early for his light rescue duty. Sally, Mrs Beaumont and Mrs Henshaw were in the sitting room. Betty and Samuel stood in front of the fireplace, holding hands. Lorna perched on the arm of the sofa. Betty's eyes were sparkling. Even the normally serious Samuel smiled broadly.

'You're all here now,' said Betty, 'so we can tell you.'

'Tell us what?' asked Sally.

Betty looked adoringly at Samuel. 'You say.'

Samuel took a deep breath. 'Betty has agreed to marry me.'

'We're engaged,' Betty exclaimed.

There were cries of surprise, then everyone jumped up to hug them.

'I know I ought to have told Dad and Grace first,' said Betty, 'but I'd have burst if I'd had to keep it secret here until then.'

'I'm glad you chose to confide in us,' said Mrs Beaumont.

'You're an only child, aren't you, Betty?' said Mrs Henshaw. 'Do you have brothers and sisters, Samuel?'

'One of each, both in the s-services.'

Lorna looked at the clock on the mantelpiece. 'I must dash.' She caught hold of Betty's hands. 'I'll want a blow-by-blow account of the proposal tomorrow.'

She was rewarded by a laugh of pure delight – a sound that was echoed the next day at the depot when Betty shared her romantic story during their morning tea break.

'I had no idea what he was building up to,' she said.

'I'm delighted for you,' said Lorna. 'You're a lovely couple and I wish you years and years of happiness.'

Betty beamed, her dimple deepening in her cheek. 'Thank you.' She paused, then whispered, 'You don't think it's too soon, do you?'

'Not if you're both sure,' said Lorna, 'and it's plain to see that you are. Things happen quickly in wartime.'

'Think of Andrew and me,' said Sally, 'and how soon we got married – and it would have happened several weeks earlier if my parents hadn't refused permission at first.'

Lorna couldn't suppress a stab of envy. Both her friends were so happy. She was glad for them, she truly was – but it was hard knowing that all she had to look forward to was an evening out for old times' sake.

It had been Lorna's Saturday for opening the depot. When she reached home after work, she had a strip-wash, and Betty helped her with her hair.

'You're lucky to have such striking colouring,' said Betty.

'Thanks,' said Lorna. 'I like your colouring too.'

'Oh, me, I'm just a blue-eyed blonde. They're ten a penny. Your green eyes are unusual as well as beautiful, and your hair is so dark. What are you going to wear?'

'I wore my WVS uniform last time.'

Betty groaned. 'Don't remind me. Why did you do that when you've got a wardrobe filled with heavenly clothes?'

'It seemed the safe option. I didn't want George to think I'd dressed up to please him.'

'How about dressing up to please yourself?' said Betty. 'Things are difficult between you and George. You should wear something you love to give yourself confidence. Not that I can imagine you in need of confidence,' she added.

'Believe me, I am where George is concerned,' said Lorna. 'A little voice in my head is telling me that seeing him again will be a frightful mistake, but...' She shrugged.

'But you don't want to listen to it.' Betty smiled knowingly. 'Let's choose something.' She opened the wardrobe. 'Where are you going?'

'It's not as though we're going out as such,' said Lorna. 'I said I'd meet him at the Claremont again, where he's staying.'

'That's a posh place,' said Betty. 'I'll bet there will be ladies in proper evening dress.'

Lorna chose her evening suit with a cream silk blouse. The suit, made of deep-green wool crepe, comprised a hip-length fitted jacket that skimmed her slender frame and an ankle-length skirt with a slight flare. She smiled to herself; she was actually more covered up wearing this than she had been in her WVS uniform.

'Enjoy yourself,' Betty said when she saw her off.

Lorna had ordered a taxi. The evening air had a bitter edge to it. There hadn't been many visitors to the depot today but everyone who had dropped in had said, 'Cold enough for snow.'

When the taxi pulled up outside the Claremont, Lorna had barely opened her evening bag to find her purse before George appeared beside the driver's window and paid him. He opened Lorna's door.

'You're here,' he said. 'I wasn't entirely sure you'd come. Let's get inside.' He cupped her elbow and escorted her up the steps and through the doors. 'I thought we could have our alcove again.'

There was an edge to his voice that put Lorna on her guard. Her skin prickled and her muscles tensed. Sure enough, after he had helped her off with her coat and handed it to a member of staff and they had taken their seats, he drew a piece of folded paper – not just paper, a sheet of newspaper – from his inside pocket and dropped it on the table between them. Lorna didn't need to see the twist of disgust about his lips to know what the newspaper article contained.

'The interview,' she said in a dull voice. She felt caught out.

'You weren't going to tell me about it,' George accused her.

She looked away. Tears stung her eyes and she blinked them back. 'Maybe I ought to have mentioned it before.'

'Maybe?' he asked. 'Only maybe?'

Lorna sat up straight. 'If I made a mistake, that's unfortunate, but I refuse to sit here meekly while you tell me off. Who gave you the article?'

George clenched his jaw for a moment. Then, with an effort, he cleared his expression. 'My mother sent it to me. It has just been brought to her attention. She thought I should see it.'

Lorna felt like saying, 'I bet she did,' but she held her tongue.

'What possessed you, Lorna?' George asked. He didn't sound angry or cold now, just baffled.

'If you must know, I was helping a friend who was in a tight spot.'

George's dark eyebrows climbed up his forehead. 'By spilling the beans about us?'

'I'd already been dragged through the mud by the newspapers. I supposed I might as well let it happen a second time.'

'To protect a friend?' George shook his head. 'It doesn't make much sense.'

'My friend got involved with a man who turned out to be a thoroughly bad lot. Never mind the details but a crime was involved. My friend was implicated, although she was innocent. Afterwards a policeman must have made a few bob by selling the information to a seedy journalist by the name of Baldwin. Mr Baldwin cornered Betty and tried to make her tell her side of the story while making it clear that, whether she cooperated or not, he was going to write his juicy story – and it would be a lot juicier without her cooperation. So I stepped in.'

George caught on at once. 'You offered an interview to make this Baldwin fellow leave your friend alone?'

'That's about the size of it. I know what it's like to be in the public glare and I wanted to save Betty that distress.'

'It's admirable that you wanted to protect your friend,' George said, 'but what a price to pay – and you aren't alone in paying it. My mother is furious. She says it shows the sort of person you are.'

'If by that she means the sort who stands by her friends, she's right,' Lorna answered at once. Then she softened. 'Look, George, if that interview has caused any unpleasantness for you or your family, I'm truly sorry. I didn't do it out of malice against you, I promise. I did it on the spur of the moment to prevent something bad from happening to a friend. And even though Mr Baldwin pressed me to give details about you and the Broughtons, I stuck to talking about myself.'

'Did you?' asked George. 'I must admit I was too angry when I read it to pay that kind of attention. I just raced through it and fumed.'

'Try it again when you've calmed down and I'm sure you'll see what I mean.'

'I ought to have read it properly before I had a go at you,' said George. 'I – well, I took my mother's word for it.'

'Your parents were never keen on me,' said Lorna. 'They wanted a titled girl for you or, if not titled, then at least someone from an ancient family. They certainly didn't want a girl who came from trade.'

'My family wanted what all families from our part of society want, but it didn't prevent me from choosing you.'

Lorna's heart twisted. 'For a time, anyway, until you took against my parents.'

'Do you still not see what they did?' George asked.

'I'm aware of what was said in London, if that's what you mean,' Lorna replied. 'I know you listened to nasty rumours.'

'Were they just rumours? I think not – and you'd agree if you would just open your eyes. Think what sort of man your father is, Lorna. Can you honestly tell me that there was no truth, none at all, in what was said?'

About to come down heavily on Daddy's side, Lorna hesitated. Had Daddy's triumph at her engagement to the heir to a baronetcy put backs up? Had her parents in fact taken her to London, not to give her the chance to fall in love, but with the express purpose of throwing her in front of eligible men of a certain type? It was a sobering thought. Daddy was the one who had instigated the breach-of-promise case against George and he'd told Lorna it was because, after shelling out a fortune to bring her to London, he wanted to get his money back.

What did that say about him?

'You haven't answered my question,' George said gently.

'I was thinking.' She stood up, needing to leave before her tears became obvious. 'I'd better go now.'

George rose quickly and leaned over the table. 'Lorna – stay – please. It hasn't been altogether easy but I think we've cleared the air somewhat. What I said to you at the Christmas kitchen still stands. I'd very much like to get to know you when it can be just the two of us. No gossips, no family. Won't you please stay for a while at least? Please. I've looked forward to it so much. Haven't you?'

Lorna's heart gave a little bump. Might they really have another chance?

Did she dare to hope?

CHAPTER SIXTEEN

It was the first full week of January and the snow had arrived, shimmering beneath the milky winter sun. The white landscape might look beautiful, but knife-edged winds forced the snow into drifts. Andrew cleared the front path first thing every morning. He did it for a couple of the neighbours too. What a good man he was. Sally's heart delivered a painful squeeze at the thought of him going off to war.

Later that morning, while Sally and Betty sorted through the daily salvage sacks indoors, Betty remarked, 'You look thoughtful.'

'I've been thinking a lot about Andrew going away.'

'Of course you have,' Betty said sympathetically.

Sally smiled at her. 'I couldn't be happier for you and Samuel. I know Lorna is taking things slowly with George, but she wouldn't want to carry on seeing him unless she cared.'

'Meanwhile you're worried about Andrew,' said Betty.

'My head can understand why he wants to join up, but my heart would give anything for him to stay,' said Sally. 'What sort of wife does that make me? I want him to stay even though I know how much he wants to go.'

'It makes you a completely normal wife, I'd say. No wife wants her husband to go to war, especially not knowing how long he'll be gone. If it's like the last war, it might be several years—' Betty's hand flew to cover her mouth. 'I'm so sorry. What a thing to say.'

'It's all right,' Sally assured her. 'You aren't saying anything that I haven't thought of already.'

Betty looked past Sally, which made Sally turn to look as well. Through the window she saw Mrs Lockwood walking across the yard, dressed in an olive-green herringbone tweed overcoat and stout lace-up shoes.

Betty frowned. 'Does the WVS have a uniform overcoat?'

'Not that I know of,' said Sally. 'She must have had it made specially.'

'You'd better not let her find you sorting through the daily sacks,' said Betty. 'Nip along to the office quick and do something that looks important.'

'Sorting the salvage is important,' Sally replied. 'All our tasks here matter.'

Mrs Lockwood appeared in the doorway. She seemed to rear up and take a step backwards, as if recoiling from the sight of Sally lowering herself.

'I might have known,' she boomed in her parade-ground voice.

She ought to be accustomed to Mrs Lockwood's attitude by this time, but Sally still felt caught out. Was Betty right? Ought she to have scuttled along to the office? But she'd have been annoyed with herself if she had.

'Good morning, Mrs Lockwood,' she said politely.

'Happy new year,' Betty added.

'Good morning, girls,' Mrs Lockwood replied. 'Is everything going well? Not falling behind, I trust?'

'We never fall behind,' Sally replied softly, 'no matter what the challenges.'

'Hm.' Mrs Lockwood loaded the sound with disbelief. 'I have a task for you, Mrs Henshaw.'

'Might I remind you that I am the depot manager,' Sally began, 'and as such—'

'And might *I* remind *you* that I was appointed by Mr Merivale and Mr Pratt at the Town Hall to oversee your performance in this role,' Mrs Lockwood said in a severe voice.

'Yes, Mrs Lockwood,' Sally murmured. Drat the woman, but what else could she say?

'Despite your obstinate attitude, Mrs Henshaw, I have decided to allow you an opportunity to show yourself in a good light. There will be a meeting at the Town Hall the day after tomorrow – Friday. Various services will be represented, and I have decided that you may attend on behalf of the depot.'

It was all Sally could do to stop her mouth dropping open in shock. 'Thank you.'

Mrs Lockwood nodded. 'Make sure you don't let me down.'

'I will represent the depot to the best of my ability.'

'See that you do.'

Having had the last word, Mrs Lockwood departed. Sally and Betty watched from the window as she left the yard.

'Good for you!' said Betty. 'She's finally showing you the professional respect you deserve. About time too.'

'I can't quite believe it,' said Sally.

Eagerness swamped her and she bounced on her toes. Was she finally getting the recognition she had worked so hard for?

* * *

Betty was glad Mrs Lockwood hadn't caused any trouble – quite the reverse, in fact. Today was a special day for her and Samuel. This being Wednesday, it was half-day closing for the local shops, and Samuel was going to go over to Salford to see Dad and officially ask for her hand in marriage.

'I'm w-worried he'll think it's too s-soon,' he had told Betty. 'I'll have to make sure he knows how d-dear you are to me and that this isn't a w-wartime fling.'

'No one could ever suspect you of one of those,' said Betty. 'You have the steadiest character of anyone I've ever met.'

'After your f-father has consented, I'll buy you a ring, Betty,' Samuel promised, 'so you must st-start thinking about wh-what you'd like.'

Betty hadn't admitted it, but she had already gazed through the window of Millington's the jeweller's, thrilled to bits at the thought that soon one of those beautiful rings could be hers. She wouldn't wear it to the depot, obviously, but she would wear it at all other times.

That evening, as soon as she'd finished her vegetable stew and jacket potato followed by steamed jam pudding, she threw on her outdoor things, grabbed her handbag and gas-mask and rushed round to the bookshop, arriving just as Samuel was about to set off to collect her from Star House.

'Sorry,' she said, laughing at his surprise. 'I couldn't wait a minute longer. What did Dad say?'

'He s-said it was sooner than he'd have expected, but he also s-said that Mrs Hughes had been talking about it as a possibility ever since I w-went round there to meet them.'

'So Grace paved the way for it.' Knowing how her step-mother wanted to get rid of her permanently, ought she to feel grumpy about this? But she didn't. She and Grace were both getting what they wanted. 'Is Dad happy about it? That's the main thing.'

Samuel nodded. 'W-we talked about my prospects and he's happy that I c-can support you and give you and any children we have a comfortable and s-secure life. He said he w-won't make you wait until you're twenty-one.'

Happy tears spilled onto Betty's cheeks and Samuel brushed them away with the pads of his thumbs.

'There's one more thing,' he said. 'Your father gave me s-something for you.'

'What is it?'

Samuel produced a ring-box and opened it. 'It's your moth-er's engagement ring. He said that if you want to w-wear it as your engagement ring then it's yours to keep.'

Betty breathed in a soft gasp. Mum's ring. Mum's engage-ment ring.

'What about you?' she whispered. 'Wouldn't you mind?'

'Not if it's wh-what you want – and I think it is. I know how much you miss her. I w-would be honoured to put her ring on your f-finger.'

Betty held out her hand, emotion swelling inside her as Samuel placed the ring on her finger.

'I'd much rather have Mum,' said Betty, 'but if I can't have her, then I'll be happy and honoured to wear her ring.' Then she threw herself into his arms.

* * *

As much as it vexed her when her mother lamented her no longer having a job that involved dressing as an office worker, Sally took pleasure the next morning in dressing smartly in a blouse and skirt and wearing her hip-length swing-jacket with stand-up collar and cuffed sleeves beneath her overcoat instead of a thick jumper. She popped her black patent leather shoes into a bag to change into at the Town Hall.

She felt brisk and professional as she entered the chess-board-tiled foyer. Just a few months ago she had worked here in the Food Office, and now here she was, walking into the hand-some building as the manager of her own salvage depot. She had to laugh at herself. Her own depot! The very idea.

The meeting wasn't due to begin yet. Sally had arrived early so she could dash upstairs to the Food Office and surprise Deborah. She did that all right. When she opened the door and walked in, Deborah squealed. Then she pushed back her chair, jumped up and gave Sally a hug.

'What are you doing here?' Deborah's bright-blue eyes shone.

Sally told her about the meeting. 'I was hoping you'd be there too, representing the Food Office.'

'You're kidding, aren't you? Since when did Mr Morland ever let his clerks do anything of the kind? He doesn't even let us testify in court. He does it for us – even though we're the ones who gather the evidence.'

Sally laughed. 'I remember it well.'

The door opened once more and Sally straightened her face in case it was Mr Morland. He liked to maintain a serious atmosphere in his office. But it was a girl Sally hadn't seen before, a pretty redhead with milky skin and a light smattering of freckles across her nose.

'This is Miss Rushton,' said Deborah. 'She joined after you left.' To the redhead she said, 'This is Mrs Henshaw, who worked here before you did.'

'Please to meet you,' said Sally.

'Likewise,' said Miss Rushton. She picked up a box of files. 'I need to take this downstairs. I won't be long.'

Sally held the door open for her, then closed it again.

'She seems nice,' she remarked.

'She's all right,' said Deborah, 'but she's not a patch on you for company. The office isn't fun in Mr Morland's absence the way it used to be.'

'Yes, we did have fun,' Sally agreed, remembering.

'I know what you're thinking,' Deborah said ruefully. 'I'm the one who spoiled it all.'

'That's long forgotten,' said Sally. 'Things worked out well for me in the end.'

'They certainly did,' Deborah said admiringly. 'From

salvage girl to depot manager. I'm proud of you.'

'Thanks,' said Sally. 'That means a lot.' She glanced at the wall-clock. 'I'd better go.'

She hurried along to the meeting, not wanting to be the last to arrive. It was to take place in a large room around a long table.

Mr Morland was already there. He looked pleased to see her.

'I understand you're doing very well at the salvage depot, Mrs Henshaw. I heard about your promotion. Very impressive.' He turned to the man next to him. He had receding hair and heavy-lidded eyes. 'This is Mr Donaldson from casualty services. This is Mrs Henshaw, the manager of the salvage depot in Chorlton-cum-Hardy.'

Being introduced as the manager was a big thrill. Sally was sure she would never take it for granted.

During the morning she met people from various services. The purpose of the meeting was to exchange information about different types of war work and civil defence. There were several speakers. A man from the St John Ambulance Brigade talked about delivering first-aid classes, after which there was a brief talk about the messenger service. Mr Donaldson spoke for some time – too much time, judging by the way the organisers consulted their wristwatches and flung meaningful glances at one another – about the various casualty services, such as first aid and ambulance work.

After that there was a tea break. Sally chatted to a young woman called Mrs Catchpole, who had accompanied Mr Donaldson. She was a little older than Sally, mid-twenties, with rosy cheeks and a pointed chin.

'Clever old you,' said Mrs Catchpole when Sally explained about being the depot manager. 'Me, I work in a wool shop, though for how much longer is anybody's guess, with the shortages biting deeper.'

'What war work do you do?' Sally asked her.

'I drive an ARP ambulance. That's an ordinary motor that tows a trailer with racks for stretchers. A local taxi driver taught us volunteers how to drive.'

'And now you pull ambulance trailers with casualties,' Sally said admiringly.

'Part of the training took place in the blackout. It involved two ambulances starting at different places a mile apart. We had to negotiate all these winding roads and then pass one another safely. It was a bit hairy, I can tell you.'

'I'd have been scared of driving into the other ambulance,' said Sally.

'You're not the only one,' said Mrs Catchpole. 'Several drivers left the road without intending to. I ended up in a field on my first try.'

Sally laughed.

After that it was time for the second part of the morning. They heard about the new Morrison shelters that would shortly become available – sturdy indoor shelters for people who didn't have a garden. A new Air Training Corps was going to be launched that year for boys aged sixteen.

When the meeting ended, most people hung about chatting. The general consensus was that the meeting had proved most useful. Sally imagined herself being approached to be one of the speakers next time. Wouldn't that be grand?

She travelled back to the depot, her mind buzzing with everything she'd learned. She couldn't wait to tell Lorna and Betty all about it. But when she walked into the depot building and saw their faces, wariness clenched inside her stomach.

'Something's happened,' she said, not bothering to make a question of it.

'I'm afraid so,' said Lorna.

'It's Mrs Lockwood,' said Betty.

'What's she done this time?' Sally asked.

'She's been here nearly all morning,' said Betty, 'showing the men from the ministry round.'

'Showing *who* round?' Sally demanded even though she had heard perfectly well.

'Evidently,' said Lorna, 'the Town Hall informed her of the official visit and instead of handing it over to you—'

'She got rid of me and did it herself,' finished Sally. 'I can't believe it.' But she could. It was just like Mrs Lockwood.

So much for her 'wonderful' opportunity to represent the salvage depot at the meeting. It had been nothing more than a ruse to get her out of the way while Mrs Lockwood acted as the Queen of the May in front of the men from the ministry.

CHAPTER SEVENTEEN

Lorna couldn't help herself. She was interested in George all over again, which was as confusing as it was exhilarating. The thought of him set her heartbeat drumming, but then she remembered how dreadfully wrong everything had gone for them, and the battle she'd fought to forge a new life for herself.

'I want to see him again, but I don't want to get swept away,' she confided in Sally as they sat together on the hearthrug in front of the fire in the sitting room. 'For a start, I don't know what his intentions are. I don't know what mine are either, for that matter. What matters most is not to – well, not to attach too much importance to this. I want to hold myself back.'

'Are you certain?' Sally asked.

Lorna nodded. 'When I met George in London, I threw myself into the relationship. George was everything I'd ever dreamed of. When he let me down...'

'You must have felt crushed,' said Sally.

'I did,' Lorna admitted.

'Would it help to build up a social life that's nothing to do with him?' asked Sally. 'Why don't you come out dancing with Andrew and me on Saturday?'

'It's sweet of you to ask but I don't want to play gooseberry.'

'You wouldn't be,' Sally insisted. 'Samuel and Betty are coming too, and we're meeting up with my friend Deborah and a couple of other girls from the Town Hall, so you wouldn't be the only single girl. Besides, there are many more girls than men these days. Do say you'll come.'

Lorna felt drawn to the idea. It sounded like fun. When she had first come to live in Manchester, she hadn't had any expectation of a real social life. It had taken a party at Star House to bid farewell to the munitions girls to make her start to see that there was rather more to pleasure than the highly organised, rule-bound social occasions that her mother had arranged for her.

The thought of Mummy made her wonder whether perhaps she ought to mention George in her next letter home, but it didn't take her long to reject the idea. Since her last conversation with him, she'd thought a great deal about how her parents had behaved during her time in London. She hated to admit it but maybe they had rather chucked her at George, only she hadn't realised it at the time because she was so besotted with him.

No, it would be better to say nothing to Mummy and Daddy for the time being. George had hit the right note when he'd said he hoped to get to know her without all the pressures of family and polite society. She wanted to get to know him too in the same way. Just the two of them, finding out about one another. Warmth cascaded through her. It would be like the first time all over again.

After all the thought that had gone into choosing her deep-green evening suit when she went to the Claremont to meet George, Lorna's attitude towards her Saturday night on the dance-floor was refreshingly different, her love of dressing up and looking her best returning with a will.

When she had moved down from Lancaster to Manchester in the autumn, she very nearly hadn't bothered to bring any evening dresses with her. What was the point with no George to squire her about? Besides, her father had sent her to Manchester to hide her away from the public gaze. But at that time both Lorna and her mother had entertained serious hopes that Daddy would change his mind about Manchester and instead make arrangements for her to move to a posh hotel in the West Country. With that in mind, Mummy had persuaded her to add a few evening clothes to her packing.

'That way, you'll immediately have something suitable to wear when you go down to dinner in the hotel, darling,' she'd said, 'and I'll send on everything else you need as soon as I can.'

Now Lorna ran her fingertips over the dove-grey silk. The last time she had worn it had been at a ball in Mayfair, but she wasn't going to cast a cloud over this evening by dwelling on that. What mattered now was establishing a life for herself, not as her father's daughter, not as anything to do with George, but simply as a modern girl with wartime responsibilities and a measure of independence she could never have enjoyed in peacetime.

'Are you ready?' came Sally's voice, calling up the stairs. 'It's time to go.'

'Coming,' Lorna called back.

Picking up her silver evening bag, she took one last look in the mirror, then left the room and went downstairs. Below her, in the hall, Sally and Betty stared, their lips parting as they gazed at her.

'What a glorious dress,' breathed Sally. 'You look wonderful.'

'Thank you.' Lorna was touched.

'You'll be the belle of the ball,' Betty declared. 'All the men will be fighting over you for a dance.'

'That's fine as long as Andrew and Samuel aren't part of the mob,' Sally teased.

Lorna was thrilled to have caused a sensation. It gave her a real boost.

Tonight's destination was the Ritz. Lorna hadn't been there before but she'd heard about the famous revolving stage.

When they got there, they slipped inside into a dark vestibule. Once the outer door was shut, an inner door was opened for them, and they emerged into the foyer.

The girls queued to hand in their coats, receiving cloakroom tickets in return that they popped in their handbags.

As Andrew and Samuel ushered them into the ballroom, Lorna paused in the doorway, her breath catching in pure pleasure at the sight of the busy room with its pillars and art deco features, as well as the balcony above. The band was playing a quickstep and couples slow-slow-quick-quick-slowed around the sprung floor.

'Let's find a table,' said Andrew.

'If we c-can,' said Samuel.

'It's always busy here,' Betty said happily.

They were lucky enough to find a table big enough not only for them but also for the others, who arrived soon after. Lorna smiled and shook hands, taking careful note of the names.

'First names this evening,' said Sally. 'We're all friends here.'

Her friend Deborah had eyes of bright blue and her hair was the darkest of browns. Amy Brelland was a good-looking girl with red-gold hair and Josephine Hill was tall and brown-eyed, while Rosemary Greening was short and full-figured with a bubbly personality. The first two worked in the Transport department and Rosemary was in Housing.

Andrew and Samuel danced with each of the girls, though

Lorna was sure they were getting their polite duty out of the way so they could devote the rest of the evening to Sally and Betty.

A couple of boys in uniform – and they weren't much more than boys – came to their table in search of partners. One asked Lorna and the other asked Amy.

Lorna wasn't short of partners and sat out now and then only when she felt like it. She enjoyed looking at everyone else. As she watched, some of the couples on the crowded floor waltzed apart, creating a clear view across to the other side—

'What's he doing here?' Lorna breathed.

'Sorry – didn't catch that.' Sally turned to her.

'George. He's here.'

Lorna's chair was at the end of the table. She swivelled so that her back was to the dance-floor. Her heart thudded. She'd been enjoying the evening, but now she felt hopelessly self-conscious.

Everyone applauded as the music ended. Many couples remained on the floor, waiting for the next dance to start, while others broke apart, thanked one another and returned to their seats. Betty and Samuel came to sit down and Betty sipped at her lemonade. Deborah's partner escorted her to her seat. Uncomfortably aware that she was using Deborah for her own ends, Lorna focused her attention on her, admiring her dress and asking her about it. Had George spotted her? Was he even now watching her from across the ballroom?

Apparently not. Surely, if he had seen her he would have approached. Or had her studied avoidance of looking at the dancers sent him a message? Ought she to leave the table and go to him? And why was she in such a dither? She was normally a confident person.

A while later, just as she was beginning to relax, Lorna realised that Sally, Deborah and Rosemary, who were all seated around the table, were looking in the same direction. She didn't have to turn her face to know what, or rather who, had caught their attention.

'Mr Broughton,' Sally said with a quick glance at Lorna. 'How nice to see you. Do you remember me?'

'Of course,' said George. 'You kindly helped me on Christmas Eve when I came in search of Lorna.'

As Lorna stirred herself to perform the necessary introductions, she couldn't help but be aware of the admiration in the other girls' eyes as they looked at George. With a little jolt, she recalled how she'd always enjoyed seeing that look on other girls' faces and how lucky it had made her feel.

'Would you care to dance?' George asked her.

Lorna rose and allowed him to escort her onto the floor, where he took her lightly in his arms and bore her off in a graceful waltz.

'Seeing you here is an unexpected pleasure,' he said.

'I enjoy dancing,' she replied as if she went to a different ballroom every night of the week.

'I remember,' said George.

As the dance ended, George twirled her round, making her laugh. Would he request another dance? But no, he returned her to her table, holding her chair for her to be seated.

'Would you like to join us?' Sally invited him.

'You're very kind, but I'm here with friends,' George answered. He bowed his head and departed.

Deborah edged closer. 'Handsome fellow. Sally says he's someone you used to know.'

Lorna cast a grateful glance at Sally for being discreet. 'That's right.'

'It's unusual to see a man – a young one, I mean – in evening dress these days. Nearly all the young ones are in uniform.'

Lorna remembered the description of George as a man-about-town, as well as what he himself had told her about losing his position at the War Office. Some of the gloss went off the evening for her. It hurt her to picture George squandering his time. It was difficult to believe he didn't feel the same need as everyone else to do his bit for the war effort.

Presently, a ladies' excuse-me dance was announced, sending a frisson of anticipation rippling around the room. The music began and girls soon started approaching dancing couples in order to tap the girl on the shoulder with the words, 'Excuse me,' which meant that the girl had to give up her partner to the excuser.

As George danced past, Lorna surrendered to impulse. Leaving the table, she slid in between some couples, following George and his partner. Touching the girl's shoulder, she said, 'Excuse me,' obliging the girl to disappear as she moved into George's arms.

'We meet again,' she teased.

The music ended amidst clapping and laughter. George hesitated, which made him look uncertain. Lorna found it endearing in such a self-assured man. Was he about to ask if they could find a table and talk?

'Lorna, there's something I have to tell you.'

She felt giddy with delight at having been correct. 'If you fetch drinks, shall I look for a table?'

'I didn't come here alone this evening,' said George.

'I know. You mentioned it earlier. Will your friends mind if you disappear for a while?'

A beautiful girl caught Lorna's eye. Dainty and graceful, she had light-brown hair that shone beneath the chandeliers. Automatically, Lorna moved slightly to allow her to go past, but instead the girl stopped beside George, sliding her slender arm through his and standing close beside him.

Slashes of colour highlighted George's cheekbones. 'Lorna, this is Virginia Lawrence. Ginty, this is Lorna West-Sadler.'

'How do you do?' said Virginia, extending a slim hand.

'Pleased to meet you,' Lorna whispered – or maybe the words didn't emerge at all. She shook hands, then stared at George. The possessive way in which Virginia Lawrence had cosied up to him told her everything she needed to know. 'Excuse me. My friends will be wondering where I am.'

So saying, she plunged into the mass of people on the dance-floor, hardly able to breathe as the extent of her foolishness became clear to her. How could she have been so misguided as to let herself hope? What a dolt she was. What a complete and utter fool.

The lightest of touches on her arm made her turn – and there was George. A small frown, a suggestion of vulnerability about the lips, made him look concerned, anxious even. Anxious about her? Well, he had no right, not any longer – not when he had a new girlfriend to worry about.

'What do you want, George?' Lorna's cool tone belied her inner turmoil.

'Look, I'm sorry you had to find out this way.'

'What way would that be?' Lorna enquired icily. 'In the way that could have been avoided if you'd bothered to say something sooner? Is that the way you mean?'

'You're right. I should have said—'

'Yes, you should!' Lorna flared. Dropping her voice, she said, 'I spent so long trying to get over what happened, forcing myself to build a new life. But you haven't had that problem, have you? How long did it take for you to replace me, George? No.' She held up her hand as if to prevent him from speaking, even though he hadn't so much as opened his mouth. 'Don't answer that. I don't want to know.'

As the evening drew to a close, the band played the familiar opening notes of 'We'll Meet Again' and everyone surged towards the stage and grouped in front of it, their voices rising in the much-loved song whose poignant words held such a profound and personal meaning. Couples stood with their arms round one another. Groups clustered close. Sally stood encircled by Andrew's arms. Betty and Samuel held hands. Everyone needed to be near to someone who mattered. Lorna's heart ached for what she couldn't have.

Then Sally's hand reached out to her from one side and at the same time Betty's did the same from the other. Holding hands with her two dear friends eased Lorna's sense of emptiness.

At the end of the song, everybody applauded warmly. After that came the national anthem, and the crowd stood up straight and sang their hearts out.

They collected their coats from the cloakroom, said goodbye to Deborah and the other girls, and waited a short while for a taxi, laughing as the two couples and Lorna all crammed in together. They dropped Samuel at his shop, then carried on to Star House.

They piled into the hallway, chuckling as they bumped into one another. Andrew shut the front door behind them and pulled the curtain across. Sally snapped on the light.

Mrs Beaumont came out of the sitting room, but, instead of smiling and asking about their evening, she looked worried.

'Lorna, a telegram has come for you.'

Everyone went quiet. Telegrams had that effect even on people who didn't have a loved one at the front.

Lorna's hand trembled as she took it.

DADDY ILL STOP IN HOSPITAL STOP COME IMMEDIATELY STOP MUMMY

Lorna went hot and cold all over.

'I'll help you pack,' said Betty.

Sally turned to Andrew. 'Go to the telephone box and send for a taxi to take Lorna to the station.'

'I don't know if you'll get a train this time of night,' said Mrs Beaumont, 'but if not, you'll be there for the milk train. Don't fret, chick. You'll soon be on your way.'

CHAPTER EIGHTEEN

Lorna sat at Daddy's bedside, perched on the edge of the uncomfortable hard chair. Leaning forward, she focused her attention on her beloved father. She still felt dazed with disbelief and every now and again fear fluttered in her belly. She held Daddy's unresponsive hand in both her own, her thumbs gently stroking his skin, willing him to know on some level that she was here, willing him to know she would do anything to help him.

Mummy sat on the other side of the bed. She looked haggard, the skin around her greeny-hazel eyes stretched taut with strain.

Lorna had never seen her parents look so vulnerable – she had never seen Daddy look vulnerable at all, full stop. He was a big man in every sense, with a beefy physique and a domineering personality, and yet now—

A weight expanded in Lorna's chest, but she had to be strong. Whatever needed to be done, she would do it. She wasn't the biddable, compliant daughter she'd once been. She had grown up a lot since that excruciatingly painful experience in court when the breach-of-promise case her father had instigated on her behalf against George had backfired so catastrophically and left her personal reputation in tatters.

Since then she had learned a lot through working at the salvage depot and being with Sally and Betty. And then there were her experiences in the Christmas Blitz. Without being big-headed, she could truthfully say she had discovered reserves of courage within herself – just as thousands upon thousands of other civilians had when they found themselves facing danger. This was a war like no other that had ever been fought before and everyone wanted to do their best and conduct themselves with honour.

Lorna looked across the bed at her mother. 'Mummy, you're exhausted. Why don't you go home and rest? I'm here now. I'll telephone the instant anything happens.'

Her mother gave her a tired smile. 'I'll stay, darling. If I went home, I'd simply pace the floor until it was time to come back again.' She looked at Daddy for a long moment before returning her gaze to Lorna. 'I'm glad you're here.'

'Of course I'm here. I came at once.'

'I know you did,' said Mummy. 'Not everyone can, you know, not these days, when everybody is engaged in war work. They can't let people have leave willy-nilly, no matter what the circumstances.'

Lorna considered that. Imagine having a family emergency and being told, 'Sorry. We can't spare you. You've got to carry on.'

She gave her head a little shake. 'Sally would never do that to Betty or me. She'd always find a way for us to do what we needed to, even if it meant she ended up doing a double shift herself.'

'She sounds like a good person,' said Mummy.

'She's the best.'

Lorna looked at Daddy once more. His features, usually so

strong and resolute, were now slack in repose. A shiver of fear ran through her. She didn't know how she would bear it if anything happened to him. If it happened? It had already happened. The reason Daddy was asleep was because he had been sedated; and he'd been sedated to calm him and bring his blood pressure down because – because he was paralysed.

'Paralysed?' Lorna had repeated when she had first arrived at Daddy's bedside, desperate for information.

'Both sides,' Mummy had told her.

'I thought a stroke happened to one side, not both.'

'I believe they can happen on both,' Mummy had replied in a brittle voice, 'but apparently this isn't a stroke. They don't know what caused it.'

Even now, several hours later, Lorna still struggled to take it in. Daddy was so strong-willed, so domineering, so... well, frankly, so annoying. And now – and now he was trapped inside a body that couldn't move.

Something must have shown in her face, because Mummy said sharply, 'You mustn't be sorry for him. He'd hate that. You and I shall have to be tough and ruthless.'

'That sounds like the way Daddy treats his business rivals,' Lorna commented.

Mummy nodded. 'He says that if you feel sorry for someone, it's because they're weak – so we mustn't be sorry for him. We have to be strong and determined and matter-of-fact. Then he'll know we still respect him and – and—' Her voice caught on a sob that she quickly stifled. She drew in a breath, sitting up straight and thrusting her shoulders back. 'And that's important because it might be all he has left.'

Lorna insisted that Mummy should go and have something to eat, telling her she had to keep her strength up. When Mummy returned, she gave Lorna the same instruction. Lorna was reluctant to obey, but it was the right thing to do. She'd be of no use to anyone if she came over all light-headed because she was hungry.

Feeling the need for fresh air, she made her way downstairs and found the front doors. The January air was crisp and sparkling. Lacy flakes drifted down softly, coming to rest upon an already white landscape. The banks of sandbags protecting the buildings had vanished under the snow. Lorna left the hospital grounds and made her way along the road. She entered a small cafe, where she ordered a savoury meat roll, but when it came she barely tasted it because she was too worried and upset.

With her heart full, and her head packed to bursting with thoughts, Lorna made her way back to the hospital. What had happened to Daddy was catastrophic. He must be terrified, but Lorna sensed that her mother was correct in her assessment of the best way for the two of them to conduct themselves. Daddy wouldn't thank them for sympathy.

When she walked into her father's private room, Lorna's instant impression was of a crowd of people. Then her eyes adjusted and she realised that, along with her mother, there were four men.

Daddy was awake. He saw her at once.

'Gentlemen, this is my daughter, Lorna.'

His voice lacked its usual booming quality, but trust Daddy to take control by performing the introduction. Lorna caught his eye, but he shifted his gaze.

The men introduced themselves. Two were doctors, though one had the title of Mr. The other two were police officers, both of them in plain clothes.

'Come and sit down, Lorna,' said Mummy.

The men parted and she resumed her seat.

'Please go back to the beginning for my daughter's benefit,' said Mummy. She pressed her hand to her cheek. 'It wouldn't do me any harm to hear it again. It doesn't seem possible.'

'It's all too possible, I'm afraid, Mrs West-Sadler,' said Detective Inspector Kent. 'As I explained before, with supplies of alcohol dwindling, the making of illegal alcohol – hooch, it's known as – is a growing industry, and a dangerous one. These men aren't brewing ordinary beer or distilling ordinary spirits. The drinks they're making look and taste like the real thing, but they can inflict unspeakable damage. We know of cases where the result has been permanent blindness or even death.'

Lorna stared at her father, unable to disguise her horror as she began to see where the inspector's words were leading.

Daddy scowled back at her. 'They think I've been poisoned by something I drank.'

Mr Swanson, the senior physician, took up the story. 'Mr West-Sadler met up with three business associates in a hotel. He and two of the others each had a whisky and soda. The fourth man had something else. Mr West-Sadler and the other two who'd had the whisky are now in a state of paralysis, which we believe was caused by consuming illegal alcohol.'

Lorna's mouth dropped open. 'How many drinks did you have?' she asked her father.

'Kindly don't make it sound as if I drank the bar dry,' he replied. 'I had one drink. One!' The final word came out on a burst of frustration.

'That can be all that is required to have a severe effect,' Mr Swanson confirmed.

'Oh, Daddy...' Lorna whispered.

'Everybody at the hotel assures us that they had no idea they had purchased illegal spirits,' said Detective Inspector Kent, 'but of course that is under investigation.'

'And there is no doubt that this is the cause of my husband's condition?' Mummy asked quietly.

'None,' said Mr Swanson.

'That leaves one question,' said Daddy. Though his voice wasn't a patch on its usual self, Lorna sensed this was the strongest he could muster. 'Am I going to get the damn feeling back in my arms and legs – or will I be stuck like this for ever? Because, if I am, you can slit my throat right now.'

CHAPTER NINETEEN

After a couple of sleety days when tiny half-melted balls of ice splattered against windows, there was a fresh fall of snow.

'Even the depot looks attractive under a layer of snow,' Betty told Samuel.

She had gone round to the bookshop for the evening and they were in his parlour-office. He had added a sideboard and a standard lamp to the room. At this rate, despite the bookcases that lined the walls, it wouldn't be long before the room simply became a parlour. Betty couldn't wait. She loved Samuel all the more because of the trouble he was taking on her account.

'That's one of the things I love about you,' he said, his hazel eyes softening behind his spectacles. 'You s-see the good side of everything.'

'There's no point in being miserable, is there?' said Betty. 'But there is one thing I've been worrying about.'

Samuel was instantly concerned. 'Wh-what's that?'

'The money I owe Dad. You know how Mr Tucker paid my fine as well as his own at the magistrates' court, and then Dad reimbursed him for both amounts minus the week's wages Mr

Tucker had already held back from me. Since then I've saved what I can and given it to Dad, but I still need to pay back...' She bit her lip before bringing out the next words on a shamed whisper. '...several pounds. I feel that I have to clear the debt before I can get married.'

'That's not a problem,' Samuel, dear Samuel, said at once. 'I'll repay it for you. Everything I have is yours.'

'You're so good,' said Betty, 'and I truly appreciate the offer but it's important that I do this myself. I want to start wedded life with a clean slate. What I did at Tucker's was wrong and I ought to pay for my own mistake.'

'Don't f-forget it will be my job as your husband to s-support you,' said Samuel. 'If I pay this d-debt, it'll mean we don't have to w-wait so long to get married.'

Dismayed, Betty pictured the length of time it would take her to repay Dad, but she refused to let it sway her. 'There's a new type of girl now because of the war work we all have to do. I know I haven't been doing war work for very long, but I understand about women doing men's jobs to keep the country going.'

'I respect that,' Samuel answered, 'but I don't w-want you to be too independent. I w-want you to need me.'

'I'll always need you,' Betty promised, 'just as I hope you'll always need me. But I have to pay this debt out of my own money, Samuel. It's a question of self-respect.'

* * *

As she and Betty sorted the contents of the daily salvage sacks, Sally was glad to chat. It helped to – well, not exactly to take her mind off the thought of Andrew joining up, because that knowledge, that worry, was with her the whole time; but chatting provided a distraction.

They talked about Lorna's family situation.

'I wonder how her father is.' A look of anxiety crossed Betty's pretty face. 'I hope he's all right.'

'He's in hospital,' said Sally, 'and that's the best place for him.'

'I know how upset I'd be if my dad was ill like that,' said Betty.

'Me too,' Sally agreed. 'Lorna is by his side and that's what matters. Being together is the most important thing.' Awareness flashed through her mind that she and Andrew weren't going to be together for much longer, and something clenched inside her chest. 'Let's talk about something more cheerful.'

'You're preparing another talk about salvage, aren't you?' Betty asked.

Sally nodded. 'When I started getting out and about in the community before Christmas, it was to a large extent to get my name rather than Mrs Lockwood's associated with the depot, but actually I love the work I'm doing, spreading the word about salvage.'

'You're the reason the local Boy Scout troops are in such hot competition with one another to collect the most,' said Betty. Bless her, she could always be relied upon to show her loyalty.

'They love it when their weight wins,' Sally agreed with a smile.

'What about this new talk you're putting together?' Betty asked.

'I don't want to tell people the same things over and over again,' said Sally, 'so I'm always on the lookout for fresh information. I try to include one thing that will make the audience sit up and take notice and that will stick in their minds.'

Betty chuckled. 'Like some parachutes being made partly out of corsets. I remember that one. Go on, what's your latest fact that's going to impress your audience?'

'It's to do with paper. Did you know it's used in construction? There is one ton of paper in every mile of concrete runway.'

Betty looked impressed. 'I'll think of that the next time I'm removing paper-clips before we send the paper off to the mill.'

When they had finished the daily sacks, Sally consulted her wristwatch.

'Time to stop for a cuppa.'

'I'll pop the kettle on,' said Betty.

Soon they were sitting in Sally's office, enjoying a hot drink and a cigarette. Sally's glance fell on the third chair – Lorna's. How were Lorna's family getting on? How were she and her mother coping?

Betty inhaled on her cigarette, then turned her head sideways towards the window to exhale. Her head gave a little jolt and she blew out the smoke at top speed.

'Crikey. I was just thinking about Lorna and I think I've magicked her up.'

Sally looked through the window and there, crossing the yard, was Lorna in a belted mackintosh and her brimless fur hat, carrying a small suitcase.

Sally and Betty jumped up and ran to the front door to bring her inside. They drew her into the office and sat her down.

'I'm just popping in here before I go to Star House,' she said.

'How are things?' Sally asked. 'How is your father?'

'Still in the land of the living,' said Lorna, 'but it's... complicated.'

'How so?' Betty asked. 'No, wait. Let me go and fetch you a drink. Don't say anything until I get back.'

'A cup of tea is just what I need,' Lorna told Sally as Betty darted away. 'It felt like a very long journey. I was on the six o'clock train this morning.'

Betty returned with a cup of tea and the three of them settled in for a natter.

'You aren't going to believe what's happened to my father,' said Lorna. 'We can hardly take it in ourselves.'

'It sounds serious,' said Sally.

'It is,' was the sober reply. 'To put it as succinctly as possible, he drank a glass of tainted alcohol and it has left him paralysed.'

'Paralysed!' Betty exclaimed.

'You're kidding,' said Sally.

'I wish I were,' said Lorna. 'He was with three other businessmen. Three of them had a whisky and soda – just one drink each. The other man had something else. The three who drank the whisky are now paralysed. The one that didn't isn't.'

'You said the drink was tainted,' Sally said quietly.

'Illegal alcohol,' said Lorna.

'My goodness.' Sally's flesh tingled as the penny dropped. 'That instruction we received before Christmas to keep empty alcohol bottles to one side to be returned directly to the breweries and distilleries – that mentioned preventing the production of illegal alcohol, but I really only thought of it in terms of salvage.'

'It's your job to see things that way,' said loyal Betty.

'I'm very sorry that this has happened to your father, Lorna,' said Sally. 'Is it... is it permanent?'

Lorna's eyes shone with tears but she lifted her chin. 'At present it's a question of wait and see.'

'If you're needed up in Lancaster—' Sally began.

Lorna shook her head. 'I wanted to stay but Daddy said there was nothing to be gained by it. He was dead set on my coming back to Manchester and, believe me, when my father tells you to do something, you jump to it.'

* * *

At the end of their tea break, Lorna rose and picked up her case.

'I'll go and explain to Mrs Beaumont and then I'll come back.'

Betty gave her a hug. 'Poppy off, chick. That's what my mum used to say to me when I was little.'

She and Sally watched as Lorna left the yard, then they turned to one another.

Betty shook her head. 'I don't know what to say. It's so horrid. Poor Mr West-Sadler.' What must it be like to lose the power of movement? Fear shivered through her.

'We'll have to hope and pray that he recovers,' said Sally.

When Lorna returned, she went upstairs to get changed into her dungarees and headscarf.

'I don't want you handling me with kid gloves,' she said when she came down. 'Let's get on with everything as normal.'

The three of them got on with their work. They had to make sure both the rubber and the metal were ready for collection.

The vans arrived early in the afternoon and the girls helped load them up. Soon the salvage was on its way. Not long after that, it was time for their tea break.

'I'd really like to go and see Dad this weekend,' Betty told Sally and Lorna as they sat together with their drinks, 'but I'm working this Saturday and he's on duty on Sunday.'

'Is he working on Saturday as well?' Lorna asked.

'No,' said Betty.

'That's easily dealt with,' Lorna said breezily. 'I'll do your Saturday for you. Don't argue. I've already told you, my father wants me down here.'

'Well, if you're sure, that would be marvellous,' said Betty, delighted. 'And I'll do yours next week.'

Lorna maintained the same airy voice but there was a glint in her eye as she said, 'No need.'

Betty looked at her sympathetically. 'I know you think that keeping busy will stop you thinking about your dad—'

'It isn't just that,' Lorna replied.

'It's George, isn't it?' said Sally. 'You can't hide away in your work just because he let you down.'

'Let me down for a second time, you mean,' said Lorna. 'Actually, that's not fair. All he said was that he'd like the opportunity to know me away from the social whirl of London. He never uttered a word about us getting back together.'

'Even so,' said Betty, 'it was rotten of him not to mention the girlfriend.'

'I don't intend to waste my time dwelling on George,' said Lorna. 'I've got plenty to keep me busy, both here and with the WVS. The WVS is organising a fundraising dance to be held at the Claremont Hotel and I've been helping with that.'

'Even though George is staying there?' asked Betty.

Lorna shrugged. 'I was involved in it before George produced Virginia Lawrence like a rabbit out of a hat. I'm not going to back out now. If I bump into him, I'll be polite, but that's all.' She stubbed out her cigarette. 'That's enough about George.'

Betty exchanged a look of concern with Sally but said no more. She hoped Lorna would let down the barrier and allow them to provide whatever support she needed when she felt ready to receive it.

'Thanks so much, Lorna,' said Betty. 'This will be the first time I've seen Dad since I got engaged—' She stopped.

'I know you want to see your father,' said Lorna, 'and it doesn't hurt me or upset me that your father is in good health and leading a normal life while mine is... bed-bound. My advice is: see your father every chance you get.'

Betty nodded. How brave Lorna was, how generous. 'I want him to see Mum's ring on my finger.'

'That'll mean the world to him, I'm sure,' said Sally.

The prospect of the trip to Salford carried Betty through the rest of the week on a wave of excitement. It was a shame Samuel wouldn't be able to come with her, but he had to open his shop.

When she alighted from the bus on Saturday, she couldn't help feeling different about herself. Before, when she went to Dad's house she'd been the unwanted stepdaughter. Now she was engaged, with a home and family of her own to look forward to.

Neighbours stopped her in the street to offer congratulations and ask her about her intended.

'Have you set the date?' she was asked.

'Not yet,' said Betty, all too aware of why not.

Grace answered the door and actually gave her a hug. Betty hung up her coat and went into the parlour, where Dad took both her hands as he studied her face.

'I hope Samuel realises what a lucky man he is.'

'And Betty's a lucky girl too,' Grace trilled from behind them. 'She's well and truly landed on her feet, hasn't she, Trevor? Who'd have thought of our Betty doing so well for herself?'

Looking down at Betty's hands, Dad raised the left one and gazed at her engagement ring.

'Oh, Betty,' he murmured.

'I'll make some tea for us,' said Grace. 'Come and help me, Betty.'

Grace disappeared, but for once Betty stayed put.

'Thank you so much for letting me have Mum's ring,' she said quietly. 'I can't tell you how much it means to me.'

'To me as well.' Dad's voice was throaty with emotion. 'It's not the same as having your mum here to be the mother of the bride, but at least you'll always carry a little bit of her with you.'

Grace appeared in the doorway. 'Betty – are you coming?'

This time Betty followed her. They made the tea and Grace arranged some biscuits on a plate.

'Honey biscuits,' she said. 'I'll give you the recipe. You'll have to start collecting recipes now. Have you and Samuel set a date?'

'Not yet. There's something I need to talk to Dad about.'

'And me,' said Grace. 'You need to talk to both of us about the wedding.' Scooping up the tray, she led the way back to the parlour. 'Trevor, Betty wants to talk about the wedding.'

'Already?' said Dad. 'She's hardly been engaged for five minutes.'

'Now then,' said Grace, 'this is no time to be the protective father not wanting to let go of his little girl. Couples aren't hanging about these days. Long engagements have gone out of fashion.'

'Actually,' said Betty, 'that's exactly what it's going to be.'

'Why?' Grace asked. 'Samuel isn't having second thoughts, is he?'

How Betty wished she could prevent the heat from staining her cheeks. 'Of course not. It's because of the money I owe Dad. I want to pay it back before we get married.'

'But, Betty—' Dad began.

'I know, Dad,' she replied. 'It's a large amount. Before you say anything else, I want you to know that Samuel offered to pay it back for me, but I want to do it myself.'

'I'm more than happy to waive the debt,' said Dad. 'All I want is to see you settled and happy.'

'Oh, Dad.' Betty's chest hitched as the thought of his generosity overwhelmed her.

'What?' Grace exclaimed, the colour draining from her face. Then she was all smiles and concern. 'That is so very generous of you, Trevor, but is it really the right thing? Can you honestly say it's the correct and proper thing for a policeman, a sergeant no less, to write off a debt just like that? You can hardly lay down the law to others and then let your own daughter off the hook.'

Betty pressed her lips together. Oh, why couldn't Grace buzz off and leave her and Dad to sort this out between them?

'I don't need to be let off the hook, thank you,' she said coolly. 'I've said I'll pay back the money myself and that's what I'm going to do.'

'That remains to be seen,' said Grace.

CHAPTER TWENTY

Sally arrived at the top of the ladder, steadying herself before pushing open the skylight above her. The night-time chill dropped through the opening, making her skin tingle in spite of how warmly dressed she was. There had been another fall of snow and the depot roof twinkled beneath the stars.

She hauled herself onto the roof.

Betty passed a broom through the skylight. 'It's a shame to spoil the snow,' she said, popping her head out. 'It always looks so pretty.' She disappeared back inside.

Taking care not to slip, Sally brushed a small area clear. Betty returned with their folding chairs, which she exchanged for the broom. By the time Sally had set them up, Betty was back with a pair of blankets, which they drew around them-selves like cloaks.

'This feels cosy now,' said Sally, 'but it won't last.'

'I wonder what sort of night we're in for,' said Betty.

It had been some nights since the last raid, and tonight was another quiet one. At six o'clock, after stamping their feet to get the circulation going, the girls folded their chairs and climbed through the skylight and down the ladder, then locked up the yard before they walked back to Wilton Road.

Lorna, who had also been out on duty, arrived at Star House at the same time as they did.

'Come in, girls.' Mrs Beaumont appeared in the hallway. 'You must be frozen. Lorna, isn't Mrs Henshaw with you?'

'She'll be back presently,' said Lorna. 'She was in the middle of something when I left.'

'Is Andrew home?' Sally asked.

'Not yet,' said Mrs Beaumont. 'I've popped hot-water bottles in your beds. Go and snatch an hour's kip.'

When Sally reached her room, she found that Lorna had followed her.

'Can I come in for a minute?' Lorna asked, hovering in the doorway.

'Of course. What's wrong?' Was it bad news from Lancaster? Sally braced herself.

'I dislike telling tales out of school,' said Lorna, 'but I think you should know that Mrs Henshaw has been talking to her WVS chums about leaving Star House.'

Sally frowned. 'What of it?'

'She's saying that when she leaves, you'll be going with her.'

'Ah.' Sally shut her eyes for a moment. 'Thanks for telling me. You've done the right thing.'

Lorna withdrew and Sally quickly got into bed and cuddled the hot-water bottle. Her muscles relaxed as she warmed up, but she didn't drop off. Presently she got dressed and went downstairs into the sitting room. When she heard the front door open, she looked into the hallway and saw Mrs Henshaw taking off her coat.

'Would you come in here for a minute?' Sally asked. 'I've got something to tell you.'

'Andrew...?' Mrs Henshaw asked at once.

'He's fine as far as I know. It's something else.'

Sally shut the door behind her mother-in-law. Mrs Henshaw's eyes were lined with strain after her long night on duty, but she didn't sit down. She looked questioningly at Sally.

'It's to do with when you go to live with Auntie Vera,' said Sally, taking a breath for courage. 'I won't be coming.'

'What d'you mean, you won't be coming?'

'I'm going to stay here at Star House,' Sally said firmly.

'No, you aren't,' said Mrs Henshaw. Then her face softened. 'Are you scared you'll be imposing? You're new to our family, Sally, but Vera has a generous heart and she'll make you welcome. You're not to worry yourself about that.'

'It isn't that,' said Sally. 'You're a wonderful mother-in-law and I love you to pieces, but – well, I'd rather stay here at Star House. It's nothing personal against you or Auntie Vera.'

'I should hope not!' Mrs Henshaw exclaimed.

'Living here is convenient for the depot.'

'So what? Vera doesn't exactly live in Timbuktu. If that's your reason for wanting to stay here, it's a pretty lame one.'

Riled, Sally said, 'I like it here. I love being with Betty and Lorna.'

'Don't be silly,' said Mrs Henshaw. 'You're not a single girl having fun in her first billet. You're a married woman and that means you stay with your family.'

'I'd go anywhere to be with Andrew,' Sally said firmly, 'but that isn't possible. He's leaving and I want to stay here.'

'Oh aye? You'd go anywhere to be with Andrew but not to be with his mother. Is that it?'

'No!' cried Sally. 'It isn't like that.'

Mrs Henshaw's mouth set in a straight line. 'It seems to me it's exactly like that.'

After a short run of days of duck-egg blue skies and bright sunshine beneath which the snow shimmered and at times dazzled, the sky filled with surly grey clouds and the snow turned to slush. Pedestrians kept as far from the kerb as they could so as not to get splashed as vehicles swept past.

At the depot, the girls took turns to sweep the yard regularly.

'Why bother?' asked one of the Corporation drivers who collected the salvage. 'You're keeping salvage here, not the Crown Jewels.'

'It keeps the depot looking smart – or as smart as it can be,' Sally told him. 'It shows we're proud to work here.'

Betty looked at her friend in admiration. No one seeing her at work would guess at the upset that lay between her and her mother-in-law.

Later, when they stopped for their tea break, Betty said as much. 'You seem very good at separating your work life from your home life.'

'You have to be, don't you?' Sally replied. 'We all have to do it.' She gave Lorna a look of sympathy. 'You're doing it all the time at the moment.' Then she looked at Betty. 'I bet when you worked at Tucker's and the customers asked after Grace, you never complained about her, did you?'

'True,' said Betty.

'Well then,' said Sally.

Betty exhaled a stream of smoke on a lengthy sigh. 'It feels as if the two sides of my life are all tangled up now.'

'How so?' Lorna asked.

Betty explained about wanting to pay off her debt to her dad.

'How much are we talking about, if it isn't a rude question?' Lorna asked.

'It started out as six pounds.'

'Six!' Sally and Lorna exclaimed in unison.

Betty's cheeks felt hot. 'I've paid back a little since I started here but I still owe more than a fiver. In fact, I owe more than five guineas.'

'That's a huge sum,' said Sally.

'That's way more than a week's wages for most people,' said Lorna. 'And that's a man's wage, not a woman's. Oh, Betty.'

'Could Samuel pay it for you?' Sally asked. 'I imagine he's the sort to have savings.'

'He's offered,' said Betty, 'but I don't want him to. It's my responsibility.'

'Good for you,' Lorna applauded her.

'But it's going to take for ever to pay back.' Betty felt deflated. 'I can't bear the thought of waiting that long to get married – which is why I've decided to look for another job.'

'Betty! You're not leaving the depot, are you?' Sally exclaimed. 'I'm sorry,' she added, looking shamefaced. 'That makes me sound so selfish. I know you could get much higher wages in a munitions factory.'

'I don't mean to leave here,' Betty said quickly. 'I love being here with the two of you. I mean that I need another job on top of this one.'

'How on earth would you fit it in?' asked Lorna. 'Don't forget you're also a fire-watcher.'

'I'm sure there must be plenty of jobs these days where the hours can be adjusted to suit,' said Betty. 'And it would only be until I'm free of the debt.' She ignored the thought that it wasn't going to be anything like as easy as she made it sound. 'Please don't try to talk me out of it,' she added, seeing the look of concern that passed between the other two.

'We won't,' said Lorna, 'as long as you promise to listen if we worry that you're pushing yourself too hard.'

Sally looked thoughtful. 'It's important to have a clear conscience before you get married. I haven't told anyone this before, but you know how, when Andrew and I got engaged, my parents – well, my mother – refused permission for us to get married because I was under twenty-one?'

'Yes,' said Betty.

'Later, Mum said we could have permission if we used Andrew's position as a teacher to get ourselves evacuated.'

'She never!' said Betty.

'Were you tempted?' asked Lorna.

'Up until that moment, I'd have said I'd have given anything to get married,' said Sally, 'but when Andrew and I talked about it, we knew it was more important to stay here and do our bit. Going off to the countryside would have felt like running away.'

'So you told your mother no,' said Lorna.

'My dad found out. He was shocked at what Mum had tried to do and he gave permission, so it worked out in the end.' Sally looked at Betty. 'The point is, I understand about not having ifs and buts hanging over you when you get married.'

'Thanks,' said Betty. 'That makes me feel better.'

'Will you go to the labour exchange?' Sally asked.

'I'd rather not,' Betty said mournfully. 'I'd sound so fussy and unpatriotic the moment I started talking about wanting to pick and choose my hours.'

'That leaves the situations vacant column in the paper,' said Lorna. 'What time is the early edition of the *Manchester Evening News* available? Sally and I will help you look for a new job.'

Betty's spirits rose instantly. With her friends by her side, she could do anything.

Betty was sent for by the very first place she applied to, which sent her straight into a state of nerves.

'C-congrats,' said Samuel, stretching out his feet to reach the tiled hearth in the parlour-office at the rear of the shop. Betty was sitting on the hearthrug, leaning against his legs.

'Thanks,' she said.

'You d-don't sound thrilled.'

'Bad case of butterflies,' she admitted ruefully.

'Wh-when's your interview?'

'The day after tomorrow. Sally's giving me time off.'

'Are you sure you'll be able to manage the extra hours?' Samuel asked. 'I d-don't want you w-wearing yourself out.'

'If it enables us to get married sooner, it'll be worth it,' said Betty.

'As long as you d-don't f-fall asleep in the middle of our w-wedding,' he teased.

Betty laughed, but the truth was that she was concerned about what she was letting herself in for. She was already tired, what with her full-time job and her fire-watching and having to drag herself out of bed when the siren went off. Well, what was a bit more tiredness?

Her interview was at a small factory in Seymour Grove, which she would be able to cycle to if she got the job. The factory was owned and run by Mr Harris, who had thinning dark hair and a sharp chin. His office was tucked away inside a long, low building with no windows. It had no heating either, and Betty's feet gradually turned into lumps of ice as the interview progressed.

'Before the war we used to build, among other things, teasmades,' said Mr Harris. 'Decent little contraptions. "The teamaking and shaving-water robot-service", is what we used to say in the advertisements. When war was on the horizon, we switched to making various engine parts and also parts for altimeters. Do you know what those are?' Without waiting for what he clearly expected to be a no, he went on, 'They're fitted in aeroplanes. They measure how high the plane is above sea level.'

'I'd like to help make them,' said Betty, determined to get a word in.

'According to your letter, Miss Hughes, you already have a job. You're simply looking for extra hours.'

'That's right,' Betty confirmed. 'I work at the salvage depot in Chorlton Monday to Friday and every third Saturday. I could work here the other two Saturdays and some evenings. I'd soon build up a routine. I wouldn't let you down.'

'You'd be out on your ear if you did,' was the blunt reply. 'The factory runs from six in the morning until ten at night. We can always do with more girls on the evening shift.' Mr Harris looked at her letter. 'Before you worked at the salvage depot, you were in a grocer's.'

'Ever since I left school,' said Betty.

'You'll find it very different here,' said Mr Harris.

'I'll do my best,' Betty answered. 'I've always worked hard.'

Mr Harris's face cracked into a brief smile. 'A grafter, are you? That's what I like to hear. But are you accurate? That's the most important thing when you're constructing parts. Do you have to be accurate in the salvage depot?'

Betty pictured herself jumping up and down on a crate of rubber items to squash them into their container. 'Not really, not in the way you mean.'

'But you had to be accurate when you were weighing in the grocery, didn't you?'

Betty went hot and cold. Was this the moment when he asked her why she'd left Tucker's?

But Mr Harris didn't appear to need an answer to that question, because he continued with, 'Have you brought a reference for me to see?'

Betty delved in her handbag. 'It's from the manager of the salvage depot.'

She handed it over. She didn't know what Sally had written, but Mr Harris nodded as he read it. Then he gave it back to her.

'Welcome to Harris's Small Robotics, Miss Hughes.'

CHAPTER TWENTY-ONE

Mrs Beaumont fetched the first post from the doormat while everyone was having breakfast. On returning to the dining room, she handed a letter to Lorna, who went hot and cold at the sight of the writing.

'It's from my mother.'

She quickly opened it and read it. A powerful wave of relief made her feel wobbly inside when she discovered that Daddy was starting to recover. The next moment, she was in tears. Her friends clustered around her, making sympathetic noises.

Lorna swiped a hand across her face. 'It's all right – it's good news. I'm crying because it's such a relief.'

She couldn't have repeated afterwards what the others said to her. All she was aware of was the kindness and compassion. It was some moments before she could control her emotions sufficiently to pass on the details.

'The feeling is coming back into Daddy's limbs and the doctors are optimistic that he will return to normal. Apparently one of the other men began to improve the day before Daddy and this gave everyone hope for Daddy and the third man.'

'That's wonderful news,' said Betty.

Mrs Henshaw nodded. 'I'm very pleased for you and for all your family.'

'Do you want to go back up there?' Sally asked.

'Daddy says I should stay here and get on with my war work.' Lorna half-laughed. It came out on a fresh spurt of tears. 'Typical Daddy. He sent me back here because he said there was no point in my sitting beside his sickbed, and now he says I should stay away because there's no point in hovering over him while he gets better.' She had to wipe her eyes once more. 'Sorry. I can't stop crying.'

'It's all the worry coming out,' said Mrs Beaumont. 'You never realise just how worried you were about something until afterwards.'

Lorna looked at the clock on the mantelpiece. 'We'd better get ready for work.'

The three girls set off together through the late-January chill. Lorna felt rejuvenated and worked with a will, her happiness and gratitude spurring her on.

'Mrs B was right,' she told her chums. 'I didn't realise how much of a burden I was carrying.'

'Now you've got the WVS ball to look forward to,' said Betty. 'I'm glad you'll be here for it.'

'Yes,' Sally agreed. 'It would have been a shame if you'd had to miss it after all the effort you've put into organising it.'

'I never gave it a thought when I was in Lancaster,' said Lorna.

'Of course you didn't,' said Betty.

'I'd better get in touch with Mrs Callaghan and see what she wants me to do,' said Lorna.

'She knows you were called away,' said Sally. 'Andrew's mother told her. I'm sure that anything you were responsible for has been taken on by someone else.'

'I'm sure it has,' said Lorna. 'The WVS ladies are nothing if not highly efficient. I'll make sure I pull my weight on the night.'

She hesitated before adding, 'It's not as though I've got a chap of my own to keep me occupied.' With a glance at Sally, she said, 'Go on, spit it out. I can tell you want to ask something.'

'It's about George,' said Sally. 'Are you going to tell him about your father, seeing as they know one another?'

Lorna considered it for a moment. 'No,' she said decisively. 'I'm perfectly sure Daddy wouldn't want me to. He and George didn't exactly part on good terms. Besides, the police in Lancaster want to keep the matter hush-hush while they do their investigation. Not to mention George is the last person whose sympathy I want. He's got a new life and a new girlfriend and I intend to keep my distance.'

The WVS fundraising dance was to be held that Saturday. Since being introduced to Virginia – or Ginty, as George had called her – *Ginty.* Lorna had tried saying the name with a sneer in her voice to build up a stock of healthy loathing towards George, but what was the point? If she hated him, that would mean she was thinking about him. It was better to cast him and Virginia out of her mind altogether, in so far as that was possible. Besides, thoughts of George had no business cropping up now that she had Daddy's health to think about.

She had written to her mother to ask her to parcel up her turquoise-and-cream satin dress with the pearl-edged neckline, her cream silk shawl with the long fringe and her cream evening shoes. She'd also asked Mummy to pick out a couple of other dresses and as many accessories as she could cram into the cardboard box.

I hope you don't mind being asked to do this, Lorna had written, *when you're so concerned about Daddy.*

To which Mummy had replied, *Quite honestly, it's a pleasure to have something else to do.*

The reason Lorna had asked for extra gowns was so that Sally and Betty could borrow something if they wanted to.

'What will the other girls be wearing?' Betty asked.

'It'll be a mixture,' Lorna told her. 'There'll be evening dresses, smart day dresses and some uniforms.'

When Saturday evening came round, Sally and Betty helped Lorna get ready. She had ordered a taxi because, being one of the organisers, she wanted to arrive early to make sure everything was ready.

As the taxi drew up in front of the hotel, staff were outside erecting an awning over the steps. It was dark blue and scallop-edged, its underneath covered in silver stars. Lorna smiled, certain the guests would love it.

Inside, she found Mrs Callaghan. A tall, spare woman with grey hair, she was in charge of the Chorlton WVS branch, a job that – according to Sally, who had heard it from her mother-in-law – had been made a good deal smoother for her when Mrs Lockwood had been diverted from constantly stepping on her toes by being appointed the branch's official salvage officer.

Other committee members soon arrived. Between them, they checked the arrangement of the tables around the dance-floor in the ballroom, ensured that the cloakroom had freed up sufficient space, and counted the quiz-sheets and the crosswords for the beat-the-clock crossword competition. Every competition entry would cost a shilling and guests would also be able to pay to request that the band play a particular piece of music. The aim was to raise as much money as possible.

When the guests started walking through the doors, Lorna helped to welcome them, pointing out the cloakroom and the entrance to the ballroom.

Sally and Andrew, Betty and Samuel, Mrs Henshaw and Mrs Beaumont all arrived together.

'I'm so pleased you're here,' said Lorna. 'That chart on the easel outside the ballroom will show you where your table is.'

'You'll join us soon, won't you?' Betty asked.

'I will if I can, but it'll only be for a while,' said Lorna. 'I'm mainly going to be floating about, keeping an eye on things.'

'What a shame,' said Betty sympathetically.

But it suited Lorna: she wasn't here to have a wonderful time. She was here to keep busy.

'I appreciate the way you're watching over everything,' Mrs Callaghan said to her some time later, 'but there's no need for you to feel you have to do everything. The whole committee is here and it's our joint responsibility.'

It was on the tip of Lorna's tongue to agree that she'd quite like to sit with her friends for a spell when she had an odd feeling, something that made her turn round – and there was George, looking across the room at her. He was seated at a table, with Virginia beside him. Also at the table, accompanied by their expensively dressed wives, were the two well-to-do men – the thin-lipped one and the one with red veins threaded through his cheeks – who had come to see George that time when she had accidentally on purpose bumped into him here in the Claremont's foyer. He'd referred to them as his business associates, whatever that meant.

George looked straight at Lorna and she looked back. She hadn't known he was going to be here, but then why would she? But it made sense. The Claremont had been asked to sell tickets to their guests, so of course he had purchased some. He had probably paid for the whole table.

He bowed his head to her, a sharp gesture rather than a cordial one, but so what? She no longer wished to be friendly. She no longer wished to have anything to do with George Broughton.

Realising Virginia was now looking her way as well, Lorna suddenly became very busy, stopping the master of ceremonies, who happened to be walking past, to ask him how he felt the event was going.

If only she could keep out of the ballroom altogether, but it wasn't possible. All she could do was steer clear of George's table. Even so, she couldn't help but be aware of him. Her heart sensed where he was. She saw him dancing with Virginia, and then with the wife of one of his 'business associates'.

When a gentlemen's excuse-me was announced, Lorna hastily quit the ballroom. It would be just frightful if George chose to dance with her.

Would it be worse if he didn't want to?

It seemed a good moment to dive into the powder room. The door closed behind her and she looked along the line of gilt-edged mirrors above the basins. At this end was a shallow wicker basket containing rolled-up hand towels, each one not much larger than a face flannel.

Lorna stood aside with a polite smile to let a couple of ladies pass her and leave. At the far end of the basins, of all people, was Virginia. Lorna's heart sank – or at least it started to. Was Virginia weeping? She was pretending to powder her nose but was she really dashing aside tears?

Lorna was on the verge of withdrawing and leaving her to it when compassion came to the rescue. She went to stand beside Virginia.

'Are you all right? Silly question. I can see you aren't. Tell me to push off if you want to, but I'd like to help if I can.'

Help George's girlfriend? Was she mad? But it was what she wanted to do, what her instinct prompted. It felt right.

Virginia sniffed. Producing a dainty hanky, she dabbed at her tears.

'It's nothing – really.'

'Forgive me, but it doesn't look like nothing,' Lorna said gently. When she received no reply, she said decisively, 'Here's what we'll do. You can't stay in here where anyone might walk in. I'm one of the organisers of this event. I'm sure I can wangle somewhere private where you can be alone for a few minutes. Come along.'

Soon they were in a cosy sitting room. The hotel manager himself switched on the standard lamp and offered tea.

'No, thanks, honestly,' said Virginia.

The manager left and Virginia perched on a chintzy armchair.

'I'll leave you to it,' Lorna said, heading for the door.

'Really? You're not going to stay and...'

'And what?' Lorna asked. 'Pump you for information? It's none of my business. I hope you feel better soon.'

She left the room quickly so Virginia didn't have a chance to say anything else. With luck, all the girl needed was a few minutes to pull herself together.

And indeed, a while later Lorna noticed her back on the dance-floor, waltzing with one of the men from George's table, the thin-lipped one. Virginia smiled and chatted to her partner, giving no sign of having been upset.

'Thank you.'

The deep voice beside her made Lorna's heart turn over.

'George!' she breathed. 'What do you mean?'

'Thank you for taking care of Ginty. She told me what you did for her.'

'I didn't do it for you. I did it for her.'

'And I'm thanking you for it, though you seem to think it's not my place to do so.'

Nettled, Lorna faced him. 'She's a lovely girl, George. I'm sure your family must be delighted with her.'

And she walked away.

CHAPTER TWENTY-TWO

On hearing a sound at the skylight, Sally walked across the depot roof. Betty had nipped down to the little kitchen to put the kettle on and now she was bringing their tea up. Sally took the mug Betty handed her and waited while Betty descended the ladder to fetch the other one. Sally took it and Betty climbed out onto the roof.

Giving one of the mugs to her, Sally wrapped her gloved hands round her own mug, grateful for the warmth seeping through to her fingers.

'Another quiet night,' she remarked.

'Don't say that,' Betty answered. 'You'll jinx it.'

'It's weird,' said Sally. 'We've suffered air raids practically every night since last summer and now, all of a sudden – nothing. It's something to be grateful for, but I do find it unsettling.'

'Me an' all,' Betty agreed. 'It's tiring too. You dare not relax in case there is a raid after all. Then the night goes by without one and the next morning you realise you were on pins for nothing.'

'That's better than facing a raid, though,' said Sally.

'Definitely.'

'And it's giving you the chance to settle in at Harris's without having to keep dashing to the shelter,' said Sally. 'That's part of why you're so tired, Betty. It's all these extra hours you're working.'

'It'll be worth it when I pay off my debt. They pay good wages in factories.'

'You aren't thinking of leaving the depot?' asked Sally, alarmed.

'I wouldn't dream of it,' Betty answered at once. 'I love the depot – well, not the depot so much, but I love being with you and Lorna.'

'Have you made friends at Harris's?'

'Sort of. There's plenty of chat and now that I've got the hang of the work, I like joining in, but there's a difference between being friendly and being friends. I'm friendly with the girls at Harris's but I'm true friends with you and Lorna.'

'I know what you mean,' said Sally.

Betty laughed. 'I'll tell you something. After I've paid my dad back, and before I get married, I'm going to award myself a jolly good sleep.'

'You'll deserve it,' said Sally. 'Have you decided what kind of wedding you want?'

'I've always dreamed of a church and Dad walking me up the aisle, but Grace says that's unpatriotic in wartime. She says the less fuss the better.'

'I hope you told her to go and jump in a lake,' Sally exclaimed, adding, 'Sorry. I know you'd never do that because you wouldn't want to upset your dad. What does Samuel say?'

'He says it isn't the wedding that matters. It's being married and spending our lives together that counts.'

'He's right,' said Sally, 'but the wedding still matters. It's important for you to have what you want.'

'Were you happy with the registry office?' Betty asked.

'Yes, I was,' Sally said truthfully. 'I was so thrilled to be getting married without having to wait for my twenty-first birthday. All I wanted was to be Andrew's wife and, so far as I was concerned, we had the perfect day.' She looked earnestly at Betty. 'You'll have the perfect day too. Whatever it's like, whatever kind of ceremony you have, you'll be so happy and excited that you'll have the perfect day too. I promise you that.'

Sally went over to Withington for the evening to see how Mum and Dad were getting on. She wished she could see more of them but it was tricky with all her commitments, not to mention theirs. Dad was an ARP warden and Mum worked for the WVS. Like other families, they were all busy doing their bit.

Mum was keen to hear about the dance at the Claremont.

'We had a wonderful evening,' said Sally. 'The band played their socks off and the refreshments were very good. There were various quizzes that you paid to enter. Lorna says they raised more money than they'd anticipated, so that's splendid.'

'I'm glad you had a good time,' said Dad, puffing on his pipe. 'What were the quizzes about? I like a good quiz.'

'Tell Sally about the new pools thing you're doing,' said Mum.

'Have you started doing the football pools?' Sally asked.

'It's a different kind of pools,' said Dad. 'You're given lists of German towns and you have to pick the ones you think will get bombed.'

'Dad!' Sally exclaimed. 'That's... well, I don't like the sound of it, that's all.'

'It's only a bit of fun,' he replied.

'Don't be so pious, Sally,' Mum chided. 'It's not like you to be holier-than-thou.'

'I'm not,' she protested.

'Now then, Mother, don't let's argue,' said Dad. 'It's a treat for us to have Sally here with us.' He gave his daughter a warm smile.

'I wish I could get here more,' said Sally.

'Do you?' Mum asked.

'Of course I do. You know I do.'

'Only I've been hearing about you from Mrs Taylor in the Withington WVS,' said Mum.

Sally frowned. 'I can't say I know a Mrs Taylor.'

'You wouldn't. It's her sister you know – or know of, at any rate. Mrs Callaghan, who runs the Chorlton WVS.'

'Yes, I've met her,' said Sally, 'but it's really Mrs Henshaw who knows her.'

'So I gather.' Mum sucked in a breath that almost turned her lips inside out. 'Mrs Henshaw has been telling the world and his wife your personal business. I have to say, Sally, I didn't appreciate hearing your news from a third party.'

'What's this about?' Sally was mystified.

'Mrs Henshaw told Mrs Callaghan she's going to leave Star House and move in with her sister – and Mrs Callaghan told Mrs Taylor, and Mrs Taylor told me.'

Sally's heart dipped. 'Obviously, I wish you hadn't heard it that way—' she began, but Mum hadn't finished.

'According to Mrs Henshaw, when she leaves you're going with her.'

'Oh, Mum.' Embarrassment crept across Sally's cheeks. 'That really isn't the plan.'

Dad removed his pipe from his mouth and pointed its stem at Mum, saying mildly, 'I told you not to say anything.'

'If it isn't true,' Mum challenged Sally, 'why is your mother-in-law telling all and sundry?'

'It's true that she wants me to, but—'

'Anyway, all that's beside the point,' said Mum, sitting up straight and pushing back her shoulders.

'What *is* the point?' Sally asked, grasping at the hope that somehow she was off the hook.

'I would have thought that was obvious,' said Mum. 'If you're thinking of leaving Star House, then you're not going anywhere with Mrs Henshaw. You're coming back here to Dad and me.'

* * *

Aside from working two Saturdays in three, Betty's hours at Harris's weren't regular, because her fire-watching nights changed from week to week. To begin with, she'd had to start again with new people each time she did some hours at the factory, but by now she'd settled in and was getting to know the other girls and women.

They were a friendly lot and as Betty had told Sally, there was plenty of chatter. When asked how come she was doing extra hours on top of her full-time job, she simply said she was saving up to get married, which sparked many a conversation about weddings, all of which Betty lapped up.

She liked Dora Eastley, a round-faced girl with a wonky front tooth, whose sister had deliberately fallen pregnant at the outbreak of war so as not to have to do war work and was now stuck at home with twins who, between them, ensured she never slept. Then there were Mrs Cave and Mrs Lewis, a middle-aged pair who always worked the same shifts and kept a motherly eye on their younger colleagues. They had persuaded Mr Harris to allow the daytime women to work split shifts if they wanted, so as to have shopping time.

'Or queuing time, as it should be called,' said Mrs Lewis.

Betty warmed to a pretty brunette called Nettie Hobson, who had a shy smile and tended to keep herself to herself.

'Leave her be, love,' Mrs Cave quietly advised Betty. 'Her

husband copped it a few weeks back and now she's working harder than anyone to win the war.'

'The poor love,' Betty murmured. 'Perhaps I shouldn't talk about Samuel and me getting married.'

'Don't be daft,' was the immediate reply. 'Of course you should. Things are hard enough all round without folk feeling they have to hide the good things. A spot of happy news cheers us all up and Nettie is the last person to begrudge you, believe me.'

Betty was pleased to see that there were bins dotted around the factory for collecting salvage, mostly metal offcuts and also masses of swarf, which was the name given to the tiny, thin spirals of metal that were pushed up when a plate of metal was drilled into. Betty found herself on the receiving end of a certain amount of ribbing along the lines of taking the salvage home with her so she could take it to the depot, which she took in good part.

'You won't have anything to do with salvage while you're here,' said Mr Parker, the floor supervisor. His tone suggested she'd been mithering to be put in charge of salvage, but actually she was glad to be left out of it because she didn't want to look like a know-all.

The salvage was gathered up on alternate evenings and got ready to be sent off to the depot the following morning. There was a big set of scales out in the loading bay, which was the grand name given to the area where vans came and went. Everyone was familiar with the loading bay because you had to walk across it to get to the privy. Betty found that embarrassing because, if there were men there, they knew why one of the girls had come outside. Betty tried not to visit the privy at Harris's, but it was impossible not to. She tried to pick her moments, when the loading bay was empty.

She was heading for the privy one evening when she got the timing all wrong. Mr Parker and his sidekick, a boss-eyed lad called Albert, were weighing the salvage. Mr Harris liked to keep all kinds of figures and statistics, which he wrote up on a huge blackboard for everyone to see.

'Keeping up morale,' he called it. 'Seeing how many parts we produce spurs you girls on to make more. And seeing what the salvage weighs keeps us all salvage-minded.'

Betty walked past the weighing machine, keeping her face to the fore as if that would prevent Mr Parker and Albert from knowing where she was going.

If she'd been asked to pick out the worst thing about Harris's, this was what she'd have chosen – except that, if anyone had asked, she would never have said it out loud because the whole point was that it was embarrassing.

Aside from that and the tiredness, she liked working here, which was just as well because she seemed to be surrounded by people with her interests at heart, who all wanted to know how she was getting on – namely all of the Henshaws, Lorna and Mrs Beaumont, as well, of course, as her lovely Samuel.

Even the collection men who came to the depot had picked up on her extra work and asked her about it. Just like her colleagues at Harris's, they seemed amused that Harris's salvage was brought here to the depot for sorting before being sent on elsewhere, and they teased her about it.

'You're right,' Betty joked back. 'We don't need to weigh the Harris salvage because I've already seen on the blackboard what the weights are.'

'You shouldn't have told us that,' said Mr Cox, the van driver. 'You should have made out that you could tell by magic.'

'Bewitching Betty,' Lorna chimed in.

With a chuckle, Betty closed her eyes and made floaty movements with her hands. 'It's coming to me,' she announced in a sing-song voice. 'The weight of the metal offcuts... the weight of the metal offcuts is...' She did more finger-wiggling. '... eight pounds ten ounces.'

Everyone laughed and after loading up their van, Mr Cox and his assistant went on their way.

'I'll weigh the Harris's salvage,' said Sally.

'No need,' said Lorna. 'We've got inside information.'

'No offence, Betty,' said Sally, 'but you know I like to do things by the book.'

And what a good thing too, because when the sack of metal was weighed it turned out that Bewitching Betty had got it wrong by over a pound.

'Good job you didn't take my word for it,' she said.

'Don't worry about it,' Sally said kindly. 'It's an easy mistake to make. You must be more tired than you thought.'

Betty certainly was tired. How long could she keep up this lark with the second job? She had to be cheerful about it too, even when she felt like death warmed up. But she needed the job at Harris's, because it meant she could get married sooner.

CHAPTER TWENTY-THREE

It was Lorna's Saturday for the depot. Yesterday had been Valentine's Day. Andrew had taken Sally to see the romantic film *'Til We Meet Again* and Samuel had given Betty a pretty bracelet. Lorna hadn't received anything. Well, of course not: she didn't have a boyfriend. Virginia Lawrence was the one with the boyfriend. Had George presented her with something? A book of poetry handed across an elegant dining table, or a trinket pressed into her hand as the waltz ended... or a ring slipped onto her wedding finger—

No. It did no good to think like that. But Lorna couldn't help remembering the ring George had once given her. Would he give the same engagement ring to Virginia? It was, after all, a family heirloom and not one that had been purchased for Lorna personally.

She had loved that ring. More than anything, she had loved what it represented, and not even Daddy's remark that it must be worth a mint had taken the gloss off her happiness.

Might George have proposed to Virginia on Valentine's Day? In her determination not to dwell on the thought, Lorna threw herself into her work that Saturday, emptying the daily sacks and sorting their contents in record time. Then she separated the string from the twine, flattened all the cardboard boxes, and stuffed half a dozen sacks full of rags – and all before it was time to stop for her tea break. As well as being used to make battle-dress and blankets, the rags would be turned into charts for submarines or roofing felt for army huts.

Shortly before midday, Mrs Beaumont popped into the depot, bringing a letter.

'This came for you by the second post. It's your mother's writing, so I thought you'd want to see it right away.'

'Thanks, Mrs B. You're an angel,' said Lorna. 'No, don't go. Stay while I read it. It'll have news of Daddy.'

'I don't want to be a nosy parker.'

'If it's more good news, I'll want to share it.' Lorna opened the letter and found what she had hoped for. 'Daddy's doing well. The paralysis is wearing off.'

'I'm pleased to hear it,' said Mrs Beaumont. 'Do send my best wishes when you write back.'

'Thank you,' said Lorna. 'I will. Mummy will appreciate it.'

Mrs Beaumont raised an eyebrow. 'But your father won't?'

Lorna smiled. 'Who knows? He might be furious at the thought of anybody knowing about his incapacity.'

Mrs Beaumont nodded wisely. 'He's a proud man, which is all well and good, but he can't expect you to keep it to yourself. You need support from your friends.' To Lorna's surprise, her landlady kissed her cheek. 'I'm glad you've had good news, dear. I'll see you later at home.'

Lorna felt warm inside as she walked Mrs Beaumont to the gates. She kept herself busy all day. Salvage work might not be what one would call intellectually stimulating, but it was essential war work and she was fully aware of its importance.

At the end of the day she locked up the depot and went home to Star House, where Mrs Beaumont had vegetable ragout and mashed potato ready for her. The others had all had this at dinnertime and now were served swede soup followed by beans on toast for their tea.

After that Lorna got ready to go out. The munitions girls had called round earlier in the week to suggest going to the pictures in town on Saturday night. Sally and Betty had been obliged to decline because of their fire-watching duty, but Lorna had accepted. It was important to support the shops, dance-halls and cinemas that had survived the Christmas Blitz.

She met up with Stella, Mary and Lottie on Oxford Road and they went to see Ginger Rogers in *Kitty Foyle*.

Afterwards they emerged into the blackout.

'Shall we walk you to your bus stop?' Stella offered.

'No need, thanks,' said Lorna. 'It's not far. Thanks for inviting me out.'

They separated, calling 'G'night'. Lorna pointed her tissue-dimmed torch at the pavement ahead as she made her way along the road. Nearby she heard laughter and apologies as some people bumped into one another, such was the depth of the darkness.

Then the siren started up, bringing Lorna out in goose-bumps as she recalled the previous time she'd been caught in an air raid in town.

Some people hurried past her. One caught her arm.

'There's a shelter down this way.'

'Thanks.'

Lorna followed, hurrying to keep up, but her heel got caught in a crack in the pavement, forcing her to stop and pull her shoe free. Beside her some young women tumbled out of a doorway.

'D'you know where the nearest shelter is?' one asked.

'That way,' said Lorna, 'but I don't know how far. I'm following those people.'

She pointed, but already the others had been swallowed up by the darkness. The girls, half a dozen of them, streamed across the pavement in pursuit. Having freed her heel, Lorna was about to go too when a voice came out of the darkness behind her.

'Lorna?'

'Virginia?' Lorna jumped and turned round but before she could say anything further, there was a great *whump* as a high explosive fell through the road, exploding underneath it and hurling it upwards. Lorna grabbed Virginia and hauled her into the doorway. They huddled together, raising their arms over their heads as earth and stones rained down, followed by a chunk of asphalt that landed right beside Lorna, cracking the ground. Debris flew everywhere. The people on the road – the ones Lorna was following and also the girls Virginia had been with – had been picked up and tossed aside like dolls as the ground heaved.

The two girls clutched one another in shock. When they moved towards the people in the road, the pavement picked itself up and shook from one end to the other before settling again, this time at an angle that tipped the girls forwards and sent them stumbling, the drop from the kerb now being at least a foot.

Virginia fell to her knees beside one of her companions.

'Isabel! Isabel! My goodness, she's...' She looked despairingly at Lorna. 'She can't be.'

Before Lorna could do anything, Virginia jumped up and sped to another of the girls. Her trembling exclamation told Lorna the tragic news. In the light cast by nearby fires, she absorbed the scene. A couple of the people moved and her heart leapt before she realised that it was the ground that had moved, causing the people to seem to be struggling to get up.

Not people – bodies. And not all of them were whole bodies. There were several limbs dotted about.

Lorna stared, transfixed. It was like the end of the world in miniature.

There was a flash of flame at the other end of the road and a vast column of earth erupted skywards. With more debris blasting out in all directions, Lorna grabbed Virginia and dragged her away.

'They're gone,' she yelled, trying in vain to compete with the noise. 'They're all gone. There's nothing we can do. We have to seek shelter.'

For a moment Virginia resisted. Lorna tugged hard and they stumbled towards the buildings.

'This way!' An ARP warden made a grab for Lorna's arm, tiny pieces of shrapnel pinging off his tin helmet. 'That doorway over there – they've got a cellar. No, not that doorway. Their cellar has been turned into a water reserve for the fire brigade. The doorway next to it.'

'Come on, folks,' shouted another warden. 'Let's be having you.'

Others crowded towards the doorway, Lorna and Virginia at the back. Lorna held on tight to the other girl so she couldn't do anything mad, like go haring off back to the bodies in the road in the desperate hope of finding someone alive.

And there was something Lorna needed to hear. She thought she knew but she had to be sure.

'Was George with you?' She made no effort to disguise the urgency in her tone.

Virginia shook her head. 'I was out with girls I used to know.'

An ARP warden was at the top of a dark staircase. 'This way, ladies and gents. Don't rush. Mind your step.'

As Lorna and Virginia hastened towards him, there was a blinding flash of light, accompanied by a massive, all-encompassing sound. Everything lurched sideways and tore apart as the floor heaved. Wrenched away from Virginia, Lorna made a wild grab for her, clinging on with all her might as they were tossed sideways. Dear heaven, they were going to be smashed into the wall. But no, the wall simply fell and they were dumped on top of it. Blood bubbled out of a gash on Virginia's temple.

Lorna was paralysed. Fear poured through her. No, not paralysed – winded. There wasn't an ounce of breath left in her body. She didn't know if she would ever breathe again. As plaster showered down on them, she found the strength to roll over and shield Virginia with her own body.

Gradually the noise stopped. Every bone in Lorna's body felt as though it had been jolted into a new position.

'Virginia?' she said – or tried to say. She had to spit dust and goodness knew what else from her mouth before she could utter a word. Voice rasping, she tried again. 'Virginia? Speak to me! Say something! Are you all right?'

The all-clear sounded while the young nurse, frowning in concentration, gave Lorna's cuts and grazes a thorough clean.

'I'm sure there are patients more in need of your attention than I am,' said Lorna.

The nurse glanced at her. 'Let's just make sure these don't get infected, shall we?'

Reaching for a pair of tweezers, she gradually teased out a splinter as if to make her point. Then she dabbed at the site with iodine, making Lorna breathe in sharply. She submitted to the rest of the treatment without a murmur.

Just as the nurse was finishing, a doctor appeared at Lorna's side. He was middle-aged, with bushy eyebrows that met in the middle above eyes that were both tired and fierce.

'Is this the cuts and abrasions who came in with the unconscious girl?' he said to the nurse. 'The ones who had to be dug out?'

'Yes, Doctor,' said the nurse.

'How is my friend?' Lorna asked.

'Don't speak to Doctor unless he speaks to you first,' the nurse admonished her.

'That's all right, Nurse,' said the doctor. 'Your friend is awake now but one arm is fractured and she has concussion. That's why I need to speak to you. I need to check her answers to see if she knows what she's talking about.' He rattled off Virginia's name, age and address.

'I know she's Virginia Lawrence,' said Lorna, 'but I don't know about the rest. You could try asking her what her boyfriend's name is. He's George Broughton.'

'It can wait until after the fracture has been set. She'll be in here overnight, so if you can inform whoever needs to know that would help. Don't leave here without speaking to somebody from the Red Cross or the ARP. They'll need to know where you were and what happened to the people you were with.'

Lorna's stomach rolled as her mind filled with images of all those people being flung into the air.

'I don't know their names,' she said, 'but Virginia will know some of them.'

'You're sure you don't know any names?' the doctor asked sharply. 'You're not trying to get out of a trip to the mortuary?'

'No,' she replied stiffly. 'I wouldn't do that.' She rose to her feet. 'If there's nothing wrong with me, please may I leave now? I'd like to see Virginia – Miss Lawrence – if possible. Is that allowed?'

She had to walk past an office with windows onto the corridor. She glimpsed a tall young woman inside, plastered in dust. Her eyes were dark and haunted. It took Lorna a moment to grasp that she was looking at her own reflection. She couldn't help but stop and stare.

'Chin up,' said a passing nurse. 'Be grateful you're alive.'

Another nurse gave a little laugh. 'Be grateful you're dressed. We have plenty coming through our doors whose clothes were blown off in the bomb-blast.'

Lorna pulled herself together. This wasn't the moment to think of herself. She went to find Virginia.

The girl lay on a narrow bed, her dainty body looking unbearably fragile. Compassion washed through Lorna. Virginia's skin was pale, her breathing shallow. Her arm was in a sling.

'I've got to wait my turn for it to be set,' she told Lorna.

'I've never broken anything,' said Lorna, 'but I believe it hurts like the devil.'

Virginia smiled briefly, though the pain was evident in her eyes. 'Would you do something for me? Can you let George know?'

Lorna nodded.

'You don't mind, do you?' Virginia asked.

'Why should I?'

'I know you and he...'

'Ancient history,' said Lorna. 'Of course I'll tell him.'

She left Manchester Royal Infirmary and walked all the way to the Claremont, calmly avoiding the rescue parties and once or twice walking round the block to keep out of the way of the fire brigade. She felt curiously distanced from what was going on around her. She kept remembering those people being hurled up into the air – and the corpses that had landed. She might easily have been among them.

But she hadn't been. She was alive. She had survived. That was how easily it happened. Some copped it and others lived to tell the tale. It was all down to pure luck.

At the Claremont, she sat in the foyer for over an hour waiting for George. Every now and again she stood up and paced the floor. She was still struggling with the thought of witnessing those deaths.

Finally, she gave up waiting. She asked at the reception desk for a piece of paper and wrote George a note, which she handed across the desk. As she turned away, he appeared on the other side of the foyer. He was covered in grime, his grey-blue eyes very blue against the filth that streaked his face.

Lorna took one look at him and all her old feelings came storming back. Her pulse raced and her skin tingled as if he had just touched her.

Of course, none of it meant anything. It was just part of being in shock, part of having witnessed those tragic deaths. These weren't her real feelings for George. They were just an emotional reaction to everything that had happened tonight.

That was all. Just a reaction caused by being in shock.

George approached her, his long stride eating the space between them. Lorna stepped backwards. He stopped in front of her, his breath ragged, his gaze searching.

'Lorna, what are you doing here? You're hurt! Are you all right?'

She'd forgotten how warm his voice could sound, how tender his eyes could be. But once she told him what had brought her here, that warmth, that tenderness would be withdrawn from her and directed towards Virginia – as was only right and proper.

She didn't want that to happen but that was just her being foolish. It was the shock.

Tearing her gaze from him, she waved her hand towards the receptionist. 'Please could I have that note back? There's no call for alarm, George. Virginia is fine, or she's going to be. Everything you need to know is in this note. I'll leave you to read it. I... I have to go now.'

CHAPTER TWENTY-FOUR

When they emerged from church on Sunday morning, Sally tugged at Andrew's arm, whispering, 'Let's go for a walk and have a bit of time together.'

He smiled at her before addressing his mother. 'We'll see you back at Star House. We're going for a walk.'

'See you in a while,' Sally said to her mother-in-law. Their previous loving relationship had cooled since Sally had made clear her intention of remaining at Star House. Sally understood what a blow this was to Mrs Henshaw, coming on top of the prospect of Andrew's departure, but she also had faith that their love and regard for one another was strong enough to withstand this rocky spell. It was a difficult time for them all.

'Where are we going?' Andrew asked her.

'Nowhere in particular,' said Sally. 'We need to talk, that's all.'

'About me receiving permission from the Education Office yesterday to join up?'

How could he be so matter-of-fact about it? Sally's heart gave a dull thud, but she pinned a brave smile to her lips. As much as it hurt her to think of Andrew going away, she was determined not to hold him back.

'I still need my other bosses to consent, don't forget,' he said.

Sally was all too aware of that. He worked for two sets of masters – in his public role as a teacher and in his secret work as a builder of coffins.

'I'm sure they'll agree,' she replied. She'd told herself from the start that it would be a colossal mistake to let herself hope that he might not be permitted to go. Of course he would.

'I'm sure they will too,' Andrew agreed. 'I can't think what the hold-up is. Sorry,' he added ruefully, squeezing her hand. 'I don't mean to make it sound as if I'm desperate to get away. I don't want to leave you, my darling Sally. No husband or father wants to say goodbye to his family but I want to do my duty.'

'I understand,' she replied softly.

'Would you rather we changed the subject?'

Sally let go a soft sigh. 'We need to discuss what's going to happen here when you leave.'

'Mum's going to Auntie Vera's.'

'And she wants me to go too. My mum wants me to go home to her and I don't want to do that.'

'I can understand that,' said Andrew. 'I know how much your parents mean to you, but going back there would be a step backwards. You're a married woman now.'

'Your mum thinks she and I should both go to Auntie Vera's so we can stay together.'

Andrew smiled. 'I must admit I like the sound of that.'

'Is that what you want me to do?' asked Sally.

He stopped walking and turned to her. 'Shall I tell you what I think? This reminds me of what you told me about you and Rod Grant. You knew in your heart that he wasn't the right man for you, but you couldn't bring yourself to tell him because you hated the thought of letting everyone down.'

'I ought to have told him long before I did,' Sally admitted, 'but it was hard with our two families always having been so close.'

'I can see that,' said Andrew. 'Is there a touch of that in this situation too? You don't want to let my mum down. You don't want to seem less of a Henshaw. But you want to stay at Star House.'

'That's it exactly.' Sally was pleased and relieved that he understood her so well.

'Sally Henshaw, listen to me! I would love it if you and Mum stayed together – but only if it's what you want. You're an independent woman and I value that in you. You've also got a soft heart that makes it hard for you to put yourself first when you know others aren't going to like what you've chosen to do.'

Sally grimaced. 'That makes me sound weak.'

'No, it doesn't,' answered Andrew, putting his arms round her and drawing her close. 'It shows your compassion. It shows you care about other people, and that's part of what makes me love and admire you. It is never weak to pay attention to other people's feelings – but that doesn't mean you have to do what they want. This war is hard on us all and we have to make the best of it in our own ways. If staying at Star House is what's best for you, then that's what you should do.'

* * *

On Sunday afternoon Lorna was in the sitting room, listening to the City of Birmingham Orchestra on the wireless while she carefully mended a tear in the lapel of the coat she'd worn last night. Not so long ago, living at home, the daughter of a wealthy family, she – or rather, the housekeeper – would have sent out the mending to be taken care of by a local seamstress. These days it was up to her to manage her own mending. Mrs Beaumont had shown her how to do it and got her started before going out to spend the afternoon with a neighbour.

Lorna was alone in the house. Mrs Henshaw was on WVS duty this afternoon and Sally and Andrew had gone to Auntie Vera's to talk about why Sally wasn't going to move in with her after Andrew left.

'It was ever so kind of her to invite me,' Sally had said to Lorna and Betty before she and Andrew set off, 'so I want her to understand why I'll be staying at Star House.'

'I'm glad you're stopping here,' said Betty. 'I'd miss you if you left.'

'What does Mrs Henshaw have to say about it?' Lorna had asked.

'She'd rather I went with her, obviously, but if Andrew is happy for me to stay here – and he is – she can't really argue with that.'

'You'll have to go and see her regularly,' Betty advised.

Betty was out this afternoon as well. She and Samuel were spending time with the Kendalls, the elderly couple Samuel helped by running their errands and doing their shopping for them. Hearing about that had made Lorna like him all the more – most men wouldn't dream of doing the shopping, no matter what the circumstances.

Lorna was just getting to the tricky part in the mending when the doorbell rang. Drat. She put her sewing down and went to answer the door.

'George!' she exclaimed, shocked.

'May I come in?' He looked tired, but his smile was true.

She stood aside. 'Here, let me take your coat.'

'Thanks.' He unfastened his buttons and let the wool overcoat slide down his arms. With a questioning glance to seek permission, he dropped his hat on the shelf and hung his scarf and gas-mask box together on a peg.

'Come in.' Lorna led the way into the sitting room, not waiting to take a seat before asking, 'How's Virginia?'

George smiled and his eyes crinkled. Lucky Virginia, generating a response like that.

'She's fine – well, she's tired and feeling a bit washed out, but otherwise she's fine. Thank you for what you did for her. Why did you rush away from the Claremont last night?'

'Have a seat,' Lorna offered, making a fuss of resuming her place and setting her sewing to one side. 'I'm glad she's all right. For a moment I thought – well, you know. The girls she was with were all killed.'

'She's very cut up about it.'

'I can imagine. Those poor girls...' Lorna shook her head as if that might dislodge the memory for ever. She didn't want to remember those people being hurled up into the air and landing any old how. 'I'm glad to hear Virginia's all right. I wouldn't have left her in the hospital if I'd thought otherwise.'

'I know you wouldn't,' said George. 'You're a good sort.'

'A good sort,' Lorna repeated in the lightest tone she could manage, as if it didn't matter in the slightest. 'Thanks ever so, George.'

He nodded. Did he really not know how little she wanted to be deemed a good sort? Oaf.

'I didn't come here just to give you a progress report on Virginia.'

'No?'

George gave her a long, steady look. 'I also came to tell you the truth.'

Lorna frowned. 'The truth?'

'You must have wondered what brought me to Manchester.'

'You said you'd been booted out of the War Office.'

'I did tell you that, yes,' he said.

'The staff at the Claremont call you a man-about-town.'

'Do they indeed?' George's eyes flickered. 'I was unaware of that.'

'Well, what d'you expect?' Lorna asked crisply. 'You've left your old life behind, a thoroughly decent and worthwhile life, I might add, in order to... to fritter away your time dressing up and gadding about. How could you, George?'

'Lorna, wait—'

'Where's your pride? Your self-respect?'

'Please let me get a word in. I can explain. That's why I'm here today – to tell you everything. Please let me. This is important. I didn't leave the War Office. I still work for them. I'm attached to the Air Ministry.'

'Then why pretend otherwise?'

'What I'm about to tell you is highly secret,' said George, 'and you're not permitted to tell anybody else. I need your agreement to that before I can continue.'

Suddenly feeling fluttery inside, Lorna nodded.

'Good,' said George. 'Then let me tell you about hooch.'

'Hooch?' she repeated. It was the word Detective Inspector Kent had used when he saw Daddy in hospital. A chill ran through her.

'It's the name given to illegal alcohol—' said George.

'I know,' Lorna cut in.

'You do? How?'

'Never mind that just now,' she said. 'I know basic information about it, but no details – and I'd like to know.' A fierce anger at Daddy's suffering mixed with a feeling of protectiveness towards him coursed through her veins.

George frowned in puzzlement. 'I can see this is important to you, Lorna, but I don't understand why.'

'Please, George, just tell me what you can. I'll explain presently.'

'Very well. With a ridiculous name like hooch, it might not sound like a serious matter, but it is, and not merely because it's against the law but because of the terrible damage it can do. Some of these men distil their own alcohol from chemically treated sugar beet and water. Others use industrial alcohol.

Then they use essences to turn pure alcohol into spirits. Some makers use methylated spirits and doctor the colour and flavour. Take gin as an example. They make that from pure alcohol, water, juniper and almond essence. Some hooch is so skilfully made that even an expert would have trouble telling that his drink was synthetic and not the real thing. Bad hooch can cause blindness, madness, death. As I said, I'm attached to the Air Ministry. The safety of the nation relies on our pilots and if one of them consumes hooch – in other words, poison – he might never fly again. Or suppose he only consumes a very small quantity and doesn't suffer the worst side effects. He might still be impaired without realising it, which means he might fly badly the next day.'

'I see.'

'Let me give you some real examples,' said George. 'A hooch incident in Glasgow left fourteen people dead. In Liverpool, after a single drink each from a stranger's bottle, two seamen were left unconscious and one of them subsequently died. There was an occasion when an airman went berserk. It took six men to restrain him.'

'Did he recover?' Lorna asked.

'Brain damage for life,' George said grimly.

'I'm sorry to hear that,' she said. Emotion rose and she was suddenly close to tears as she added, 'I've got another example for you.'

'Lorna...' George leaned towards her, the expression on his handsome face softening in concern.

'Goodness.' Lorna pulled out her hanky and dabbed her eyes. 'Sorry, I don't know whether that came from. Well, I do. It's because of Daddy. He's my example. He had a whisky and soda in a hotel bar, just one, and he ended up paralysed.'

'Lorna! What a brutal thing to happen. Is he – is it permanent?'

'No, thank heavens. He's recovering – and so are the men he

was with. That's how come I've heard of hooch. It was dreadfully frightening when it happened.'

'I can imagine.' George shook his head. 'For your father of all people to be paralysed. He's so...' His voice trailed off.

Lorna couldn't stifle a smile. 'I think the word you're looking for is "bombastic". Or possibly "overbearing".'

George smiled too. 'I'm glad he's getting better.'

'Thank you,' she said softly. 'What's your role in all this?'

'Those men I was meeting when you first saw me in the Claremont,' George began.

'Your "business associates", you called them.'

He nodded. 'Their names are Lennox and Richardson. They have an illicit still. Please don't imagine them making hooch in a bathtub. They've got a hundred-gallon tank and they employ men with a considerable degree of engineering ability. I can't prove it – yet – but they've probably got an underground printing press so they can produce their own counterfeit labels.'

'And your job was to befriend these men?'

'Hence my so-called parting of the ways with the War Office. Hence my new man-about-town persona.' George hesitated. 'And hence Virginia as my new lady friend. She's an agent in this operation too, though obviously she can't continue in her current state. Her role was to play the part of my new girlfriend, just to round out the character I was presenting to the world. To be honest, the powers that be were thinking of pulling her out anyway because she's pretty vulnerable at the moment and we can't afford for anybody to be distracted on the job.'

'Has she got problems?' Lorna asked.

'Her chap is an RAF fly-boy. He was shot down. After a month or so of silence, she finally had word that he's a POW in Germany.'

'Don't tell me,' said Lorna. 'That was the reason I found her in tears.'

'That's right – a mixture of profound relief that he's still alive and a whole new set of worries as to what will become of him,' said George. 'It all got a bit much for her and it didn't help that she had to pretend in public to be my girl. But now that she's been injured, she's out of the game anyway.'

'So it's just you on your own,' said Lorna. 'What do you have to do?'

'Expose Lennox and Richardson as the villains they undoubtedly are, but they're slippery customers and known to be dangerous. We know of someone who had a go at double-crossing them and he didn't live to tell the tale.'

Lorna's insides quivered. 'Oh, George, do be careful.'

'I'm careful every minute of every day.' He looked grim. 'That's how it has to be.'

'If you're going to live to tell the tale,' Lorna finished in a brittle voice beneath which she hid her fear. Drawing in a breath that failed to rein in her stampeding heart, she added, 'How will you expose Lennox and Richardson?'

'They seem to have accepted me as an investor in their business,' he told her. 'Now I need to be at a meeting with them in one of their places of operation – and I have to know about the meeting sufficiently far in advance so that the police and the military police can also be there in order to take everyone into custody.'

'Ri-i-ight.' Lorna dragged the word out as thoughts raced through her mind. 'Something tells me this isn't as straightforward as you make it sound.'

George gave a mirthless laugh. 'You can say that again. It was meant to happen a couple of weeks back. Everything was set up and our blokes were all in position. Then, at the last minute, Lennox and Richardson took me to a different place. I don't mind telling you it was pretty unsettling. I thought I'd been rumbled.'

'But you hadn't?'

'The simple fact that I'm sitting here talking to you means I wasn't,' he said lightly.

Lorna swallowed. 'What happens next?'

George tilted his head sideways for a moment in a manner that conveyed a shrug. 'We do the same thing all over again and hope that next time there won't be any last-minute change of venue.'

'Did they tell you why they changed?'

'They called it caution,' he said. 'I said, "Don't you trust me?" and they said, "We don't trust anyone." It's only to be expected.'

Lorna didn't know what to make of that. Did these villains now really trust George? And what would happen to him if they didn't? She couldn't bear to imagine the answer to that question.

'These places – the one you were meant to go to and the one they took you to instead,' she said. 'Where were they?'

'A couple of different places in Manchester,' he replied. 'Both of them were warehouses.'

A chill skittered through Lorna at the thought of what could have happened to George at the second warehouse when his colleagues were positioned around the first one.

'There's one thing I don't understand,' she said. 'Why are you telling me? Why are you *allowed* to tell me something so secret?'

'Because,' George said soberly, 'if something happens to me—'

'You mean if...'

'If I cop it, yes. I wanted you to know the truth and I've been given permission to tell you. You won't ever be able to tell anyone else, Lorna. You understand, don't you?'

An idea began to take shape in her head. Even before it was fully formed, she knew she was going to act on it.

'I'll tell you what I understand, George,' she said crisply. 'I can't let you do this alone.'

'I'm sorry?'

'You heard me. These men have to be stopped. Believe me, I understand that better than most. I want to take Virginia's place. It's no secret we used to be engaged. Tell these men we met up again during the Christmas Blitz – which is true – and since then we've realised that we're meant to be together. That way I can be by your side when you meet with them. The hooch-poisonings in Lancaster were kept out of the papers, so Lennox and Richardson won't know about them. They won't know I have a vested interest.'

'Lorna, no! The last thing I want is for you to be involved in this.'

'I'm not asking you, George, I'm telling you. If your bosses thought it was a good idea for you to have Virginia as your so-called girlfriend, then it makes sense for you to be "reunited" with me.'

'I can't deny that, but—'

'Good,' said Lorna. 'That's settled.'

'It most certainly isn't.'

'Yes, it is, and I'll tell you why.' She met his gaze squarely. 'I'm doing this for my father and I'm doing it to prevent other people, other families, from having to face catastrophic medical situations.'

'That's very honourable,' said George, 'and I do understand—'

'And I can also provide you and your colleagues with a place to meet Lennox and Richardson that is a lot safer than going to a massive warehouse – and that they won't be able to change at the last minute.'

CHAPTER TWENTY-FIVE

After working alongside Lorna to sort out the contents of the daily sacks, Betty made a start on preparing the next consignment of paper for the paper-mill. Paper that had come from offices had to be checked for staples and treasury-tags, which, if left in, could snarl up the machinery in the mill. Then all the scraps of paper had to be thrust into sacks, while the sheets had to be bundled up and tied with string. One of the first things that Betty had learned about paper when she started working here was that when it was stacked it was surprisingly heavy, so it was important not to make the bundles too big for the girls to heave around.

In a deliberate effort to keep her spirits up, Betty hummed to herself as she worked. The truth was, she felt increasingly dragged down by all the work she was doing. It was all very well telling herself that her factory hours were in a good cause and without them her marriage to Samuel would vanish over the distant horizon, but she was tired all the way down to her bones, and not just physically either. Her full-time salvage job plus her hours at Harris's, all put together, felt like a dreadful grind. But if she intended to pay Dad back, what choice did she have?

The worst bit was that she felt she couldn't talk about it, not even to Samuel. He would worry about her and would want to use his savings to sort out her problem, and she didn't want that. She would just have to grit her teeth and get on with it.

On her wedding day, she would look back and it would all be worth it.

Just now, though, her brain felt as if it was full of cement as she stood at the table fastening string around bundles of paper. It was a job that had to be done standing up, unless… what if she formed a low 'table' out of several bundles? Then she could sit down to work.

She did this, but, instead of easing her weariness, it seemed to make it more intense. Waves of fatigue swept over her and for a moment she felt ill. She just needed to put her head down for a moment. The table was beside her. Swivelling on her chair, she placed her arms on it and rested her head on top. The sensation of nausea receded. Good. She knew she ought to sit up and get on with her work, but before she did that she might just rest her eyes for a minute…

'Betty? Betty!'

She came awake with a start. She felt groggy and then sharply awake. Lorna's hand was on her arm, and she looked up into her friend's face.

'I'm so sorry. I never meant to drop off. What must you think? I've never done it before, I swear.'

'Betty, sweetheart, are you all right?' Lorna's green eyes held nothing but concern. 'Are you ill?'

Betty thought of how unwell she'd felt before she put her head down, but she wasn't going to hide behind that. Lorna was her friend and she deserved the truth.

'I'm not ill. I'm…' The sentence remained unfinished because something was clogging her throat.

'Worn out, I expect. Worn to a frazzle.' With a sigh, Lorna

crouched down and slipped an arm round her. 'You can't keep this up. It's too much.'

Betty tried to make light of it. 'We're all tired these days.'

'We are, but there's a difference between being tired and running yourself into the ground. You're doing too much.'

Betty shut her eyes and breathed in and out before she opened them again. 'I've had this debt hanging over me since last summer. I need the factory job or I'll never repay it.'

'And you feel you can't in good conscience get married with the debt hanging over you,' Lorna said softly. 'I understand that, I really do, but you can't be falling asleep at work, Betty. You know that. Apart from anything else, it's not fair on Sally. What if she'd been the one to find you? She's your boss as well as your friend. It would have put her in a deuced awkward position. Or what if Mrs Lockwood had marched into the depot unexpectedly and come in here?'

'You don't have to rub it in,' said Betty, immediately adding, 'Sorry. You've every right to rub it in. I know I'm in the wrong.'

'No harm done.' Lorna stood up. 'Just go easy on yourself. That's my advice.'

Go easy on yourself. That was easy for Lorna to say but she wasn't the one with the debt nagging away at her – a debt that was well over a week's wage for a well-paid man. Throughout the rest of the morning, Betty thought seriously about asking Samuel to pay back the money on her behalf. He would do so willingly, she knew that, but she also knew she wouldn't ask it of him. It wouldn't make him think any less of her, but it would make her think less of herself. Her self-esteem had taken a huge knock after the business with the magistrate's fine and this was the only way of putting it back together.

She worked extra-hard for the rest of the morning, feeling

she had something to prove. She pushed the bundles of paper outside on the sack-trolley and Lorna helped her to load them onto the scales for Sally to make a note of the weight.

'Stack them inside the front doors, please,' said Sally. 'It's too damp to leave them out here until they're collected.'

Mrs Lockwood came swanning in through the gates and planted herself in the centre of the yard, looking all round and taking her time about it, as if intending to seek out the smallest sign of incompetence.

'Good morning, Mrs Lockwood,' Sally said loudly.

At last Mrs Lockwood deigned to notice them. She walked closer. 'Good morning, Mrs Henshaw. What is happening here?'

'We're weighing the paper before it goes to the mill,' said Sally.

'So I see. And it requires all three of you to achieve this? How inefficient. I shall be sure to add it to my list of remarks when I next see Mr Merivale and Mr Pratt at the Town Hall.' Without pausing for breath, Mrs Lockwood ploughed on. 'I have come to inspect the premises.'

'I'll be glad to show you round,' said Sally.

Mrs Lockwood looked down her nose at her, actually looked down her nose. Betty had read that in stories but she'd never seen it in real life before.

'Yes,' said Mrs Lockwood. 'Then you can give me your excuses as we go. I'm sure they'll be most inventive. I met the postman on my way along Beech Road. Here's the post.'

Sally held out her hand. 'You mean you didn't open it?' she asked sweetly.

'I would have done but it isn't actually for the depot.' Whisking the letter away from Sally's outstretched hand, Mrs Lockwood thrust it at Betty. 'This is addressed to you, Miss Hughes, though I can't say I'm pleased at your receiving mail at work. Kindly furnish your acquaintances with the address of your billet in future.'

'Yes, Mrs Lockwood.'

Who on earth could it be from? The envelope felt tightly packed and the address was typewritten. MISS E. HUGHES, CHORLTON SALVAGE DEPOT, BEECH ROAD, CHORLTON-CUM-HARDY. Aware of Mrs Lockwood's disapproving eyes on her, Betty hurriedly shoved the letter into the big pocket in the bib of her dungarees, where she intended it to stay until after Mrs Lockwood had gone. Presently, Mrs Lockwood departed, leaving Sally quietly fuming.

Betty didn't feel any need for privacy when she opened her letter. As the three of them settled down with the sandwiches Mrs Beaumont had made for them, out it came and Betty opened it – and found a second envelope inside.

'It's addressed to me care of the *Manchester Evening News*,' she told her friends.

'It must be from someone who saw the piece about you in the newspaper,' said Lorna.

'That was ages ago,' said Betty. 'Before Christmas.'

'It could be a fan letter,' teased Sally.

'Don't be daft,' said Betty.

The inner envelope was typewritten. Inside was a typed letter addressed to *Dear Miss Hughes*. Betty read it quickly, then had to read it again because she couldn't believe her eyes.

'Who's it from?' Lorna asked.

Betty opened her mouth to answer, then shut it again. It couldn't be from who she thought it was from – could it? Was she about to make a massive twit of herself?

'It's from...' No, she couldn't risk it. She pushed the letter across the table to Lorna. 'Here, you read it.'

'If you're sure,' said Lorna.

Betty held her breath, watching her friend closely. Uttering a small gasp, Lorna lifted her face, her green eyes shining.

'*Betty*,' she exclaimed. 'This is astonishing.'

Sally leaned forward. 'What is it?'

'Go on, Betty,' Lorna urged. 'Tell her.'

'You know Radiance, the face cream?' said Betty. 'This is from the Radiance people. They saw my picture in the paper and—' A laugh burst from her, a sound of pure amazement.

'And what?' Sally asked eagerly.

'I can't say it,' said Betty. 'It can't possibly be true.'

'It is true,' Lorna said jubilantly. She addressed her words to Sally but Betty lapped them up every bit as eagerly. 'The Radiance people want Betty to appear in an advertisement for their face cream.'

'*Never!*' breathed Sally. 'Oh, Betty, that's marvellous.'

Finally, Betty allowed herself to start to believe it, though it hadn't quite sunk in. 'They want me to write back if I'm interested.'

'If you're interested?' said Lorna. '*If?*'

Betty pressed a hand to her chest. 'I can't take it in. They want *me*.'

'And why wouldn't they?' Sally asked loyally. 'You have a lovely face. Gosh. Imagine opening a women's magazine and seeing yourself. Lorna, where are you off to?' she asked as Lorna pushed back her chair and stood up.

'Brown's the stationer's,' said Lorna. 'We need nice writing paper and an envelope so Betty can write back.'

'What – now?' Betty squeaked.

'Yes, now,' said Sally. 'And then we'll walk with you to the pillarbox to make sure you post it.'

'The boss has spoken,' said Lorna, 'so you can't get out of it.'

Betty wafted through the following days in a happy dream. She had begged Sally and Lorna not to say a word to anyone in case nothing came of it, though she did of course tell Samuel, or rather she didn't tell him exactly but gave him her letter to read. That seemed safest, because it still felt like it might all turn out to be a huge mistake.

'My goodness.' Behind his glasses, Samuel's hazel eyes filed with a mixture of surprise and delight. 'Wh-what an offer.'

'You don't mind, do you?' Betty asked.

'Mind? W-why would I mind? I'd be s-so proud.'

'Would you really? I don't mean to fish for compliments – well, I do.' Betty laughed. 'But I want you to be happy with this.'

'Happy that the f-future Mrs Atkinson is c-considered a beauty?' Samuel pretended to think about it. 'I s-suppose I could learn to live with it.'

That was the moment when Betty began to believe fully in what might lie ahead. Knowing Samuel was as thrilled as she was meant the world to her.

When she'd written back to Mrs Inglis, the lady from Radiance, Lorna had suggested that she include the depot's telephone number, looking at Sally for permission.

Sally had readily agreed. 'It makes sense. Tell her this is your place of work and it should be fine.'

Betty was up to her elbows in mucky rubber when Mrs Inglis rang up. Sally came rushing from the office to fetch her and she hurriedly cleaned herself up.

'Don't go.' She pulled Sally back when she would have left. 'I need you to listen in case I forget every word.'

Mrs Inglis couldn't have been nicer. She was complimentary about the photograph that had appeared in the *Manchester Evening News*.

'The picture of you sitting on top of the stack of tyres was just right. It caught all our imaginations here in the office. It was good enough to be a war work poster. You're a pretty girl, Miss Hughes – good skin, good smile – and you have something more. You have character and appeal. Put together, they make you charming. You're just what we want for our next Radiance advertisement.'

'I can't believe this is really happening,' was all Betty could think of to say.

The smile in Mrs Inglis's voice was audible. 'I'm sure it must feel very exciting. Can I take it that you're interested in appearing in our next advertisement?'

CHAPTER TWENTY-SIX

The Radiance photographer, Mr Tichenor, came to the depot on Saturday, the first day of March. It was Betty's day to work, but Sally and Lorna both came with her to make sure the work got done and Betty was free to have her picture taken.

Mrs Inglis, a beautifully dressed lady who looked as if her costume had been pressed minutes before her arrival, accompanied the photographer, as did a young lad who was weighed down by lamps and boxes.

While Mr Tichenor prowled around with narrowed eyes, Mrs Inglis explained what was going to happen, though her explanation was frequently interrupted by her breaking off to dart here and there as if some murky corner of the yard was of consuming interest, or to have a low-voiced but heated discussion with the photographer. She returned from each of these arguments with a serene smile, showing by an airy flutter of her hand that what had just happened was of no moment at all.

Sally and Lorna kept out of the way – sort of – but it was obvious they were dying to watch.

Betty went over to them.

'Mrs Inglis wants to have the pictures taken here at the

depot because she loved the one of me on the tyres. Apparently, the daylight is good enough today, or it will be when they've added the lamps.'

'I imagined you going to a proper studio,' said Lorna.

'No such luck,' said Betty.

'What do they keep fighting about?' asked Sally.

Betty had to laugh. 'You won't believe this. Never mind me, the new Radiance girl. They can't decide which bits of salvage to include.'

Mrs Inglis walked over. 'Miss Kathy will be here in a minute to prepare you, Miss Hughes. She'll do your face and your hair.'

That sounded promising. 'Should I go and change out of my dungarees and back into my dress?'

Mrs Inglis looked at her in surprise. 'Good heavens, no! You're a salvage girl. We want our customers to see you in your dungarees. A nice-looking girl with good skin, dressed for war work, is exactly the image we wish to project. And the best thing is you really are a salvage girl, not a model. Radiance will generate additional publicity out of that.'

Miss Kathy arrived, a leggy girl who looked about fifteen but was presumably older. Introductions were barely accomplished before she swept Betty indoors.

'We need a room with good natural light if possible, Jimmy,' she called over her shoulder to the photographer's lad. 'Bring a lamp, will you?'

Sally and Lorna gave up all pretence of work and followed Betty. Miss Kathy sat her down and scrutinised her face closely until Betty was ready to squirm.

'I'll cleanse your face and then smooth on lots of lovely Radiance. While that's sinking in, I'll do your hair and then I'll do your make-up. How does that sound? Ooh, you've got a dimple. Jimmy, go and tell Mr Tichenor that Miss Hughes has a dimple.'

It was surprisingly relaxing having her skin cleansed and creamed.

'Now let's sort out your hair,' said Miss Kathy. 'It's a beautiful shade, truly golden, and I can tell from your roots that it's real. Keep still while I wrap it up in a turban.'

'Shouldn't you leave it loose?' asked Lorna.

Miss Kathy shook her head. 'We're advertising face cream, not shampoo.'

She put the turban on Betty and then applied some make-up before giving her a hand mirror. Betty caught her breath. Her eyes looked bright, her complexion creamy, her skin soft and smooth.

'You look gorgeous,' said Sally.

They all trooped outside.

Mrs Inglis took Betty's arm. 'We've decided on the sack-trolley. We'll have you pushing it loaded with boxes full of saucepans. Everyone remembers the "Saucepans for Spitfires" salvage drive, so that will create a nice patriotic message within our advertisement.'

'I'll take some full-length pictures,' said Mr Tichenor, 'and some from the waist up and also some head-and-shoulders pictures. Who knows what will be used in the end? The important thing is to give Radiance a choice. Give us a smile, Miss Hughes. No, a real smile. I want to see how photogenic your dimple is.'

'I can't switch my dimple on and off,' said Betty.

To her surprise, Mr Tichenor chuckled. 'Of course you can't, love, but if it's on display that'll tell me you're relaxed. That's what I need from you. It will show in the photograph if you're uncomfortable. That was what was so good about the picture in the paper. You looked...'

Pretty? Beautiful? Fetching? Charming? Possible compliments raced through Betty's mind and her heart fluttered.

'...natural,' Mr Tichenor finished. 'Don't look so disappointed. Shall I tell you something about yourself, Miss Betty Hughes? You have no idea how pleasing you are to the eye. Trust me. It's my job to look at people professionally and I like what I see when I look at you. Shall we get started?'

Betty entered the new week feeling as if a huge weight had been lifted from her shoulders. The Radiance people were going to pay her five guineas.

'Five whole guineas!' she said to Sally and Lorna, having dragged the pair of them into her bedroom. 'Can you believe it?'

'That's a small fortune,' said Lorna.

'Not so small,' said Sally.

'It means that, with the money I've already paid back, I'll be able to clear my debt and even have a bit left over.'

'It must be a massive relief,' said Sally.

'It is,' said Betty. 'I can't tell you how much it means to me. I'll be able to hand in my notice at Harris's as well and finally be able to get some sleep,' she added with a glance at Lorna.

'Congratulations, Betty,' said Sally.

Betty waved the letter she'd received from Mrs Inglis. 'They've chosen two photographs. If the first advertisement is well received, they'll use the other picture in a second one later in the year.'

'Will you get paid extra for that?' Lorna asked.

'No. The five guineas covers everything.'

'When will you hand in your notice at Harris's?' Sally asked her.

'How much notice will you have to give?' Lorna added.

'Two weeks.' Betty smiled widely. 'Two weeks!'

'It'll fly by,' said Sally, 'and you'll have your evenings and your non-salvage Saturdays to yourself again. Won't that be champion?'

'And it's all thanks to Radiance,' said Betty.

'No,' said Lorna. 'It's all thanks to that photograph in the *Manchester Evening News*.'

'No,' said Betty. 'It's all thanks to Sally letting me take the credit when the *Evening News* wanted to write about how Eddie's thieving scheme was foiled.'

'It was my pleasure,' said Sally, looking pleased.

'It's thanks to you an' all,' Betty told Lorna.

'Me?' said Lorna. 'I didn't do anything.'

'Yes, you did,' said Betty. 'You gave that interview to that horrid Baldwin man. If you hadn't done that, he would have plastered the story of me and Eddie all over the newspapers. Radiance wouldn't have touched me with a bargepole if that had happened.'

'Unlike Sally,' said Lorna, 'I'm not going to say, "It was my pleasure", because it emphatically wasn't. But I'm glad I did it.'

'Thank you for helping me.' Betty hugged them both, a tear in her eye. 'You're the best friends I've ever had.'

The days were getting longer. In the corners of their gardens that householders were saving for their favourite flowers, having given up the rest of their outdoor space to growing vegetables, golden daffodils and hazy-blue grape hyacinths were often to be seen, as well as pretty primulas in a range of hues. Betty appreciated the sight of them as never before, her pleasure heightened by being engaged to Samuel, by knowing that she was the new Radiance girl and by the end being in sight at Harris's.

Mr Harris wasn't best pleased about her handing in her notice.

'We've gone to a lot of trouble to train you, Miss Hughes,' he said. 'I wouldn't have taken you on had I known you would stay such a short time.'

'I'm sorry, sir,' Betty said. 'I never meant to let you down, but my circumstances have changed and I don't need the extra hours any more.'

Mr Harris shook his head but his face softened. 'Ah well, it can't be helped. I wish you well, Miss Hughes. You're a good worker, I'll say that for you.'

'Thank you, Mr Harris,' she answered.

Although Betty looked forward to leaving, she surprised herself by feeling a touch of sadness too when the other women said they would be sorry to see her go.

'You fit in here,' Mrs Cave told her.

It made Betty realise how fond she had become of some of her new colleagues.

There was just one thing niggling at her and spoiling things. She wished she could dismiss it from her mind, but she couldn't.

When she had taken her resignation letter to the office, she'd had to wait outside for a couple of minutes, and she'd glanced at the daily, weekly and monthly totals on the blackboard that showed how much work the factory had done. The figures included how much had been salvaged, counted by weight.

Betty knew how much the most recent lot of metal offcuts and swarf had weighed because Lorna had laughed when she'd dumped the sack on the scales.

'Look at that – dead on seven pounds.'

But Betty's gaze fell on the relevant figure on the board. It said *8lb 7oz*. Betty frowned. She must have misheard Lorna – but she knew she hadn't. Even if Lorna had said 'Eight pounds' and not 'Seven pounds', she had definitely said 'dead on'. They almost never got something that weighed to the exact pound or stone or hundredweight. That was why Betty remembered it. So what about the other seven ounces? In fact, what about the other one pound seven? Betty was certain Lorna had announced the weight as seven pounds.

She remembered that other time when there had been a

discrepancy in the weight when she'd pretended to do magic, and how she had assumed it must be her own mistake. She'd thought it was because she was tired.

What was going on? She vowed to keep an eye on the recorded weights, both here and at the depot. Did one place have a faulty scale?

Since then there had been one delivery to the depot from Harris's and there had been no discrepancy, which had made Betty glad she'd kept her doubts to herself; but, if she had hoped this would dispel her unease, she was disappointed.

Now she was in her final week at Harris's. The previous night, Tuesday, she had been on fire-watching duty with Sally and it had been a bad one. Today they had learned that twenty-six had died in Manchester, most of them in Hulme, which wasn't far from Chorlton. According to Mrs Henshaw, there had been quite a few casualties in Chorlton, who had been taken to Manchester Royal Infirmary or Withington Hospital.

Tonight, Betty was to work at Harris's. She hoped for a quiet night because, as a casual worker, she only got paid if she was actually on the assembly line, not when she was sitting in the cellar waiting for the raid to be over. Not that she was anxious to earn the money any longer, but, since she had to be here, she wanted to get paid for it.

She got her wish about the quiet night. Later on, when the other girls went to get a cup of tea, Betty dashed out to use the privy, passing the salvage containers on her way. When she came back, she heard the door open and a couple of men came outside. She heard voices but not what they were saying.

Drat. They'd come outside for a fag. She didn't want to walk past them because they would know where she'd been and that would be embarrassing. She hesitated, hovering at the corner, just out of sight. Then she chided herself. She was being ridiculous. Everyone had to use the privy, even the King and

Queen. All she had to do was stick her nose in the air and walk straight past.

She took a step forward – and stopped. There were two faint lights. Not the tiny glow of cigarettes, but torchlight dimmed by tissue as per the national regulations. What were the men up to? Were they...? Yes. They were leaning over one of the salvage drums – the one containing metal offcuts and swarf. Betty could hear soft chinking and scraping sounds.

Then the men laughed quietly and stood up straight. In the faint light, Betty saw one of them disappear round a corner for a moment or two. When he came back, they both laughed, then one gave a warning 'Shh!' – and the door shut behind them.

What had just happened?

CHAPTER TWENTY-SEVEN

George had given Lorna the chance to change her mind about posing as his girlfriend, or at least he had tried to. She had refused in no uncertain terms before he'd got all the words out.

'Besides,' she finished, 'you know perfectly well that my idea is better than what the Air Ministry came up with. They were happy to let Lennox and Richardson choose the meeting place.'

'It was the only way,' said George. 'It had to happen on their turf.'

'Until I came up with something better – and before you decide you can use my plan without my being involved, ask yourself this, George. Isn't it better, safer, to organise this quietly with Sally rather than having the Air Ministry go through a lot of red tape? It'll be quicker too.'

So, after consulting with his bosses, George asked Lorna to arrange a meeting for him with Sally.

'It's to do with the depot,' he said, 'but I want to meet up somewhere else – and nobody else must know.'

'Betty will be working at Harris's on Wednesday and Thursday evenings,' Lorna told him, 'so how about Thursday? I know that Andrew – Sally's husband – has a meeting at his school then.'

It turned out that Mrs Henshaw and Mrs Beaumont were both due to be out as well, Mrs Henshaw on WVS duty and Mrs Beaumont at her knitting circle, so the simplest thing was for George to come to Star House.

The two girls were sitting on the hearthrug in front of the fire when the doorbell rang. Lorna got up to answer it. George slipped into the house and Lorna tugged the door-curtain across before switching on the hall light. Once George's things had been hung up, she took him into the sitting room.

He and Sally greeted one another and Lorna offered him a seat.

'Thank you for agreeing to see me,' he said to Sally. 'I know it must seem very mysterious.'

'You could say that.' Clearly, Sally wasn't sure whether to laugh or frown.

'Let me explain the real reason why I'm here in Manchester,' said George. He went on to tell Sally everything about illegal alcohol and the terrible damage it could inflict.

'That's like what happened to Lorna's father,' Sally exclaimed.

'Exactly,' said Lorna.

George continued telling Sally everything she needed to know.

'These men need to be brought to justice,' she declared.

'I couldn't agree more,' said George, 'but actually they're more likely to be up in court for defrauding the Inland Revenue than for causing poisoning.'

'Why?' asked Lorna. 'That's outrageous.'

'Easier to prove,' said George. He looked squarely at Sally. 'That's where you come in – or rather, your salvage depot.'

The glowing firelight cast golden flickers into Sally's tawny eyes as she looked from George to Lorna. Lorna held her tongue. This might be her idea, but if it went ahead, it would be an Air Ministry operation.

'I'm sorry,' said George, 'but you know how important secrecy is in this matter. Let me explain the plan. Hooch men can run big operations. They have access to printing presses to produce fake labels to stick on bottles. Even so, they'll pay good money for the real thing.'

'Real labels?' Sally asked.

'Real labels on real bottles. It doesn't matter how good the fake is. Nothing beats the real thing. Real bottles are the holy grail to these men.'

'What do you want the depot to do?' Lorna asked.

George looked at Sally. 'The two hooch men I've been cultivating are called Lennox and Richardson. As far as they're concerned, I'm interested in joining them. As a sign of the seriousness of my intent, I have offered to provide them with two gross of genuine Scotch bottles complete with labels. If they take possession of the bottles, that, together with other evidence, will prove beyond doubt that they are involved in the illegal alcohol trade. Believe me, that is far preferable to their simply being had up for defrauding the Inland Revenue.'

Sally nodded, absorbing the information, before she asked, 'And the depot?'

'Lorna will play along so that Lennox and Richardson believe I've got back together with her. She works in the salvage depot, so where better to hand over the bottles? It adds depth and credibility to my story. It's better than handing them over in an anonymous bombed-out warehouse. Lorna has told me about empty alcohol bottles being stored in the depot ready to be returned to distilleries and breweries.'

'What's going to happen?' Sally asked.

'It will take place quickly,' said George. 'A van will deliver the crates of empty bottles to the depot. That evening, before the fire-watchers arrive, I'll bring Lennox and Richardson to examine the merchandise and satisfy themselves that they're receiving the real thing. They'll have their own men with them in a van to take everything away – except that they won't get the chance to do that.'

'I don't know if I have the authority to give you permission for this,' said Sally.

'I apologise for putting you on the spot,' said George, 'but secrecy is essential. The fewer people who know, the better. It really is up to you, Sally. What d'you say?'

Sally drew in a breath and let it out again. 'Deliver the bottles on Saturday. It's my day to open the depot, so that will make it straightforward. Can you make sure everything happens on Saturday evening? Or Sunday at the latest? That way, no one else ever need know that the crates of Scotch bottles were there.'

On Friday afternoon, Betty asked Sally if she could see her in the office.

'Of course,' said Sally. 'What's it about? You look serious.'

Betty waited until they were in the office with the door shut. They sat on either side of the desk.

'Is there a problem?' Sally asked.

Betty nodded. 'Yes – but don't worry. It isn't here, it's at Harris's.'

'Then shouldn't you be having this conversation there instead of with me?'

'It's because I belong here that I've worked out what someone at Harris's is doing,' said Betty. 'Listen. Harris's is like lots of other factories. They're constantly counting things and displaying the figures to spur the workers on to do even better. At Harris's, they count up everything that can possibly be counted, including weighing what they send for salvage.'

She waited for the penny to drop.

'Their salvage comes here,' said Sally.

Betty nodded. 'There was an occasion when there was a discrepancy between what they said the weight was and what we said it was. I assumed I'd made a mistake, but then it happened again. I worked at Harris's on Wednesday evening and again yesterday evening. On Wednesday I saw a pair of men sifting through the metal salvage and at least one of them seemed to take something out. I say "seemed" because it was dark and I couldn't really see.'

'Go on,' said Sally.

'This was after the metal salvage had been weighed, so I looked at the board and made a note of the weight. I did the same again yesterday, so I know exactly how much metal salvage Harris's believe they've sent here.'

'We had a delivery from them earlier on,' said Sally.

Betty took a scrap of paper from her pocket and passed it across the desk. Sally looked at it, then pulled one of the ledgers towards her and opened it. After a moment she looked up.

'We received a smaller amount than they supposedly sent. This is a serious matter.' She frowned. 'It could be that their scales are faulty. I know our machine has nothing wrong with it because it is calibrated regularly. It has to be Harris's scales.'

Betty shook her head. 'If that was the reason, then the paper salvage figures would be wrong as well, and they aren't. Remember what I said about the two men. What if they're smuggling small items out of the factory by slipping them in with the metal salvage? Later, they remove the smuggled goods and hide them ready to be taken off the premises, and then they flog them on the black market.'

'That's a serious accusation,' said Sally.

Betty was undeterred. 'It's a serious thing to happen.'

'If it really is happening,' said Sally.

'I know what I saw,' Betty replied. 'And you've seen for yourself the difference in the figures.'

'Have you reported this at Harris's?' Sally asked.

'No – because I've thought of a better idea.' Betty felt a flutter of excitement. 'I want you to report it. I want you to see Mr Harris and tell him that, because I work here at the depot, I've taken an interest in the salvage figures on his blackboard. Say I told you that the scales at Harris's might be wrong, but you realised that they can't be because the paper weights are correct. Tell him you've thought about it and you're concerned that the reason for the metal weights always being lower when the salvage gets to the depot could be because someone in the factory is using the salvage bin as a means of stealing things and getting them outside the building.'

'Why can't you tell him?' Sally asked. 'I'll come with you if you're worried about it.'

'When the *Manchester Evening News* wanted to write a story about what happened here when Eddie used the depot for his ill-gotten gains, you let me be the heroine of the hour,' said Betty. 'I want to repay you for that, Sally. I want you to take the credit for solving this crime.'

Lorna felt she ought to work on Saturday at the depot alongside Sally as a thank-you for Sally's cooperation in the matter of tricking Messrs Richardson and Lennox, but Sally refused.

'Everything has to continue as normal,' she pointed out.

Besides, George wanted to spirit her away as part of the scheme.

'We're going to have lunch with the Lennoxes and the Richardsons.'

Lorna was horrified. 'Do we have to? Knowing what's going to happen this evening—'

'This meal is by way of cementing the new partnership,' George said gently. 'I need you to be present, Lorna. I'm the host and I need you there as hostess.'

'Very well,' she replied. 'I can do that.'

'I'll need you at the depot this evening as well to unlock. Everything must look as it ought.'

'Of course.'

Lorna was determined to play her part to perfection. She went early to the Claremont to be by George's side as he greeted his guests when they came into the gracious foyer. Mr Lennox was the thin-lipped one. His wife was tall and elegant, with pale-blue eyes and a chin that was just a trifle too prominent. Mr Richardson, with his cheeks threaded with the red veins of a drinker, was accompanied by a smiling, motherly woman who was only too delighted to meet Lorna.

'It's so romantic that the two of you have got back together,' she whispered when they shook hands.

The group went up the stairs to the dining room and were shown to a table. They examined the menus and discussed the relative merits of devilled fish, roast sheep's heart and fillets of pork.

'Pork fillets – that's sausagemeat mixed with mash and fashioned into the right shape,' said Mrs Lennox.

'Doesn't mean it's not tasty,' her husband replied.

'I fancy the mince slice with vegetables,' said Mr Richardson.

As soon as the waiter had taken their orders and withdrawn, the motherly Mrs Richardson leaned forward to address George across the table.

'Well, young man, I hope you've decided where your heart truly lies. Poor little Miss Lawrence. Was she dreadfully upset?'

'Agnes!' her husband exclaimed. 'Don't ask personal questions.'

'That's quite all right,' said George. 'It's a dashed shame about Ginty and I'm awfully sorry, but Lorna...' He looked at her, holding her gaze for a moment before returning his attention to Mrs Richardson. 'As you may know, we used to be engaged. We met up again during the Christmas Blitz and realised that – well, Lorna has decided to take another chance on me.'

'Old spark still there, is it?' Mr Lennox asked with a chuckle.

Lorna treated the others to her most dazzling smile. Adopting a light-hearted tone, she said to George, 'You'd better not let me down.'

It was the right thing to say. Mrs Richardson and Mrs Lennox tilted their heads and smiled indulgently.

'Talking of the Christmas Blitz,' said Mr Richardson, 'it's a damn shame about the Free Trade Hall.'

'The ruins are being used nowadays as a centre for distributing ration cards to people who lost theirs in air raids,' said George.

'Timpson's shoe shop reopened this week,' said Mrs Lennox. 'It was reduced to a shell in the Christmas Blitz.'

'Oh, air raids!' said Mrs Richardson. 'It's all anyone talks about these days.' She turned to Lorna. 'Tell us about yourself, dear. Where are you from?'

'Lancaster,' said Lorna, 'but George and I met originally in London – though you probably already know that if you read the newspapers.'

'Well...' Mrs Richardson uttered a breathy laugh. 'One can't help but be aware.'

'It was vile for Lorna, being dragged through the mud by the newspapers,' said George. 'She didn't deserve it. The judge made her appear unpatriotic and that's the last thing she is. What was written about her angered me – made me want to protect her, as a matter of fact.'

Lorna hid her surprise. She'd had no idea that George had felt that way about the coverage.

'It was a profoundly unpleasant time,' she murmured. 'I'd prefer not to discuss it.'

'Of course,' said Mrs Lennox, and her husband and the Richardsons made suitable noises of agreement.

'I apologise if I've trodden on any toes,' said Mrs Richardson. 'The main thing is that the two of you are together again.'

'It's how things were meant to be,' Lorna said recklessly. She might never have the chance to say it to George for real, so she might as well say it now as part of this strange conversation when they were pretending to mean the world to one another. 'The ending of our engagement was most unfortunate. There were reasons – well, never mind. We see things clearly now.'

'Indeed we do,' George chimed in. Then he stilled for a moment before his gaze locked with Lorna's. 'We know that reuniting is the best thing for us. It will be the making of me.'

Lorna couldn't help but catch her breath, but then their meals arrived and the moment was lost. Once the plates were on the table, Mr Lennox firmly steered the conversation in a different direction.

At the end of the meal, the three men excused themselves to talk business, leaving Lorna with the wives. It came as no surprise when Mrs Richardson once again wanted to talk about her and George.

'It's like something off the silver screen,' she declared. 'An adoring couple torn apart by circumstances, then brought back together in a time of peril.'

Lorna faked a laugh. 'You make it sound very dramatic.'

'You wait,' Mrs Richardson said archly. 'In years to come, it'll be your children's favourite bedtime story.'

'Don't embarrass the poor girl,' Mrs Lennox chided.

The men returned, and presently the Lennoxes and the Richardson made their farewells.

'I do hope we'll see you again soon,' Mrs Richardson said to Lorna.

'I'll look forward to it,' Lorna replied.

'Well done,' George murmured as the others walked away.

'What now?' Lorna asked.

'Now we go to the pictures.'

'You're kidding.'

'I'm not,' said George. 'Just in case I'm not as trusted as I think I am, we need to spend a blameless afternoon together. Is there a film you'd specially like to see?'

'I don't think it'll make any odds which film it is,' said Lorna. 'I can't imagine concentrating on anything.'

'Just a few more hours,' said George, 'and it will all be over.'

Lorna nodded. And what of her and George after that?

Lorna spent all afternoon with George, though what in other circumstances could have been pure pleasure became increasingly tense. She worked her way through several cigarettes.

'As I said before,' said George, 'I can't guarantee that they fully trust me. I *think* they do, but in case they don't, I'd rather keep you close by. If they have any reservations about me, and you're on your own, who knows what might happen?'

A little chill pattered down Lorna's spine. 'Such as?'

'They might make off with you.'

She started. 'As in – kidnap me?'

'You're safer if you're with me.' George shot his cuff and looked at his wristwatch. 'The Scotch bottles will have been delivered by now – along with a squad of men in the back of the van. They'll hide in the depot. Your connection to the salvage depot has been a real bonus.'

'Glad to be of service.' Although her voice was cool, Lorna meant what she said. 'These hooch men are devils who make a fortune out of putting other people's health at grave risk. If my small part in this helps put Lennox and Richardson behind bars, I'll do anything that's asked of me.'

She and George had a light meal at teatime and then settled down to wait in the Claremont's gracious foyer. Presently

Richardson and Lennox walked in, and George stood up to shake hands. The other two men were affability itself, but was it just pretence?

Outside, a motor was waiting. They set off. Richardson looked back through the rear window a few times, then nodded and settled down to face forward.

Lorna twisted round to peer out of the window, but George nudged her and frowned a warning, though not before she had glimpsed a van travelling behind them.

As they approached Chorlton, Lorna provided directions.

'You'll have to pull in over here for a minute,' she instructed as they drew level with the rec. 'I have to nip into my billet and fetch my keys.'

'Don't you have them on you?' growled Lennox in displeasure that he made no effort to conceal.

'I wasn't expecting to be out with George all day,' she replied.

George got out of the motor to hold the door for her. The fresh green tang of the rec's privet hedge surrounded Lorna as she hurried to Wilton Road. Inside the house she called, 'Only me. I'm not staying,' as she ran upstairs. She was back out of the house in no time and hurrying back to the motor. In the darkness she could make out the van that had pulled in to the kerb behind it.

Before Lorna could get into the motor, Richardson asked, 'How far is the depot?'

'Just down the road,' she told him.

'Go and unlock the gates,' he ordered. 'We'll drive round the block and when we come back, we'll drive straight into the yard and you can shut the gates behind us – not you,' he added as George made to accompany her.

She walked briskly past the shops and unlocked the door in the fence before unbolting the large gates and pulling them wide open, one at a time. She chewed the inside of her cheek as she waited. Was she being watched by the men who had arrived in secret earlier with the crates of empty bottles? It took all her willpower not to peer into the darkness.

Hearing motor engines drawing closer, she grasped the edge of the gate, ready to heave it shut. The two vehicles swung into the yard and, by the time Lorna had closed the first gate, a man had jumped from the van and secured the other one.

'Let's see these Scotch bottles,' said Lennox. 'Where are they?'

'In the cellar,' said Lorna.

There had been some discussion between Sally and George as to the best place, and the cellar had been chosen because it was the most secure hiding place.

'I had to have them put there,' said Lorna, 'so that there'd be no chance of my colleagues stumbling across them. I'll be very glad when you remove them, as a matter of fact.'

'Let's go and have a butcher's, then,' said Lennox. 'Lead the way.'

He stepped aside for Lorna to take the lead. She opened the door that gave on to the cellar steps.

'There's no electric light but we have candles down here,' she said over her shoulder, 'and everyone has a torch.'

The crates of empty bottles were stacked over by a wall. Shining their torches, Lennox and Richardson went across and picked out a number of bottles, scrutinising them closely. They looked at one another and nodded.

'Yep,' said Lennox. 'They're the real thing.'

'Did you doubt me?' George asked, lifting one eyebrow as if amused.

'If we did, we certainly don't any longer,' said Richardson. 'Welcome to the firm. We'll gladly pay the price you asked for these.'

'And we look forward to you providing more,' Lennox added.

'It will be my pleasure,' George replied smoothly.

Lennox addressed the men who had come in the van. 'Start carrying these crates up. Let's get the van loaded.'

'Aren't you forgetting something?' George asked. 'The small matter of payment.'

'We'll pay when our van is loaded,' Lennox replied.

'I'd prefer it if you paid up now,' George said in a voice of perfect civility, 'if it's all the same to you.'

Richardson nodded to Lennox, who, with an elaborate sigh, unfastened his coat and reached into an inside pocket. He brought out a plump envelope and offered it to George.

'It's all there.'

George flicked it open and glanced at the wad of notes. 'Received with thanks.' Stepping away from the empty bottles, he waved a hand. 'Help yourselves, chaps,' he bade the men from the van.

While the men went up and down the steps, carrying the crates, the bottles chinking, George caught Lorna's eye and, with a small jerk of his chin, indicated that she should quit the cellar. He followed her up the steps.

'Not long now,' he breathed into her ear at the top, then casually turned aside as the two hooch men appeared behind them.

'That's it, guv,' one of the men said a few minutes later. 'Those steps were a bit of exercise I wasn't expecting.'

'That's everything, then, Broughton,' said Richardson. 'Until next time.' He held out his hand to shake George's.

'There's just one last thing,' said George. As he took the proffered hand, he made a swift movement that twisted it up behind Richardson's back.

'Hey! What?' yelled Richardson.

Lorna was jostled out of the way as the yard sprang to life. Men appeared from nowhere to seize Lennox, Richardson and their minions, quickly subduing them. Lorna had hardly caught her breath before it was all over.

As the wrongdoers were handcuffed and taken away, a man in a uniform Lorna was unfamiliar with shook George's hand.

'Well done, Broughton. Jolly good show. With the evidence we've already got, plus now having them pay you and load up their van, this gives us what we need. They'll get prison sentences for this, no question.' He turned to Lorna. 'Using the depot made a substantial difference. It kept the situation contained, d'you see?'

'It would have been a far trickier thing to pull off if we hadn't had access to this place,' George added.

'What happens now?' Lorna asked.

'I have to go with these men,' said George.

'Should I come too?'

'No need,' he said. 'You've done your bit. You can go home – with the thanks of the Air Ministry.'

CHAPTER TWENTY-EIGHT

When Sally walked into their bedroom, Andrew was standing at the window, looking out. He turned to face her and, as soon as she saw his face, she knew. Her heart plummeted but she forced herself to hoist a smile into position. She had come this far without crumbling and she wasn't going to give in now.

Quickly he crossed the floor and took her hands. 'Sally...' he began.

'You've heard, haven't you?' Catching the sharp note in her voice, she took a moment to adjust her tone, saying softly, 'You've got permission to join up.' She didn't make a question out of it. She didn't kid herself that there was any doubt.

He nodded. 'I'm going to see out the school term. With Easter being mid-April, that's not long for me to wait, and it'll make life easier for the school.'

For the school? Sally wanted to ask, 'What about me?' but she didn't.

What she said was, 'Yes. It makes sense to stay until the end of term.'

Her mouth went dry as despair washed over her. Andrew was leaving. He really was leaving. So much for the gratitude she'd felt at having her darling husband in a reserved occupation. But she would bear the sorrow with the same fortitude as the thousands upon thousands of other wives who were in the same situation, virtually all of whom had been obliged to wave their husbands off well over a year ago.

Sliding her arms round Andrew's waist, she laid her head against his chest.

'I know you have to go. I understand why. You're a good man, Andrew Henshaw. I'd give anything to keep you here, the same as any wife would, but that isn't the right thing for you. You have very particular reasons for wanting to fight for king and country. I respect you and I respect your reasons. All I ask, all I will pray for every day, is that you come home safe.'

It was good to see Betty looking bright-eyed now that she had finished working all those extra hours at Harris's. It had worried Sally that her friend was overdoing things, and she was relieved that Betty had been released from that strain.

Mr Harris called at the depot to see Sally. She took him into the office and closed the door before she sat down, inviting him to do the same. He politely removed his trilby.

'I've come to thank you, Mrs Henshaw,' he said. 'You were right about the thieving that was going on in my factory. I'm ashamed to think that anybody working for me would do such a thing. Along with the caretaker – a trusted fellow, who worked for my father for years before I took over the business – I arrived earlier than usual each morning and re-weighed the metal salvage to compare it to the previous evening's weight. As you suspected, parts were being smuggled out of the factory via the salvage and were then removed from the salvage bin once it was outside.'

'I'm glad the matter has been dealt with,' said Sally. 'How very unpleasant.'

'Yes, indeed,' he replied, pressing his lips together, which made his sharp chin jut forward. 'I put it in the hands of the police. They soon had all the evidence they needed and the wrongdoers were carted off. They will stand trial and I hope they get the sentences they deserve. It angers me to think of what those scoundrels did.'

'It must be distressing to be let down by people who work for you,' Sally acknowledged.

'Well, I mustn't take up any more of your time.' Mr Harris came to his feet.

Sally rose also. 'Thank you for coming to tell me.'

'It was the least I could do.'

They shook hands across the desk. Mr Harris put his hat on and departed.

Sally sat down, feeling satisfied. She appreciated the courtesy of the visit.

But the matter didn't end there. To her surprise, she had a visit from Mr Merivale and Mr Pratt the following day. They were the men from the Town Hall who had, against Mrs Lockwood's wishes, appointed her to the post of depot manager. Pinstriped and bowler-hatted, they walked across the yard. Portly Mr Pratt was puffy-cheeked with a trim moustache. Straight-backed Mr Merivale used his rolled-up umbrella like a walking-cane, tapping the metal ferrule on the ground with every step.

'Mrs Henshaw, might we see you in the office, please?' Mr Merivale asked.

Both he and his colleague looked flustered, which in turn affected Sally. What had happened? Was she about to be sacked? Was Mrs Lockwood going to get her own way at last?

When they were all seated, Sally took the initiative.

'What brings you here, gentlemen?'

'Mrs Henshaw,' Mr Pratt began, 'we have received a letter from Mr Harris of Harris's Small Robotics.'

'At the Town Hall, we had no idea you had been instrumental in uncovering a thieving operation,' Mr Merivale added.

'I didn't see any need to report it to you,' Sally replied, 'since the thefts occurred elsewhere.' She bit her lip. Had she put herself in the wrong?

'Mr Harris was most appreciative of your assistance and what he called your – what did he call it, Mr Pratt?'

'He praised your keen observation, Mrs Henshaw, and your powers of deduction.'

'He said that, without them, the thefts would have continued indefinitely,' said Mr Merivale. 'This is most impressive, Mrs Henshaw.'

'Most impressive,' his colleague echoed.

'Thank you,' she answered, managing to keep her voice steady even though she felt overwhelmed. Betty was the one who deserved this praise, but dear Betty had handed it to her on a plate.

'And that's not the only letter we've received,' Mr Merivale continued. 'There was also a short and frankly rather cryptic missive from the Air Ministry commending you personally for your patriotism and professionalism in allowing the Ministry the use of the salvage depot for an important operation.'

'Nobody in the Town Hall has any idea what this refers to,' Mr Pratt hinted.

Sally didn't take the bait. 'Which is as it should be,' she murmured.

'Of course, dear Mrs Henshaw,' said Mr Merivale. 'Keep mum, and all that.'

Dear Mrs Henshaw?

'You are clearly an asset to the salvage service,' said Mr Pratt.

'And we have decided,' said Mr Merivale, 'that you are more than capable of running this depot without the need to be watched over or guided by anyone else.'

'You mean, by Mrs Lockwood,' said Sally. 'Has she been informed of this decision?'

'Not yet,' said Mr Pratt.

Sally's heart dipped. 'You are going to tell her, aren't you?'

The gentlemen squirmed. They weren't going to wimp out of it, were they?

Mr Merivale turned to look at his colleague. 'Do you know, Mr Pratt, I rather think that, considering the praise Mrs Henshaw has received, it is only right to bring these letters to the attention of the Lord Mayor's office.'

'Yes, indeed.' Mr Pratt's eager tone showed he had caught on at once. 'I'm sure the Lord Mayor will wish to write a few lines to Mrs Henshaw—'

'—and at the same time we can prevail upon him to write to Mrs Lockwood, thanking her for her service and for the way in which she has trained and guided Mrs Henshaw—'

'—to the point where Mrs Henshaw is henceforth fully capable of standing on her own two feet,' finished Mr Pratt.

They beamed at one another.

'I think that will do very nicely,' said Mr Merivale.

Sally walked the two Town Hall gentlemen to the front door and watched as they made their way across the yard to the gates. Was it her imagination or did she detect a spring in their steps? She grinned. They must be jolly pleased with themselves at having found a way of sliding out of having to contact Mrs Lockwood themselves, and who could blame them?

Betty and Lorna stopped what they were doing and came over to her.

'What did they want?' Betty asked.

With a light heart, Sally explained.

'So you've had two letters of praise,' said Lorna. 'Congratulations.'

'Don't look so innocent, you two,' Sally scolded. 'Those letters didn't write themselves.'

'Mr Harris wrote one,' Betty answered with a cheeky smile, 'and an important bod at the Air Ministry wrote the other.'

'Very funny,' said Sally. 'I was thinking more along the lines of *why* they wrote them. Could it be that they received a little prompting?'

Betty shrugged. 'I might have suggested to Mr Harris that it wouldn't do you any harm if the Town Hall knew how clever you'd been.'

'And I might have dropped a word in George's ear,' Lorna added.

Sally felt an inner glow of gratitude. 'You two are the best friends anyone ever had. Where would I be without you?'

Betty laughed. 'Under Mrs Lockwood's thumb!'

CHAPTER TWENTY-NINE

Betty's heart swelled with love and pride at the sight of the additional pieces of furniture that had appeared in the parlour behind Samuel's shop. It was definitely a parlour now and not a parlour-office, and she'd come to love the bookcases that still lined the walls. Now there was a gateleg table with its flaps folded down, and a pair of dining chairs, as well as a green baize-covered card table.

Samuel had even dug out a couple of pretty china orna-ments and a cut-glass vase to place on one of the over-mantel shelves.

'I f-found a box of things packed up in newspaper tucked away in a c-corner upstairs,' he said when Betty commented approvingly. 'If you like, I can bring the box d-down and you c-can have a look.'

'I'd love that,' said Betty. 'But not just now. Let's have a cup of tea and a chat first.' She opened the kitchen door. 'Daffodils!' she exclaimed in delight, seeing the rich-yellow blooms in a jam jar.

Samuel appeared by her side. 'They're f-for you to take home to Star House.'

Betty gazed lovingly at him. How thoughtful he was. 'Thank you. I love daffs. But would you mind if I left them here?' She glanced at the cut-glass vase. 'I'd love to do that.'

Samuel fetched the vase and Betty filled it with water from the tap in the scullery, then arranged her daffodils.

'There.' She returned the vase to the shelf and stood back, slipping her hand into Samuel's. 'My first flowers in what is going to be my new home. I can't wait. Now that I have the promise of the fee from Radiance, I can let myself look forward to it wholeheartedly instead of dreading how far away it is.'

'It c-can be as s-soon as you like as far as I'm concerned,' said Samuel. 'I w-want nothing more than for us to be married.'

'I feel the same,' Betty whispered, tucking herself into his side. 'I need to go and see Dad and tell him I'll soon be able to pay him back. Then we can start planning our wedding.'

'W-we'll go to Salford on S-Sunday.'

Betty shook her head. 'Dad's on duty then, but he'll be at home on Saturday.'

Samuel frowned. 'I have to open the sh-shop. Anyway, isn't it your S-Saturday for the depot?'

'It's meant to be,' Betty told him, 'but after the Saturdays I worked at Harris's, Lorna offered to swap. She'll work this week if I do her Saturday next week, so I can go to Salford. It's a shame you won't be able to come an' all, but I don't want to put it off.'

'I understand,' said Samuel, and bent to kiss her.

A happy sigh made Betty feel as if she was glowing. Samuel always wanted what was best for her and he always understood. She was the luckiest girl in the world.

Betty was filled with anticipation as she headed to Salford on Saturday. Dad was going to be so surprised when she told him she would shortly be able to give him his money back – and even more surprised when she told him how. She wished Mum could have lived to see her as the Radiance girl.

'Your dad isn't here,' were Grace's not-so-welcoming words as she let Betty in.

'Oh.' Betty would have been disappointed in any circumstances, but it felt worse after she had looked forward to it so much.

'Well, that's very flattering, I must say. Your face just fell a mile.' Grace's light-brown eyes narrowed and she tossed her conker-brown hair. 'You might at least pretend you're glad to find me in.'

Betty forced a smile. 'Of course I am. I thought Dad would be here too.'

Grace sighed theatrically. 'He was meant to be, but he had to go into work.'

Leaving Betty to hang up her things, Grace went to put the kettle on. Soon they were sitting in the parlour with cups of tea and slices of Grace's home-made carrot cake.

'This is delicious.' Betty was being truthful as well as polite, but she felt obliged to say it because she knew from experience that she would end up in Grace's bad books if she didn't praise her baking.

'I'm very resourceful with the humble carrot,' said Grace. 'Cakes, scones, jam, croquettes, you name it. I'm making sardine pancakes and veg for dinner – but I don't suppose you'll be staying now that your father isn't here.'

'What time are you expecting him home?' Betty asked.

Reaching for her cigarettes, Grace shrugged off the question. 'You grew up in this house. You know what long hours a policeman works.'

Betty nodded. It was one of the reasons she and her mum had been so close. They had always spent a lot of time together. She smiled. It was also one of the reasons why she loved Dad so deeply. Having him at home had always felt special.

'Of course, it'll look good to the neighbours, you and me being here together, just the two of us,' Grace added. Her lips formed a shape that was less a smile than a smirk.

'Will it?'

'Oh aye. I am the mother of the bride, after all. All the neighbours want to know when you're getting wed.'

'What have you told them?'

'That with it being a quick engagement, you want time to be sure of one another before you take the plunge.'

Betty was offended. 'We're perfectly sure of one another. We're only waiting because of—'

'—because of the debt. You know that, and I know it, and your father knows it, but we can't have everybody else realising there's a problem, can we?'

Betty swallowed. 'I don't want folk reminded of what I did.'

'And neither do we.' All of a sudden, Grace's face was all sharp lines. 'You brought such shame on this house, Betty. I don't mind for my own sake, but the hurt you caused your father...'

'I never meant any harm,' Betty said for what felt like the hundredth time.

'I'm not just talking about the magistrate's fine. Heaven knows, that was bad enough at the time, but we had no idea what was coming next.' Grace shuddered elaborately, closing her eyes as if the sight of Betty pained her. 'When you were accused of organised crime...'

'I was innocent,' Betty said stoutly. 'I was duped by Eddie. He accused me because he thought it might get him off the hook, or at least muddy the waters. I was never more frightened in my life than when I was kept at the police station, and I felt perfectly dreadful about what it might do to Dad's reputation.'

'You weren't the only one. The worry you caused me!'

'Believe me, I'm aware of that. Did you really have to come to Star House and tell me to steer clear of here?'

'Yes, I did,' Grace snapped, unrepentant. 'If your name hadn't been cleared—'

'But it was, thanks to Samuel and my friends,' said Betty, 'so there's no need to mention it again. I've put it behind me.'

'That's as maybe,' Grace replied, 'but you can't dismiss your magistrate's fine so easily, can you? That'll be hanging over you for a long time to come – and not just you, Betty, but over your dad and me an' all. Your poor dad.'

'Grace, about the fine—'

'Yes, about the fine,' Grace steamrollered on. 'I think you should come here less often.'

'*What?*'

'I've fobbed off the neighbours with a reason for your long engagement, but they won't stay fobbed off. They'll begin to smell a rat, and the more you're round here the more obvious it will be to them that your engagement is dragging on and on.'

Betty went icy-cold. 'So you want me to stay away?'

'It makes sense.' Grace blew out a stream of smoke.

'Just like it made sense for you to tell me to stay away when you thought I was in trouble with the police.'

'I've got your father's best interests at heart,' declared Grace.

'Have you?' thundered Dad from the doorway.

Betty's gaze flew to him as he stepped into the room.

Grace's face went white. 'Trevor – you're back.'

'Aye, and not a moment too soon by the sound of it. I cleared up what needed doing at the station. I knew you'd have told our Betty not to expect me, so I thought I'd creep in and surprise her, but it's me that's surprised. Flabbergasted, I should say. Did I hear you right? Have you been telling my Betty not to come to my house – to her own home?'

'It was for her own good,' Grace blustered. 'And yours. You have your reputation to think of.'

Standing up, she tried to take Dad's hands, but he side-stepped her.

'I can hardly take it in.' He rubbed a hand across his moustache. 'My wife telling my daughter, my own flesh and blood, to stop away from her own home.'

'It's not as though this is her real home any more,' Grace trilled desperately. 'She's in digs and she's happy there.'

'Which is just as well if you didn't intend to make her welcome here,' said Dad. 'This will always be her home as far as I'm concerned. Any loving father would say the same.' He looked at Betty, his serious features blurring with emotion. 'You can live wherever you like, love. You can move into Buckingham Palace, but this will always be your home if you want it.'

'Trevor,' said Grace, 'I only meant for her to keep her distance during her long engagement. It's for her own sake – so the neighbours don't realise the real reason.'

'They won't have a chance to realise,' said Betty. 'They'll be too busy gossiping about the wedding, which is going to take place soon.'

'Don't be ridiculous,' said Grace. 'Or have you decided to let Samuel pay the debt for you?'

'There's no need,' said Betty.

'Oh – so you mean to prevail upon your father to write off the debt?'

'My Betty has no need to prevail upon me,' said Dad. 'I freely set the debt aside. It's the least I can do after my wife has tried to make her unwelcome under my roof.'

'You're so generous, Dad, and I love you for it,' Betty told him emotionally, 'but there's no need, honestly. I'm going to pay you back myself.'

'*You* are?' Grace spluttered in disbelief.

Betty and Dad ignored her. 'Have you heard of Radiance face cream, Dad?'

'Radiance?' Grace asked, startled. 'That's a very good product.'

'I'm glad you think so,' Betty replied, keeping her gaze on her father. 'They've chosen me to be the new face of Radiance. That's where the money is coming from. I'm definitely going to be in one advertisement and I might be in two.'

Dad sat next to her on the sofa, angling himself towards her as he reached for her hands.

'You're going to be in a face-cream advertisement? How did that come about? Not that anyone should be surprised. You're the prettiest girl there ever was – just like your mum. Well! My Betty in an advertisement. Tell me all about it, love. I have a feeling I haven't paid you enough attention, but that's about to change, starting right now.'

CHAPTER THIRTY

Lorna had been happy to suggest swapping Saturdays with Betty. Goodness knew, Betty deserved a bit of breathing space after working several Saturdays in a row. She'd gone over to Salford to give her dad the good news about paying off her debt.

'And after that it'll be full steam ahead to the wedding,' Lorna had said to her. 'At least I assume it will be, though maybe you want to luxuriate in building up to it.'

'We want to get married soon,' Betty confirmed.

'That's understandable,' Lorna had said encouragingly, sensing there was more to this.

'Not just because it's what we want for ourselves,' Betty had confided, 'but also so that Andrew can be there. He's leaving right after the Easter weekend. It would be so sad for Sally if she attended our wedding without him by her side.'

'That's true,' Lorna agreed, 'but Easter is only three weeks away. You mustn't rush your wedding for Sally's benefit. That's the last thing she'd want.'

'I know,' said Betty, 'but after believing we'd have to wait to get married until goodness knows when because of the debt, we're now so happy to have that worry lifted and all we want is to be together.' Her blue eyes shone, but then her dimple vanished and she looked serious. 'I want Sally to share some of our happiness. This is such a difficult time for her.'

Lorna had enfolded Betty in a warm hug, whispering, 'You're such a kind person.'

Now, as she came to the end of the morning in the depot, Lorna remembered that conversation. She had grown deeply fond of Betty and she admired her too. Her sweet nature and kind heart brought warmth into other people's lives. Samuel was a lucky man. Their future children would be fortunate to have such loving, steadfast parents.

It was almost time to stop for something to eat. She just had to strip out the inner tubes from these old bicycle tyres first. She grinned to herself. Not so long ago she would have been horrified at being expected to do such a thing, but now she regarded it as normal. And to think she had once hoped to live out the war in comfort in a posh hotel. She was a very different person now.

'That's a big smile. What's the joke?'

Lorna's heart stuttered as she lifted her head from her task. 'George! What are you doing here?'

'Calling on you, of course.'

He carried a wicker picnic basket, which he shifted to his other hand to raise his hat. There he stood, tall and handsome, his jacket sitting well on his broad shoulders, a teasing smile on his lips.

No. Lorna stiffened her spine. It was no use responding. She would only open herself to being hurt, and she had no desire to live through that again.

'I haven't seen you since the night of the arrests,' she said.

'I've been up to my neck in writing reports and logging evidence.' He lifted the hamper a little. 'Is it time for lunch shortly?'

'You've brought a picnic?'

'Courtesy of the Claremont. I thought we could have a bite together – if you're not too busy.'

'I just need to get these finished,' said Lorna.

George set down the hamper. 'What are you up to? Removing the inner tubes? I'll give you a hand.'

'What about your suit? There's a reason why we wear dungarees and old jumpers.'

George removed his jacket and waistcoat and draped them over the wicker basket. Then he unfastened his onyx cufflinks—

'You're wearing the ones I gave you for your birthday,' Lorna exclaimed.

'Yes. I'm rather fond of them.'

He didn't meet her eyes as he dropped them into his pocket. But once he'd rolled up his pristine shirt-sleeves, he gave her a smile that made his face light up.

'Shall we?' he offered.

They stripped out the remaining inner tubes, chatting companionably as they did so, then added the tyres to a crate of various pieces of rubber. When they'd finally finished, they washed their hands. Then George straightened his appearance and picked up the picnic basket.

'It's a cool day but it's dry. We could cut along to the rec if you like and find a spot in between the allotments.'

'I can't leave the depot,' said Lorna, 'but we have a staffroom. We spent the winter using Sally's office for tea breaks and dinners so that we used only the one fire, but now that the temperature is kinder we're using the staffroom. It's not as warm as it might be, but it's better for Sally if we don't eat in her office.'

'Lead the way!' George said with a smile.

Betty had given the staffroom a good clean yesterday and the scent of lavender polish lingered. The room was bare aside from a table and chairs and some cupboards and shelves. The fireplace, which had been boarded up when Sally and Betty started working here, had been unboarded. It was a shame they couldn't make use of it because of the need to conserve fuel.

Placing the hamper on the table, George flicked open the catches.

'Let's see what we've got,' he said.

He took out a pair of starched linen napkins and two glasses, followed by white china plates and matching cups. Then came small parcels wrapped in waxed paper. Lorna helped him open them, revealing cheese-and-egg tartlets, potato-and-carrot balls in breadcrumbs and tuna in puff pastry.

'This looks lovely,' she said in delight.

'And the last packet has...' George said dramatically as he opened it. 'Ta da! Fruit shortcake.'

'Gorgeous,' said Lorna.

'We have a Thermos of tea and a twist of sugar, and a small bottle of white wine.'

Lorna burst out laughing. 'White wine? We're having this in a salvage depot, not at the Ritz.'

'The Ritz? Wash your mouth out, Miss West-Sadler. What would the staff at the Claremont say if they knew that the name of another establishment had passed your lips?'

'I apologise profusely to everyone at the Claremont,' Lorna replied, mock-serious.

George drew back a chair for her and, with a flourish, laid a snowy napkin across her lap. He took his place opposite her and carefully picked up the waxed sheets one by one, offering them to her so she could fill her plate. Then he opened and poured the wine, before helping himself to food.

Lorna sampled everything, closing her eyes in pleasure as she enjoyed the savoury treats.

'I'm sorry if I'm supposed to pick delicately at my food and pretend not to have anything as unladylike as an appetite,' she said as she tucked in. 'Working here always leaves me as hungry as a hunter.'

'Ginty told me that, before the war, every time she was being taken by her parents to some posh function or other, her mother would make her consume a plate of sandwiches beforehand so she wouldn't eat more than the odd morsel when she was out.'

'Really? Mummy did the same to me. It's a relief, actually, to know I wasn't the only one.' Lorna polished off a potato-and-carrot ball. 'How is she?'

'Healing well, I'm pleased to say. She's a sweet girl and I'm fond of her.'

Lorna couldn't prevent herself from saying, 'You looked good together as a couple.'

'That was the whole idea,' said George. 'It was essential that Richardson and Lennox believed in the persona that had been created for me. Ginty was part of that. Something I'm sure you'll be glad to hear: she's had a letter from her boyfriend via the Red Cross.'

'That's wonderful news,' Lorna said sincerely. 'Is he all right, or is that a stupid question to ask about a POW?'

'It isn't stupid at all. I imagine POWs will have very different experiences depending on who has captured them. In Bernie's case – he's Ginty's boyfriend – he's incarcerated every night but in the daytime he works for a farmer in Austria. The farmer's family is good to him.'

'I'm pleased to know that,' Lorna said quietly. Bernie's fate could have been so much worse. 'And what will happen to the hooch men?'

'They're going to stand trial.' George spoke with evident satisfaction. 'They've been charged with defrauding the Inland Revenue of a sum that will result in fines and penalties of six or seven hundred pounds—'

'*How* much?' cried Lorna, startled.

'I know,' George said sombrely. 'When you think that many working men earn around three quid a week and consider themselves fortunate if they get four, and a well-paid man earns five, it shows how much money these hooch villains are raking in.'

'I thought the purpose of what you did was to gain further evidence against Lennox and Richardson so they could be accused of more than cheating the tax man.'

'They're being charged with all the other crimes as well,' George confirmed. 'We found their still and we've tracked down some of the men who provided ingredients like juniper essence and what have you, so they'll stand trial as well. And we've got the underground printing press. We've got them for buying the genuine Scotch bottles – though their solicitor is trying to claim that purchasing them doesn't prove an intent to fill them with illegal alcohol, but we'll see what the jury thinks of that.'

'It sounds like you have amassed plenty of evidence,' said Lorna.

'We're as certain as it's possible to be that lengthy prison sentences will result,' said George.

Lorna raised her wine glass. 'I'll drink to that.'

George held her gaze. 'I'd rather drink to you.'

She deliberately placed her own interpretation on his words. 'Oh, me, I didn't do much. I was just polite to the wives.'

'Your working here at the depot made all the difference. That alone was far more convincing than anything I could have come up with.'

'You're welcome,' Lorna said lightly.

'I still want to drink to you,' said George.

'George, don't—'

'When I met you again because of the Christmas Blitz, I said I wanted to get to know you without all the social pressures we had to contend with last time. I've found that you're clever and funny and loyal and courageous. You're a girl in a million, Lorna.'

Lorna's heart expanded but she kept her tone light and dismissive. 'Thanks. You're not so bad yourself.'

'I hope I'm rather better than "not so bad". In case you feel like reassuring me on that point.'

'George Broughton, are you fishing for compliments?'

'No, as a matter of fact,' said George. 'I'm hoping for the truth. I've told you what I've discovered about you, the real you. I was hoping you might have learned something about me... something that might urge you to get back together with me.'

'George...'

'I apologise,' he said. 'I shouldn't put you on the spot. That's not a gentlemanly thing to do. I hope you'll hear me out, Lorna. I called off our engagement because I came to realise that your parents, especially your father, had been set upon your marrying a title. You were so... young, for want of a better word, back then. You weren't the independent girl you are now. I'm sure you'd be the first to admit that you were under your father's thumb. Then there was all the gossip, and my family were upset and angry. In the end, calling it off seemed the only thing to do.'

'I really don't need you to rub it in,' Lorna said with asperity. 'I'm well aware that my parents and I aren't perfect.'

To her surprise, George smiled.

'I don't know about your parents, Lorna, but you most certainly are – perfect, I mean. In my eyes you are. The Lorna I've come to know since the Christmas Blitz is the best girl in the world. You're strong and capable and worthy of everyone's respect. I was never happy without you. How could I be? Letting you go was the maddest thing I ever did. Now that I've met you again, I realise just how mad and stupid I was. Will you give me another chance, Lorna? Will you give *us* another chance?'

As he gazed at her, his eyes darkened, making her bones melt. Lorna realised she had stopped breathing. She had to manufacture a little gasp to get started again. Before she could utter a sound, George pulled his chair round the table so that, instead of being opposite one another, they now shared a corner. He took her hand in his.

'Lorna West-Sadler, you have made me fall in love for the first time all over again. The things I said when we dined at the Claremont with the Lennoxes and the Richardsons were true. I wasn't playing a part when I said them. Do you remember what I said? That reuniting was the best thing for us. That it would be the making of me. That is truly how I feel, Lorna. Do you feel the same?'

With delight coursing through her, Lorna nodded, her eyes filling with happy, astonished tears. Then she and George were kissing and everything in her world shifted back into the right position. Ending the kiss, she held George's face in her hands, leaning her forehead against his.

'You didn't actually say, "Yes", my love,' he murmured.

'I nodded as loudly as I could,' she answered with a gurgle of laughter. 'But for the record, yes, yes, yes!' The atmosphere changed then and she felt serious. 'We have to take things slowly. Everything was such a rush last time. I couldn't wait to get engaged.'

'Nor could I,' said George. 'That was how we ended up being vulnerable to all the gossip. Even though we were in love, there wasn't a strong, solid relationship behind us to help us weather the storm.'

'So,' Lorna whispered, 'we'll take our time.'

'Do you remember what you said to me during lunch at the Claremont?' George asked. 'You said, "You'd better not let me down," and I won't, Lorna. I swear I won't.' His gaze dropped to the hand in his as his thumbs softly rubbed her fingers. He hesitated before saying, 'I'd like to tell you what happened to the heirloom ring I gave you last time.'

'Please, George, don't. I don't think I was ever more embarrassed in my life than when Daddy demanded I should keep my engagement ring. Then, when it was pointed out that I wasn't entitled to keep it because it was a Broughton family heirloom, he had to go and demand recompense for being deprived of something of such high value. Honestly, I don't know how I didn't sink through the floor.'

'It wasn't your fault,' said George.

'I think your father believed in that moment that all West-Sadlers are tarred with the same brush.'

'Leave him and my mother to me. I'll make sure you're made welcome by my family,' George said, a trace of grimness in his tone. 'Let me tell you about the heirloom ring. I sold it.'

'But it was an heirloom.'

'An heirloom that nobody with any good taste would choose to wear after our broken engagement, and especially after the fight your father put up to get it returned to you. With the family's consent, I sold it and gave the proceeds to the Red Cross.'

'George, that's perfect.' Lorna laughed. 'When Daddy made you pay up the value of the ring as compensation to me for not being allowed to keep it, that's what I did with the money – I gave it all to the Red Cross. I think that's a case of great minds thinking alike.'

'No,' said George. 'Two hearts thinking alike.'

CHAPTER THIRTY-ONE

Dad seemed determined to push the boat out when it came to Betty and Samuel's wedding.

'I popped into the florist's on the high street and said you'll be along to choose what you want for your bouquet,' he told Betty. 'Don't you be worrying about the cost, mind.'

'Honestly, Dad, I'd be perfectly happy with flowers from the garden,' she said.

'I know there's a war on and we're all meant to be tightening our belts,' he replied, 'but when you've only got one daughter, you want to give her the best wedding you can.'

He flicked a glance at Grace as he spoke, which made Betty do the same. Grace sat there with her smile frozen in place, uttering not a single objection.

Things had changed in Dad's house since he had overheard Grace speaking to Betty and realised the truth of their relationship. He had tried to apologise to Betty afterwards. 'I had no idea. She always seemed so fond of you.'

Tempting as it was to have a good old grouse and drop Grace well and truly in the soup, Betty had restrained herself. Dad might be all riled up now but at heart he was a softy and a peace-lover who liked his home comforts. Once this had blown over, it wouldn't take Grace long to get him back where she wanted him. While part of Betty was miffed at that thought, the last thing she wanted was for Dad to be miserable. He meant far too much to her for that.

Dad was still going on about wedding flowers. 'Don't forget you'll want smaller bouquets for your bridesmaids, and button-holes for the men, and what are those upside-down buttonholes called that women wear?'

'Corsages,' said Grace.

'Aye, them an' all,' said Dad.

'This will cost a fortune,' Betty protested.

'And well worth every penny,' he replied, looking satisfied.

'Trevor,' said Grace. 'The time.'

Dad looked at the clock. 'Aye, I'd best get changed.'

He was due to go on duty. When he went upstairs to put on his uniform, Grace was about to collect the cups and saucers, but Betty stopped her.

'Grace, I want my wedding to be a happy occasion – for everyone – and that means you and me need to clear the air.'

Grace looked as if she was about to speak, but then she didn't. Her light-brown eyes were wary.

'As far as I'm concerned,' Betty continued, 'what's done is done and I'm prepared to put it behind us.'

'I never did anything other than for your father's benefit,' Grace declared.

'That's not true,' Betty answered quietly. 'You wanted rid of me. You know you did – and my dad knows it an' all now, so don't try to deny it.'

Lifting her chin, Grace looked away. She had a perfect profile, thanks to her daily chin-exercise regime that prevented unsightly sagging.

'Like I say,' Betty persevered, 'I want my wedding to be a happy occasion all round, and so...' She hesitated. This was her last chance to change her mind. She blurted out, '...and so I want to ask if you'll be the mother of the bride.'

Grace's jaw dropped and she gawped. 'You want me to be your mother of the bride?'

'Well, no,' Betty said frankly. 'The person I want to be my mother of the bride is my mum, only she's not here – but you are, and if you throw yourself into the wedding preparations, I think that would make my wedding a happier occasion than if you don't. It would mean a lot to my dad – and to me an' all. What d'you say, Grace?'

'Did Samuel get the special licence without any trouble?' Sally asked Betty as the three salvage girls settled down to eat their midday meal together. Mrs Beaumont had packed three barm cakes with different filings and three different scones – carrot, potato and sultana – 'for you to squabble over,' she'd said with a smile.

Normally, the three girls spread out their dinnertimes so as to have someone on duty at all times, but today they were all keen to enjoy wedding talk.

Betty beamed with pure happiness. 'Yes. We're getting married on Easter Saturday.'

'I bet you can't wait,' Lorna said, pouring tea.

'I hate to sound selfish,' said Sally, 'but I'm glad you're having the wedding while Andrew is still here. Knowing we have a special occasion to look forward to before he goes away is giving me something good to focus on.'

'And something happy to look back on afterwards,' Lorna said softly.

She glanced at Betty, who smiled back. She hadn't told Sally that this was one of her reasons for wanting to marry promptly. There was no need for Sally to be told. It might sound like Betty was asking for gratitude.

'From what you've said,' Sally remarked, 'it sounds like your dad is determined to throw you a huge occasion.'

'Not exactly,' said Betty, smiling affectionately as she pictured her darling dad, 'but he certainly wants it to be special. He keeps saying I'm his only daughter so it's his one chance. I think it's partly because he's trying to make up for the way Grace behaved towards me.'

'That's understandable,' said Lorna.

'But he's not just doing it because of that, is he?' Sally added. 'He's doing it because he loves you so much.'

'I know,' said Betty. 'Give her her due, Grace is busy organising everything the way I've asked. After Dad heard the way she talked to me that time, she went all frosty afterwards.'

'Guilt,' said Lorna unsympathetically.

'But now we've sorted things out between us,' said Betty, 'and she's enjoying boasting to the neighbours about "our Betty's wonderful wedding". You should hear her!'

'As long as you're happy with the way things have turned out,' said Sally.

Betty sighed happily. 'Yes, I am. As long as I can marry Samuel, Grace fades into insignificance.'

'What else has your father arranged?' Lorna asked.

'The police choir, would you believe?' Betty announced with a chuckle. 'And don't ask me how he did it but I'm to be driven to the church in the deputy chief constable's Daimler.'

Her friends stared and then burst out laughing.

'It's going to be champion,' said Sally.

'The last word in splendour,' said Lorna.

'Not if I haven't got a beautiful dress,' Betty mourned.

As she had quickly learned, the biggest downside of organising a wedding so quickly was finding the perfect dress. It was hard to find wedding dresses these days. Many brides were wearing smart suits with hats to which they added a bit of froth. These ensembles were regarded as patriotic in these times of hardship, but Betty, caught up in the excitement of Dad's ambitious wedding plans, had set her heart on a white dress.

Sally's friend Deborah had kindly borrowed a couple of wedding dresses from colleagues at the Town Hall for her to try on. One had been all frills and ruffles.

'I look like I'm covered in Christmas cake icing,' had been Betty's disappointed assessment.

'Lucky you,' Sally had joked, jollying her along. 'Rationing means there'll be no more icing until the war is over.'

The other dress had been lovely but had been bought for a girl who was significantly taller.

'The only way to alter the gown properly,' said Mrs Beaumont, 'would be to take several inches from the hem, and then the skirt would need taking in. Otherwise the proportions would be all wrong.'

But the dress's owner hadn't wanted to agree to such a major change, which was understandable.

Now, Betty changed the subject. She didn't want to end up all doleful because of being worried about not having a wedding dress.

'Have you heard from George since the night of the arrests?' she asked Lorna.

Lorna took such a long time answering that Betty and Sally both looked at her.

'He came here to the depot, actually, the day I worked your Saturday,' she said at last. 'He went to Star House and Mrs Beaumont sent him here.'

Betty sat forward, her attention hooked. 'You never said.'

'I didn't like to.' Lorna looked uncomfortable.

'Whyever not?' Sally demanded.

'Yes, why not?' Betty pressed. 'Come on, Lorna. You have to tell us now. You can't leave us dangling.'

After a moment Lorna said, 'I didn't want to steal your thunder.'

'I don't understand,' said Betty.

'I do,' said Sally. 'At least, I think I do.'

'Since I'm the only one in the dark,' said Betty, 'you'll have to say it straight out, Lorna, whatever it is.'

'We weren't going to say anything until after your wedding,' said Lorna, 'but... George and I are seeing one another again.'

Sally jumped up and hugged her. 'That's wonderful news.'

Betty hugged her too. 'Yes, it is. Congratulations.'

Lorna laughed in obvious relief, her green eyes sparkling. 'Thanks. It's been killing me not to say anything.'

'Say as much as you like, starting now,' Betty commanded.

'Begin with the Saturday when George came here,' Sally added.

She and Betty listened in increasing delight to the tale of the impromptu picnic that had taken place right here in the depot's staffroom.

'We're going to take things slowly,' said Lorna. 'We rushed everything last time and it all came tumbling down around our ears. George will be going back to London soon, so we'll have to make do with letters and the occasional telephone call, and a few visits if we're lucky.'

'Being apart won't be easy,' Betty said sympathetically.

'No, it won't,' Lorna agreed, 'but it will prove how strong our feelings are. That's the most important thing.'

When Samuel came to collect Betty from Star House to take her out, Andrew called them into the sitting room, where he indicated a shoebox on the table.

'I made these for you.' From the box he removed a wooden star with a small hole in the top of one of its points, through which a piece of string had been looped. 'I wondered if you would like to present them to your wedding guests as a keepsake. I know they're not exactly appropriate,' he added, 'with these being Christmas tree decorations and your wedding being at Easter, but...'

Betty stood over the box, gazing into it at the wooden stars. 'You did this for us?'

'And your guests – but that's up to you, of course.'

Betty lifted her eyes to his. 'You've gone to all this trouble for us.' Her eyes filled and so did her heart.

'That's a w-wonderful gesture,' said Samuel. 'I d-don't know what to s-say.'

'Well, I do,' said Betty. 'How about "Thank you from the bottom of my heart" for starters?'

'Both our hearts,' Samuel added, shaking Andrew's hand.

'It was my pleasure,' said Andrew.

Later, when she was with Sally and Lorna, Betty said, 'Andrew made the stars for us even though his mind must be full of his impending departure. What a thoughtful and generous person he is. You're a lucky girl, Sally Henshaw.'

'Believe me, I'm well aware of it,' said Sally.

'Did you know he was making the stars?' Lorna asked.

Sally nodded. 'I didn't say anything because I didn't want to spoil the surprise.'

'It's lovely to think that every time your wedding guests decorate their trees,' said Lorna, 'they'll be reminded of you and your special day.'

'I know,' said Sally. 'Think of all the stories behind some of the decorations on Mrs Beaumont's Christmas tree. As a matter of fact, while we were decorating it, I thought that the three of us ought to get her a tree decoration next Christmas to remember us by and add to her tree's special stories.'

Betty caught on at once. 'So that in years to come, when she's a proper theatrical landlady again, she'll be telling her guests about the salvage girls who stayed here with her during the war.'

'And now she's going to have a Christmas star from Andrew,' said Lorna.

'But that won't be a present from the three of us,' Sally pointed out. 'It'll be a wedding keepsake, not the special tree decoration I originally thought of.'

They all looked at one another. Betty loved the idea of the three of them presenting their dear landlady with something special from the three of them.

'I know!' she exclaimed. 'What about a special wedding day photograph of her and us together? Dad has hired a photographer and he wants me to have a whole album.' Warmth filled her cheeks. 'I know. It's a huge extravagance these days.'

'Don't feel guilty,' Lorna said at once. 'Your father wants to give his only daughter the very best wedding he possibly can. Everyone understands that.'

'The photographer said that there are certain pictures he takes at every wedding,' said Betty, 'but since Dad is stumping up for a whole roll of film, I can choose some extra pictures. Us with Mrs Beaumont could be one of them.'

Sally gave her a hug. 'That sounds perfect.'

The only issue clouding Betty's happiness and excitement was the question of her wedding dress.

'And that's the worst possible problem a bride can have,' she wailed as she knitted in the sitting room along with the other Star House women. Then her words sank into her mind and she realised what she'd said. 'Oh, hark at me. How selfish I sound when Sally and Mrs Henshaw are facing up to Andrew leaving.'

'Don't fret about us,' said Mrs Henshaw. 'Your wedding is important and it's natural to worry about it.'

'It's not like being in the music hall,' Mrs Beaumont added, 'when if your act goes wrong today, you get another chance tomorrow.'

'And your wedding dress matters most awfully,' said Lorna.

Betty released a tiny sigh, grateful for their understanding.

'I remember how difficult it was for me to find something I loved for my wedding,' said Sally, 'and I was only looking for a suit.'

'Don't say "only" like that,' chided her mother-in-law. 'That costume was the perfect colour for you. Andrew was so proud.'

Lorna said to Betty, 'And Samuel is going to be proud of you too. You could wear one of the daily salvage sacks and he'd think you're the most gorgeous girl he's ever seen.'

'We'll have to make sure it doesn't come to that,' Mrs Beaumont said with a throaty chuckle. 'I might have something up my sleeve. No – don't ask questions. Let me see what I can do.'

Betty was intrigued and it was easy to see her chums were too, but Mrs Beaumont wouldn't utter another word on the subject.

'What's she thinking of, d'you suppose?' Betty whispered as the three of them headed upstairs to get ready for their night duty.

'No idea,' Sally answered.

'I'll say one thing,' Lorna added. 'She must be fairly certain of it, whatever it is, or she wouldn't have said anything.'

That gave Betty food for thought. It kept creeping back into her mind all through fire-watching duty that night, and again the next day at the depot, but she didn't say anything because she didn't want to be a bore.

When the girls got home, Mrs Beaumont greeted them with a huge smile.

'Come straight into the sitting room,' she said. 'I want to talk to you. No, it's nothing to worry about. Quite the opposite. It's good news. Sit down and let me tell you.' Smoothing her skirt under her, she sat in her armchair. 'As you know, I'm a theatrical landlady by profession, but there was a time when I thought of being a wardrobe mistress. I've always stayed on good terms with all the backstage people I've known and so I was able to ask about wedding dresses in the costume store.'

Betty caught her breath in surprise.

'You've got a stage wedding dress for Betty?' Lorna asked. 'Forgive me but won't it be rather... well, larger than life? Everyone on stage has to be clearly visible from the back of the gods. That's why actors wear a lot of make-up.'

Mrs Beaumont gave her a look. 'Are you suggesting I would dress Betty as a pantomime dame?' she demanded and Lorna subsided. 'As a matter of fact, the dresses I was shown this afternoon were all beautifully made, with lots of detail such as embroidery.'

'Have you brought me a dress to try on?' asked Betty.

'I've brought you six. They're on your bed.'

'Six!' squeaked Betty.

'And with them being theatre dresses, there's no problem about doing alterations,' said Mrs Beaumont. 'Now get up those stairs and start trying them on. Your audience awaits.'

Betty, Sally and Lorna had a whale of a time with the dresses. One was floor-length satin with a flattering boat neckline lined with tiny rhinestones, and a short train. Another had a dramatic slash of a neckline and a long line of fabric-covered buttons down the back.

'The back matters,' said Lorna, 'because that's what everybody will see when you're standing at the front.'

Another dress had a high neckline with a small stand-up collar and long panels of fabric that created a fitted bodice and then spread into a flared skirt.

Lorna and Sally helped Betty into each dress and Betty carefully held up the skirt as she went downstairs to the sitting room, where she paraded up and down while each gown was discussed at length. Mrs Beaumont had brought downstairs not one but two long mirrors so Betty could see herself from various angles.

There were headdresses as well – one of wax orange blossom, a sweet little tiara of wired pearls, two different ones of silk flowers – and a selection of veils, from shoulder-length to floor-length.

'I don't think I've ever had so much fun in my life,' said Betty as a giggle spurted out of her.

'It's wonderful to see you so happy,' said Sally.

Betty loved all the dresses and couldn't imagine how she could possibly be expected to choose one over the others – until she tried on the sixth dress and knew instantly that this was the one. Made of ivory satin, it had a wide scooped neckline edged with teeny-tiny pearls, and a semi-fitted bodice that fell to her hips and then flared to floor-length, including a short train.

Betty had already decided when she saw it – as much of it as she could – in the small mirror in her bedroom, but when she came downstairs and saw it properly in the long mirrors she simply couldn't stop gazing at herself.

'This is it,' she said. 'This is the one. I love it. Oh, thank you, Mrs Beaumont.'

'You're welcome, dear,' said her landlady. 'Now, which headdress and veil? I suggest the pearl tiara.'

The others agreed and Lorna positioned it carefully on Betty's head.

'Which length of veil would you like?' Mrs Henshaw asked.

Betty hesitated. In her heart of hearts, she longed for the full-length one. What could be more romantic? But she knew she mustn't.

'The waist-length,' she said.

'Are you sure?' asked Mrs Beaumont. 'I saw the way the way you looked at the long one. It would look lovely with this dress.'

'Yes, but...' Betty's voice petered out.

'But what?' Sally asked gently.

'Well, it's not exactly patriotic, is it?' said Betty. 'Not when most brides are getting wed in suits they can wear for best for years.'

Placing her hands on Betty's shoulders, Sally looked her in the eye. 'Listen to me, Betty Hughes. I'll tell you what's patriotic. An ordinary girl having the wedding of her dreams. That's one in the eye for Hitler and that's patriotic. If you want the full-length veil, then jolly well wear it and we'll all be proud of you.'

They all looked round, startled, as the sitting room door opened and Andrew walked in.

'Look who I found on Wilton Road— oh.'

Samuel, following Andrew in, stopped dead as all the women shrieked.

'Get out!' cried Mrs Beaumont. 'You mustn't see Betty in her dress.'

'Too late, I'm afraid,' said Andrew. 'I'm sorry. I had no idea—'

'It's not your fault,' said his mother. 'It's just one of those things.'

'Samuel, you're standing there like a lemon,' Lorna said in exasperation. 'You might at least pretend to withdraw.'

Removing his glasses, Samuel swiped his handkerchief across his eyes. Then he stepped across and took Betty's hands, gazing at her lovingly.

'D-does it matter that I've seen the d-dress? It looks beautiful on you and I w-want you to wear it.'

'It's unlucky—' Mrs Henshaw began but Sally shushed her.

'How c-can it be unlucky when it's you and me?' Samuel's hazel eyes never left Betty's. 'You're the loveliest girl I've ever s-seen and I've never seen you look more beautiful than you d-do now. I c-can't think of anything better than marrying you looking like this.'

CHAPTER THIRTY-TWO

Betty barely slept the night before her wedding, or at least that was how it felt.

'By rights I ought to look like death warmed up,' she told Sally and Lorna.

They had come with her to Salford yesterday and had stayed the night at Dad's house, sharing the spare bedroom. They'd come into her old bedroom this morning. All three of them were clad in their dressing gowns, with rollers in their hair.

'But I don't look too bad.' Betty leaned nearer to the mirror that stood on the chest of drawers, fingering her face and eyeing it critically.

'Stuff and nonsense,' Lorna said. 'You look positively radiant.'

'As befits the Radiance girl,' Sally added.

Betty stepped away from the mirror. The advertisement had appeared for the first time in a selection of women's magazines that week. Samuel had bought a copy of each magazine for her and, when she'd arrived at Dad's house yesterday, it turned out that Dad had done the same – except that he'd bought two copies of each, one for Betty and one for him.

'You truly do look radiant,' Sally told her seriously. 'You'll make a beautiful bride.'

Betty looked at her wedding dress, which hung from the picture rail. Grace had wanted to hang it in her and Dad's wardrobe last night, since Betty's hanging-cupboard wasn't tall enough, but Betty had refused. She couldn't bear to be parted from it. How she was going to hand it back to Mrs Beaumont, she didn't know. It was going to be a real wrench.

The girls went down to breakfast. When they'd arrived yesterday, Lorna had brought with her a shopping bag containing a fresh loaf, a jar of marmalade and a bottle of milk as a contribution to the breakfast table.

'You didn't need to do that,' Betty had whispered. 'My dad would have been only too pleased to provide food for us.'

'He might,' Lorna had murmured back, 'but would Grace?'

Grace had accepted the offerings with thanks. To give her due credit, she had certainly bucked up her ideas since Dad had discovered her true attitude to Betty. Betty's offer to accept her wholeheartedly as the mother of the bride had done the trick too, giving her the opening she'd needed to start making amends.

'Let's hope it lasts,' Sally had commented.

'She's being as nice as pie to me about the wedding,' Betty had answered, 'which is all that matters at the moment.'

'And afterwards?' Lorna had asked.

'I'll leave afterwards to look after itself,' Betty had said firmly. 'I'll be Mrs Samuel Atkinson and Grace won't be half so important in my life.'

Mrs Samuel Atkinson. That was who she was going to become this very day. The thought left her breathless with happiness. Samuel had been practising saying his vows to try to iron out the stammers.

'I d-don't want to let you d-down,' he'd told her.

Betty's heart had expanded with love. Every time she thought she couldn't possibly love him any more than she already did, he said or did something that made her do precisely that.

'You could never let me down,' she'd assured him. 'As for stumbling over your vows, I don't mind *how* you say them as long as you *say* them... as long as we end up married. That's the only thing that matters.'

After breakfast Dad and Grace went upstairs to get ready first. They came down again presently, Dad looking handsome and upright in his newly pressed uniform, and Grace wearing a cream jacket over a bronze-coloured dress with a tiny floral pattern. Her hat and gloves waited on the table.

'That's a lovely dress, Mrs Hughes,' said Lorna.

'Thank you,' said Grace. 'It goes with my colouring.'

Betty went to Dad and hugged him.

'It's a big day for me,' he said, 'giving away my only daughter in marriage.'

'Thank you for everything, Dad,' said Betty.

'You're a wonderful girl, Betty, the best daughter a man could wish for.'

Betty realised she was poised for Grace to utter a tinkling little laugh and say, 'Let go of your father, Betty. You don't want to crease his uniform,' or some such, but Grace did nothing of the sort. Betty relaxed.

'My turn to get ready now,' she said, smiling up at Dad. 'The next time you see me, I'll be in my wedding dress.'

Dad cleared his throat and swiped his handkerchief across his eyes.

'Sergeant Hughes,' Lorna said, her tone both teasing and kindly, 'are you shedding a tear? What would they say down at the police station?'

The girls were laughing as they ran upstairs.

'When Sally got married,' said Betty, 'the bridesmaids got changed first and then we helped Sally. That's what I want to do today.'

'What, you two fuss around me, you mean?' Sally's hazel eyes twinkled.

Betty shook her head in mock-exasperation. 'You daft ha'porth. I mean bridesmaids first and then me – as you know perfectly well.'

They started by doing one another's hair. Out came the rollers, then they carefully brushed out each other's curls to create fashionable waves that they scooped away from their faces with hairpins.

Mrs Beaumont had offered to ask her friend the wardrobe mistress for matching dresses for Lorna and Sally, but Betty had liked the idea of them wearing their own things. She'd been very touched when Sally had asked her permission to wear her forget-me-not-blue suit.

'Would you mind?' she'd asked. 'With it having been my wedding suit, I mean.'

'Why would I mind?' Betty had responded. 'It's perfect on you.'

Sally's blue suit had a jacket with padded shoulders and a buckled belt that emphasised her slim waist. The skirt was knee-length with a panel of pleats down the front. When Sally had told Lorna that she was going to wear a suit, Lorna had said she would as well. Hers was moss green with a peplum waist.

Betty looked at her bridesmaids. 'You both look gorgeous.'

'Your turn now,' said Sally.

The others turned away as Betty slipped off her dressing gown and nightie and put on a brassière with ribbon shoulder straps. She quickly added her suspender belt, followed by a pair of camiknickers with a side-button fastening and wide legs edged with machine-lace. She pulled her suspenders out of the knicker-legs and gave the others permission to turn back round. She didn't mind being watched putting stockings on.

Excitement trembled inside her as Lorna lifted her wedding dress down from the picture rail. Lorna held it up for Sally to undo the buttons down the back, then slipped the gown from the hanger and looked at Betty.

'Wait,' said Betty. 'Should I ask Grace to help an' all?'

'She doesn't deserve it,' said Sally.

'I shan't argue with that,' agreed Betty, 'but I think Dad would appreciate it. Grace would love it too.'

'Today is about what *you* want,' Lorna said quietly.

Betty's face broke into a smile. 'What's the use of me being as happy as I am if everyone else isn't happy too?' She walked onto the landing and called down the stairs. 'Grace! We need the mother of the bride.'

Moments later Grace entered the bedroom, looking pleased and a bit flustered.

The others helped Betty into her dress. Then Lorna, who was the tallest, positioned the tiara, which now had the full-length veil attached to it. Sally and Grace fluffed out the veil and it floated mistily.

'You bridesmaids will have to do this at the church before Betty walks in,' said Grace.

Feeling like a princess, Betty made her way downstairs. The look of love and pride on Dad's face made tears rise behind her eyes and she had to blink them away.

'Goodness me, Betty,' Dad said. 'Look at you. Just look at you. No offence to Grace, but if your mum could be here now...'

At that, Betty's tears really did spill over, and Sally leapt to the rescue with a hanky to dab them away.

The doorbell rang.

'That'll be the flowers,' said Grace, and went to fetch them.

When Dad had offered to pay for whatever flowers she wanted, no expense spared, Betty had originally intended to choose something modest because she didn't want to take advantage. But then she'd decided to have the same flowers that Mum had had in her wedding bouquet – pink roses and white freesias.

There were also smaller bouquets for Sally and Lorna, as well as the corsages and buttonholes.

Sally helped Grace with her corsage while Betty attended to Dad's buttonhole. Grace was going to take the corsages for Mrs Beaumont and Mrs Henshaw, together with the groom's and best man's buttonholes, with her to the church when it was time for her to go. Samuel's sister Valerie hadn't been able to get leave to be there today, but his brother John had and he was the best man.

The doorbell rang once more.

'That can't be the motor already,' Grace exclaimed.

It was the photographer.

'I wanted to be sure of getting here before the motor,' he said.

Soon the deputy chief constable's Daimler pulled up outside the house, and the neighbours spilled out of their doors to watch Grace and the bridesmaids come outside and climb in, being very careful of their dresses. The driver handed in the box of flowers before he shut the door.

Betty watched from the window. She couldn't go outside yet because of keeping her dress under wraps until the last moment.

She and Dad looked at one another.

'Please don't say anything to make me cry,' said Betty.

Dad blew out a breath. 'I'm feeling fairly emotional myself – so *you'd* better not make *me* cry,' he added, which made Betty smile.

She looked at the clock. 'It won't be long now.'

'It'll be the proudest moment of my life,' said Dad.

Was he about to say something about Mum? Betty knew she

would burst into tears if he did, but he didn't – possibly for that very reason.

The Daimler returned.

'Ready?' Dad asked.

Betty nodded and they went outside. Once again, the neighbours appeared, calling their good wishes. Some of them clapped when they saw Betty's gorgeous dress and veil, which rippled in the gentle breeze.

The photographer got Betty and Dad to stand beside the motor's open door, angling himself to get the best photograph.

Betty handed her bouquet to the driver and climbed carefully into the motor, while Dad held the long veil out of the way, giving her time to settle herself before he got in beside her. The driver handed in the flowers.

Moments later Betty was waving to the neighbours as they set off the church.

Lorna and Sally were waiting outside and they hurried forward to give Betty whatever assistance she needed. As she and Dad made their way into the church porch, Betty could hear the police choir coming to the end of 'All Things Bright and Beautiful'. Oh, wasn't Dad marvellous to have arranged the posh motor and the choir specially for her!

And that wasn't all.

'When we go inside, Betty,' he said quietly, 'don't be surprised when you see a dozen bobbies sitting at the back. They're there to give you and Samuel a guard of honour when you come out of church. You know how fancy military couples come out of church to walk under an archway of swords? Well, Mr and Mrs Samuel Atkinson will come out through an archway of truncheons.'

In the porch was a bobby with a big grin his face. He waited for Lorna and Sally to finish fussing around Betty, settling her veil and arranging her train. Then, at a nod from Dad, he disappeared inside.

The hymn was over. Only the organ was playing now. The bobby must have tipped someone the wink because the organ stopped, then a moment later started up again, this time playing the opening chords of 'Here Comes the Bride'.

Dad took Betty's arm, patting it as he placed it within the crook of his arm. They walked into the church with Sally and Lorna behind them. There was a rustle of movement up ahead on both sides as the guests turned round to look at Betty.

And at the front Samuel turned to face her. Betty walked towards him, knowing that in a few minutes she would be the wife of the best, most steadfast and loving man in the world.

A LETTER FROM SUSANNA

Dear Reader,

I loved writing *Christmas for the Home Front Girls* and I hope you loved reading it and catching up with your friends at the salvage depot.

If you did enjoy my book, and want to keep up to date with all my latest releases, please sign up at the following link. Your email address will never be shared and you can unsubscribe at any time.

www.bookouture.com/susanna-bavin

This story includes the Christmas Blitz, which took place in Manchester and Salford on the evenings and nights of 22 and 23 December 1940. Afterwards, thirty-one acres of buildings lay in ruins around Albert Square in the centre of Manchester. What made the Christmas Blitz worse was that, on 21 December, there had been a blitz over Liverpool and firefighting resources from Manchester had been sent there. When Manchester was bombed the following night, many of the local fire brigades were still over on Merseyside, but with typical wartime determination, fire brigades from all over the North-West sent their fire engines to assist in Manchester's desperate struggle.

Lorna's involvement in the rescue of Mrs Flowers is based on a real event. The work done by Sally and Betty during the second night of the Christmas Blitz is typical of the work under-taken on a regular basis by the brave women of the WVS when-ever there was an air raid in progress.

Thank you for choosing to read *Christmas for the Home Front Girls*. I hope you enjoyed finding out what happens next to Sally, Betty and Lorna. I would love to hear your thoughts on the story in a review. These are not only valuable to me as the author but they also help new readers choose their next book.

I love hearing from my readers – you can get in touch through social media.

Much love,

Susanna xx

www.susannabavin.co.uk

facebook.com/MaisieThomasAuthor
x.com/SusannaBavin

ACKNOWLEDGMENTS

Huge thanks to my wonderful editor, Susannah Hamilton, whose insights added extra depth to one of the plot-lines. I am grateful to my agent, Camilla Shestopal, for everything she does behind the scenes; and to Nadia Michael, Jess Readett and Ria Clare. Jen Gilroy and Jane Cable are always there when needed.

Thanks also to Beverley Ann Hopper, Sandra Blower, Julie Barham, Karen Mace, Zoe Morton, Jackie Russell and Meena Kumari whose support has helped to get the series off to a great start.

PUBLISHING TEAM

Turning a manuscript into a book requires the efforts of many people. The publishing team at Bookouture would like to acknowledge everyone who contributed to this publication.

Commercial
Lauren Morrissette
Hannah Richmond
Imogen Allport

Contracts
Peta Nightingale

Cover design
Nick Castle

Data and analysis
Mark Alder
Mohamed Bussuri

Editorial
Susannah Hamilton
Nadia Michael

Copyeditor
Jacqui Lewis

Milton Keynes UK
Ingram Content Group UK Ltd.
UKHW042005240924
448733UK00005B/267

9 781837 907908